Moscow Nights Return

Book 1 of the Moscow Nights Series

By

Beth H. Macy

Edited by Dori Harrel

E-book ISBN: 979-8-9896791-0-2
Paperback ISBN: 979-809896791-1-9
Hardcover ISBN: 979-8-9896791-2-6

Acknowledgments

I want to thank my personal trainer, Sierra, who kept me going with my writing every week through her enthusiasm, encouragement, and requests for more chapters each week.

I'd also like to thank my friend, Corinne, for reading the book for consistency and realism. And for putting up with how I treated her double, Korinna.

And, a thanks to a freelance editor, Ellie Nalle, who pointed out some last-minute copy edit changes.

And last but not least, I'd like to thank my wonderful editor, Dori Harrell, who did an amazing job of cleaning up this book, keeping the action going, and encouraging me to do my best! Thank you Dori for believing in me, for your positive encouragement, and your gentle instructions

Prologue

12 February 1981

The four-ton, canvas covered truck skidded around the corner. The driver struggled with the wheel. "I'm sorry. We are too overloaded this trip. There's at least five tons of burn bags back there," he apologized to the United States Navy officer sitting beside him.

Her teeth chattering from the cold in the cab of the truck, Lieutenant Elda Ainsworth replied, "No worries, but can we stop at this address to pick up some blankets before we leave this area? Also I'd like to use the phone to call ahead and see if we can get the heat and defrost repaired in Cardiff." The wind was blowing snow in through the windows, which were slightly open to keep the front windshield from fogging up.

The shivering driver agreed. "I'd like to check the load when we stop too. Our careers will be over if we lose one of these burn bags."

Elda reached down and touched her pistol in the holster by her side. She knew that it was loaded and resisted the temptation to check again. She gazed out at the accumulating snow and hoped that it was just a passing storm without much depth. She feared the ice they would encounter with an empty truck on the way back.

The driver pulled the truck up and pumped his brakes to stop in front of the address Elda had given him. Elda noticed that his knuckles were white on the wheel. She jumped down out of the truck and dashed into the warm house. In a few seconds, she returned with an armload of wool blankets. The driver gratefully took two and wrapped them around his torso. She handed him a pair of gloves. "They are Al's, so we have to remember to return them." She jogged around the truck and pulled herself back up into the cab. "Do you want the good news or the bad news?"

"The good news," he replied, blowing on his fingers, then slipping them into the warm gloves.

"There is none."

He shrugged fatalistically. "Okay, the bad news."

"The repair facility is closed. And the storm is expected to go all night, so we will hit icy roads when we return to Wales from London."

"Shit. Oh, excuse me, ma'am."

Elda took her cover off and carefully placed it on her lap and pulled a blanket around her shoulders and over her head before responding, "That's okay. It sucks."

They both laughed sadly. With the driver now focused more on steering than the cold, the trip towards London was uneventful. As they headed into the outskirts of town, Elda glanced at her watch and noted that it was 09:00; they were right on schedule for the incinerator. She glanced over to a pub they were passing and saw a man stagger out, heading in their direction. She nudged the driver. "Look—it's the guy who is going to be burning these highly classified documents for us." He chuckled. Their mood fell when they arrived at the facility and shortly after, the same man walked through the yard and opened the door for them. Elda wondered if this mission could get any worse.

While the bags were being tossed into the incinerator under Elda's watchful eyes, the driver left to call in their status. Elda was sweeping up the ashes when he returned.

"Do you want the good news or the bad news?"

"The good news."

"There is none."

"Okay, the bad news."

"We have to pick up a passenger for the ride home and then head into the United States Embassy in London to pick up some stamps."

"Did you say, stamps?" Elda asked incredulously.

"Yes, ma'am."

Shortly after this conversation, a tall, slender teen, dressed impeccably in black with a grey greatcoat and leather gloves strolled into the facility. "Are you my ride?" he asked Elda, his voice cracking.

"Apparently. And you are?"

"Let's just call me your passenger."

Elda sighed and thought, *Perfect. Now I'm babysitting.* Out loud she stated, "All right. We have to stop for stamps at the Embassy and then we'll be heading back to the cookie factory."

"Good."

The three crammed into the cab with Elda in the middle. Elda was relieved to have some body heat for the ride home, though she thought she'd still never feel her fingers or toes again. Even the heat of the incinerator had seemed insufficient.

There was no place to park the truck by the embassy, so the driver hopped out while Elda slid over to take the wheel. In a tired daze she circled the block.

Crash. The rear impact woke Elda up. Cursing, she stopped the truck and climbed down to survey the damage. A battered farm truck had rammed the United States vehicle from behind. Elda groaned at the thought of all the paperwork she would have to fill out. Still, the truck was so old and beat up that there was no obvious sign that it had been in an accident. The farmhand pulled over his truck and walked over to chat with Elda.

"I'm so sorry," he said. "My foot slipped and caught the accelerator instead of the brakes. There's really no damage to my truck and it was all my fault. Do you have to report it?"

Elda glanced at the traffic that was having difficulty getting by and theorized that the police would soon be there. She really did not want to go through all the red tape, nor did she want to stay up any longer, since they had already worked the day shift before leaving, packed the truck, and traveled for over eight hours. "I'm alright with turning a blind eye to this, if you're okay with us just getting out of here quickly. The traffic is starting to pile up."

Before Elda had even finished her sentence, the other driver sprinted away. Elda jumped up into her truck and carefully pulled away from the curb to circle the block again. Her passenger looked at her with interest. He handed her a card with a number on it. "If you ever decide to leave the military, you might find that you fit in with some other like-minded people better than going to some civilian job. So if that happens, call this number and ask for Ed."

"Are you Ed?"

"I'm just an unknown guy going for a ride."

The driver appeared holding a locked bag. Elda took the bag from him and slid over so he could hop up to take the controls. She looked to her right, and the stranger was leaning against his window with his eyes closed. Noting the bluish tint of his lips, she took her lap blanket and put half of it on his lap. She glanced again at the card she was holding in her hand and placed it carefully in her inside jacket pocket.

The rest of the trip was a sleepy blur as the empty truck slid sideways down the Welsh hills.

***

26 November, 1990

Anatoly Petrov crept through some woods in northeast of Moscow, Russia. A ground fog lifted off the snow-covered leaves as he slowly and soundlessly moved along. The final rays of sun thinly streamed through the tall trees. He breathed the dry, cold air through his nose to limit the sound and any sign of his breath. He breathed evenly as he tracked his prey.

Anatoly heard a short, sharp sound to his left and watched as a rabbit hopped toward him. He noted the location and then veered left, ensuring each footstep landed silently as he crept along hunched over to keep from being sighted. He drew closer to the origin of the sound and dropped to the ground to listen for signs. *There!* A slight rustle just to the right of him. He peered through the underbrush and saw a shadowy figure heading in his general direction.

Khorosho. He will be here soon. Anatoly calculated the distance between the two of them, factoring in his own reaction time. Though a large, muscular teenager, Anatoly could move much faster than a smaller man. He sank farther into the freezing leaves and stilled his breath to become one with the forest floor.

A foot came down within his reach, and Anatoly grabbed it and brought the other man to the ground as he leaped on top of him, shoving his head into the underbrush with one hand and snaking a noose around his neck with the other. He held the man down with his body weight, feeling him struggle as Anatoly cut off his breath. He relished the sensation of the death throes beneath him.

Anatoly checked the other man's pulse and rolled off him. *Aga! My mission is accomplished. Now I can go to the KGB school.* He glanced down at the body of his fellow cadet. The trainers had warned all the cadets at the indoctrination that only one-third would graduate from pre-cadet training. At the time they hadn't realized that the other two-thirds would be brought out in body bags. *It is good. They guarantee our training is kept secret. Only the strong make it through.*

***

Moscow, 1997

The taxi ride to the hotel was frightening, as the car slid on bald tires across the snow-packed roads. Aurelio sank into the backseat, hoping he would make it to the hotel in one piece. This was his first trip overseas. It would stink to die in a taxi. What if the driver kidnapped him? He had heard that they did a lot of kidnapping over here. He felt like he would throw up from the stale cigarette smell in the cab.

He was shaking by the time the taxi dropped him off at the hotel, and he headed right to the bar after checking in and sending his luggage up to his room. He had never been in a nice hotel before. The bar off the lobby had a steady supply of vodka in shot glasses. After a few drinks, he observed a number of women up on the balcony surrounding the lobby. *Are they prostitutes?* He checked his wallet and counted his money. He wandered out to the middle of the lobby and leered drunkenly at a pretty brunette. She pointed to the glass elevators across the way and gestured for him to come up. He weaved his way to the elevators and punched the button for the balcony floor.

When he stepped off, the brunette waved at him. He advanced timidly. She held out her hand for money.

"Dollarov, pozhaluysta."

"How much?" He pulled out a few ten-dollar bills and handed them to her.

"More."

He kept placing bills in her hand until she nodded and closed her fist around them.

She then handed him a room key. He returned to the elevator and pressed the button for the eighth floor.

As he waited in the room, he wondered if he'd had too much liquor to get it up. He tried to calm his nerves with a shot of vodka from the minibar. He was innocent about sex. His wife had been the first and only girl he had fucked. Suddenly, he wondered if he was being set up. With shaking hands, he poured another drink.

The door opened, and a tall, slender, blonde prostitute sauntered in. He was disappointed. He had always been more attracted to brunettes resembling his mother. The blonde noticed his hesitation and quickly took control. She pushed him back onto the bed and unzipped his pants and went to work. It didn't take long for him to come. Although the prostitute didn't understand English, and he didn't comprehend Russian, it was clear she could communicate. She slowly slipped off her clothes and watched as his penis stiffened again. After a short while, he lay on the bed, exhausted, a big smile on his face. He vowed to get more sales calls in Russia.

Chapter One

Summer 2018

Aurelio Ainsworth's half-sister Elda leaped over the railing of the stairwell and onto the ground floor, leaving a swirl of concrete dust where she landed. She heard the clang of a metal stairway door closing somewhere above her, and footsteps started rapidly descending. She hurried to move outside where she had more room to maneuver. She dashed through the front door and ran in an evasion pattern, hunched over and low to the ground, across the long open expanse of field. *He's sure to get me before I can reach safety.* The long grasses and ruts conspired to take her down. She stumbled and bobbed her way across. A shot rang out behind her, but it missed. She scrunched her body as low as she could while still remaining upright. With a sigh of relief, she disappeared into the dense forest beyond. They were now in her habitat.

Elda ran through the woods, gripping her rifle tightly. A shot hit the tree next to her. Her heart leaped and pounded against the walls of her chest. *Damn, that was too close.* She changed her running pattern and zigzagged to reach her goal. Branches cracked under her steel-tipped combat boots. Her mouth was dry and her breathing ragged, echoing loudly in her ears. With all this noise, a child could track her. She'd trained to be better than this.

She ran behind a large tree, threw herself to the ground, and rolled away to change direction. Her brown and green camouflage blended into her surroundings. If she could only reach her destination, she'd be safe. This would not be the week she'd die.

She slathered her face with mud and obscured her protective head covering with leaves to hide her from air surveillance. She listened for the sounds of vehicles and was met with silence. Good. Her tracker was on foot. Looking through her gun scope, she quickly surveyed the surrounding area for her attacker.

A red-tailed hawk flew out of a tree and onto a branch farther into the woods. Something had spooked that bird. Elda calculated a line of direction using the bird's path and ran perpendicular to it. She stopped again and lowered herself to the ground, slithering to get distance between herself and the shooter. She heard faint sounds of movement. He didn't seem any closer, but he was still moving. She mapped out his locations thus far in her head, trying to triangulate his positions.

Another shot rang out. Where was he? She picked up a rock and flung it at the tree on her right to flutter the lower branches. Another shot. There! She had his location. Elda took three deep breaths and slowed her breathing and heart rate down to make less noise. *Now to get him before he shoots me.* A shot hit a nearby tree, scattering leaves down. Too close! But she needed to ensure she moved to within range.

She quietly and slowly mud crawled through the trees toward the shooter. She spied a swatch of black-and-white camouflage about twenty feet up in a fir tree. *Aha! There you are.* Sighting carefully, she aimed and fired and was rewarded by a curse. *Got you!*

A lanky, paint-covered man scrambled down out of the tree. "Damn ya, Elder. Yah got me again."

"Sorry, Jim," Elda replied insincerely, removing her helmet and shaking debris out of her short, brown-and-gray hair. She switched her paint-gun rifle to her other arm and reached out to take Jim Martin's proffered hand. "You nearly got me this time."

"Aye-yup. you wait until next week. Ah will get you good."

Elda smiled at her down east neighbor and old friend. "One of these days you will. You learned a lot during your tour in Vietnam, and you've kept them up nicely. You know I only train with the best."

"Aye-yup."

Elda watched as her old friend loped away to return his gun, and she sighed heavily. She resented her promise to stay at home. She missed the action of being in the field.

Chapter Two

15 October, 2018

A man sat in his office in the Kremlin, studying the orders in front of him. He adjusted his horn-rimmed glasses and leaned back in his chair. Too bad. She was such a good translator. He selected a Montblanc pen and wrote carefully and legibly on the orders: *Execute. Make it look like an accident. Preferably outside of Moscow to make it less obviously the work of the Kremlin.* He slipped the order into a brown routing envelope, wrote a name on the front, and threw it into his outbox for further routing. Pleased with himself, he poured a vodka. He lifted it high and toasted, "To Korinna."

***

Aurelio Ainsworth checked the date on his watch: 27 November, 2018. He was glad November was almost over. It was his birthday month, which reminded him of how old he was and how little he had accomplished. It also reminded him of Thanksgiving. He missed those wonderfully warm family get-togethers where his mother cooked amazing feasts. His life in St. Petersburg, Russia, was sterile and cold in comparison.

Aurelio adjusted himself in his tighty-whities while he took another hit off his joint. As he sucked the smoke deeply into his lungs, he contemplated a pee stain on the front of his briefs and considered getting dressed but shrugged the thought off, since there was no one, aside from Natasha Sokolov, to notice. *My wife, the lovely Natasha. Bitch.*

He regarded Natasha through the veil of smoke in front of his face. She sat sipping a glass of white wine and pouting while watching the forty-two-inch LED television across the living room. *My TV.* Her laughter echoed in his ears. His limp dick had failed him again. She should get him some cocaine or bath salts. That would perk him up again. As if she read his mind, Natasha flipped her long blond hair off her face and scowled.

He settled deeper into the overstuffed leather couch. Picking up his crystal scotch tumbler from the glass-and-marble table, he took a heavy slug of scotch. Natasha laughed.

"You bitch! You're nothing but a Russian-run prostitute. I know you're trying to kill me!"

Natasha turned and taunted him. "*Eto luchsheye, chto vy mozhete sdelat'? Vy zvuchite neobrazovannym.*"

"English, you bitch!"

"Oh that's right. Russian is hard for you to understand. Let me repeat in English. Is that the best you can do? You sound uneducated. I bet your sister has a better vocabulary."

Aurelio stood in anger. She knew that made him mad. He threw the scotch glass at the wall. It bounced off and onto the fireplace mantel, breaking into a shower of crystal shards. Scotch dripped down the wall and onto the rug.

Aurelio sat sipping scotch, toking on a joint, and glaring at Natasha. Enraged at his memories, he yelled, "I never picked you, you whore. I wanted the brunette."

The TV volume increased.

He picked up his laptop from the side table to send emails to his half-sister, Elda, and brother, Carlo. He was mad at them. He deserved their love and praise, but instead they had told him he was nuts and needed help. They'd even told him he was paranoid.

"There is nothing wrong with me!"

They were just out to get him. How ineffective all those killers were.

"I am a great man!"

Why then did he feel that he had failed in life?

"They will not get me!"

The sound of a blaring TV was the only response.

He gazed outside at the snow still falling. Winter in Russia—that would stop them in their tracks. If it stopped the Germans, it would devastate the nincompoops they had been sending after him. He picked his joint back up from where he had carelessly dropped it on the coffee table and relit it to help him think about his problems.

Perhaps Dad hadn't really passed away and was still masterminding the whole operation. Aurelio would defeat them all: his wife, his siblings, the FBI, the CIA, and all the black-op agencies spying on him.

The front door opened, and Aurelio's heart jumped. He spun around on the couch to see who was entering the apartment. Were they coming to get him?

Yuri Kuznetsov entered the apartment confidently, as though he owned it. Yuri was a large, well-built man in his early forties. He had a square jaw, which appeared even squarer because of his buzz cut. His bright blue eyes were clear and moved quickly around the room, observing everything at a glance. His coat was opened, revealing a tight sweater straining at his pecs and a gold chain around his large neck.

Aurelio burped and staggered off the couch to greet Yuri. As he passed by a mirror, he viewed his receding hairline and the grey hairs on his sagging chest. His thin hair was completely white, adding to his aged look, although he was only in his fifties. Boy, he still looked good. He'd show Natasha who was boss. He'd get some speed and pound her all night long.

"Yuri, man, great to see you," Aurelio said. "Got any cocaine or bath salts?"

Yuri took the small gilded mirror off the wall, sat on the couch, and laid out a number of lines on the mirror. Aurelio grabbed a straw and dove to snort up two lines before he sat back, beaming. Looking up, he observed Yuri and Natasha looking at him and smiling back.

His heart stopped for a beat, and he was sweating profusely. What was in those drugs? *Did they slip me something to kill me?* Sweat rolled down the middle of his back, and his hands shook. A few minutes went by, and he was still breathing. No, they failed again. He had outsmarted them.

Yuri handed Aurelio a lit joint and then went into the kitchen to speak privately with Natasha, who rose from watching the TV and accompanied him. Aurelio thought he heard money being counted out. *His money.*

He yelled toward the kitchen, "*Prostitutka! Shlyukha*! You won't get the rest of it. I have it stashed offshore in Cypress!"

He took another hit of the joint and felt the smoke strike the back of his throat and his brain at the same time. He stared at his laptop. *Why is that there?* He lifted it to one side and placed it on the couch and took another line from the mirror. Smiling, he savored the rush flowing through his body. He rose, padded barefoot across the plush rug, and poured himself another scotch. He held it up and admired the Christmas tree lights through the amber liquid, then emptied the glass, feeling it cool off his throat as he poured another.

***

Natasha returned from the kitchen to find Aurelio face down in his own vomit. She felt for a pulse and then turned him on his side so he wouldn't suffocate. She addressed him with scorn. "You wait, you small-dicked insufferable man. Soon I will be free of you. You have no information left that the government wants." She looked down at him and spit on his face. "*A ty plokho v posteli.*"

Yuri walked up behind her. She turned and kissed him passionately and entreated, "Aurelio will eventually kill himself with all the drugs and drink, and then I will be free and, even after giving the government their cut, very rich. We could go away together."

"Do you have access to his money yet?"

"I have almost all the information I need. He'll slip and tell me the rest one night when he's out of it."

Yuri kissed Natasha and murmured, "Then I'll be the boyfriend of a rich sexy woman. For now, let's go out and spend his money."

"Yes," Natasha readily agreed, "Anything to get away from this piece of trash."

Natasha had long ago passed on any information that Aurelio had from his days in the navy and his job working with electronic equipment. She had given Aurelio the information about the insider trading so that, through him, she would be rich and could route Aurelio's money to her government handlers and Yuri.

She laughed at the body lying on the floor and remarked, "What a little man. He thinks he is so smart and so superior, but he has done nothing on his own. I even manipulated him into marrying me."

She left the lights on and went out with Yuri.

Chapter Three

27 November, 2018

Elda Ainsworth holstered her weapon. A sharp, pungent smell filled the air. Despite her earplugs, the ring of the revolver retort still echoed in her head. She pushed the button to bring the target to her, and as she changed the sheet of paper, she admired the grouping around the bull's-eye. She then sent the target back. She opened her box of ammunition and reloaded her revolver.

Smith & Wesson made a fine weapon.

Elda had worked in intelligence in the navy and still kept up her skills. She was coy about telling her age but was physically fit. Her face showed the lines of active living, though her short brown hair was graying around the temples. She'd been blessed to inherit her mother's high cheekbones, since they helped keep her face youthful. She grinned, remembering winning first place in her age group in her last race. That wouldn't happen again this year, since two of her younger and faster running buddies had just entered her age group.

Elda rapidly fired off five shots at the target. Again, a great grouping. She holstered her empty weapon and then packed it and the holster into a lockbox for the ride to her home on the Maine coast.

"Honey, I'm home," Elda shouted as she entered the front door.

Simultaneously, her partner, Dawn, hugged her; the cat rubbed her leg; and her dog, Vee, jumped up her other side. Elda stepped back and admired Dawn, a stunning woman with a mane of brown hair framing her square face. Her blue eyes drew Elda into another world when she gazed into them. It was nice, too, that they were about the same height and could stare into each other's eyes so easily.

"How is it that you take my breath away every time I look at you?"

Dawn bantered back, "Are you getting COPD?"

Elda laughed and kissed her partner. She strode across the wide, wooden planks of the living room floor into the kitchen to clean her gun.

"Honey, I wish you wouldn't do that here," Dawn yelled after her.

"But it's so therapeutic. You should try it," Elda retorted.

She didn't acknowledge Dawn's soft whisper of, "I hate that you have that gun. You would think that after twenty-five years together, you would know that by now."

Elda sat at the old farmhouse kitchen table and laid out the cleaning equipment. She dipped the bore brush in the solvent and fed it through the barrel. She followed that with a patch dipped in solvent. The rhythm and familiarity of cleaning the gun relaxed her. Using a toothbrush, she brushed around the muzzle and then worked on her favorite part: the cylinders. She ended her ritual by polishing the Smith & Wesson logo, then she placed the gun into the lockbox, pocketing the key.

Elda sauntered back into the living room and admired the Christmas tree tucked in the corner. The twinkling white lights reflected off the windows, mirroring the white of the snow on the ground.

"Honey, you did an excellent job decorating the tree."

"It was all those years of practice alone, while you were away on secret missions."

Elda remembered the Christmases she'd spent with her mother and sister. Her mother had always insisted on a perfect Christmas tree, every light equidistant from the other, ornaments evenly spaced and tinsel laid on piece by piece. What a contrast to Christmases at her father's house, where they threw tinsel onto the tree in handfuls. What a noisy, frenetic group that was. No surprise the mental illness and addictions from their mother's side was showing up in later years, she concluded.

Elda wondered what had happened to her half-brother's brain. Aurelio was triggered by holidays and his birthday. The inflow of emails from him increased during those times, but she never read them. She had an auto-filter that automatically forwarded the emails to the FBI and deleted them from her account. She suspected her half-brother Carlo Ainsworth did the same thing. Aurelio obviously hadn't factored into his thought process how technically savvy Elda and Carlo were.

She guessed that after his mother died, he'd started taking synthetic drugs, causing delusions and paranoia. If that was true, his brain would never recover. Ah, well. He was dead to her anyway. As a therapist, Elda understood Aurelio's personality disorders were caused by his inner insecurity and his mother's constant praising of his small deeds. The drugs had layered on top of this, resulting in an intense, incurable paranoia. He was a sad case, but not worth spending much energy thinking about. Aurelio was definitely a small fish and a pawn in the larger game. She did hope her informants would keep him from betraying his country any more than he already had. She didn't care what happened to him, but she did care about her country.

She was glad to have Yuri to report back on him. Any of Aurelio's information was so stale it should be useless by now. But Russia was spying on him, and Natasha worked for the Russian government, so it was only right that America also had the same information.

Elda had had a strong sense of patriotism from the time she had been selected in third grade to raise the flag every day. She'd felt a sense of pride at knowing the rules for displaying the American flag and folding it into that tight triangle. Even now, the sound of the ropes and hooks clanging against a flagpole filled her with a sense of honor and duty.

Elda looked out the windows at the falling snow and the waves crashing against the rocky coast. She turned to Dawn and remarked, "I'm so happy living here with you, honey."

Knowingly Dawn responded, "Were you thinking of your family again, Elda?"

Amazed that Dawn knew her so well when she felt that, even after all these years, she hardly knew Dawn, Elda opened up and answered, "Yes, I was thinking about Christmas at my father's house. I remember Aurelio tiptoeing around giggling to himself. There were indications he wasn't right even then. Perhaps that was why his mother protected him so much."

"Do you miss them?"

Dawn's question stopped Elda in her tracks. She cocked her head and thought about the answer, struggling to bring forward her feelings. Finally, she shook her head and replied, "Not really. I miss my long talks with my father. We used to stand in the driveway each time before I left and chat for at least an hour. I remember one time, he mentioned with regret on being forced to marry Aurelio's mother. Apparently, she was a Catholic and faked being pregnant to lure my dad into marriage."

Dawn voiced the obvious question, "Was Aurelio his own child?"

Elda cleared her throat and smirked. She shrugged and stated, "My dad had doubts. Aurelio definitely didn't look at all like the rest of the crew. The grapevine had said that one of the neighbors and Aurelio's mother had had an affair. No wonder my dad was obsessed with riding around with the police and observing the neighbors' antics. He was elated when Carlo was born, since he was a dead ringer for my grandfather."

Elda rarely talked about herself or her family. Dawn prompted Elda to continue, "Who do you think the rest of those kids look like?"

"Oh, they definitely have the brown eyes and the prominent cheekbones that run in the family. Family lore says it's from my Wapanoug Indian blood." Elda pointed to her own cheeks and brown eyes and plopped down on the couch.

"Ah, that's where your warrior instinct came from!"

Dawn rose from her chair, strolled over, and sat by Elda, wrapping an arm around her shoulders. They silently surveyed their land and the ocean, absorbing the quiet of the evening. The peace of their life together washed over Elda.

"Shouldn't you check in so we can have the night to ourselves?" Dawn asked.

Elda knitted her brow and retorted, "Drat, do I have to?"

"Did you hear me say 'the night to ourselves?'" Dawn kissed Elda on the cheek.

Elda winked and smiled. "That I like. I much prefer that to working."

Dawn gently took Elda's head between her hands and turned her to look into Dawn's eyes. She stated emphatically, "Quit then. We're all set for retirement, and you promised me no more trips. Why stick it out?"

Elda recoiled from Dawn, shaking herself loose. She was horrified at the thought of leaving her job. She said in a pleading but certain tone, "It makes me feel vital and alive."

Dawn angrily snapped at Elda, "Some days I think you love your job more than you love me."

Elda reached out her hand to touch Dawn's arm and stated lovingly, "You know that's not true, honey."

"Do I?"

Dawn rose and stomped away. Elda regarded her quizzically and then reluctantly picked up her MacBook Pro from the coffee table. She logged into the VPN and performed her daily check for emails from her agency. She was proud to help the United

States government in any way she could, as long as it was ethical and humane. Although she was at an age where she rarely did field work anymore, they had the occasional need for her expertise and business connections.

Elda had accomplished much in her life. She had served in the military, been a teacher, an artist, a personal trainer, a programmer, a therapist, a coach, an author, a videographer, and through it all had managed to fit in a number of covert operations for her government. She had an advanced degree and many certifications, and she kept actively learning every semester. It was her plethora of talents and active, analytical mind that had kept her as an asset for so long.

She looked at her computer screen. "Nothing there! I'm a free woman. Want to celebrate?" Elda leered at Dawn, who scowled back but then laughingly tossed a throw pillow at her.

Vee jumped on the couch in an attempt to catch the pillow. Her antics broke the remaining tension.

Elda glanced at her Garmin watch and calculated that they had a couple of hours before dinner. "Let's walk the dog and then go to the gym."

"That's how you celebrate?"

"Later, honey, later . . ." Elda winked at Dawn and circled her tongue, which resulted in a pillow landing on her head.

***

Elda startled at the unexpected sound of the secured landline phone ringing. She hopped across the room with one sneaker on and another in her hand, nearly falling over the cat. She grabbed at the receiver and breathlessly gasped a hello. Her heart dropped when she heard the secure line click in and the deep tones of her boss.

"How's your Russian?"

"*Privet, Ed. Moy Russkiy khoroshiy.*"

"Do you remember Korinna Fedorov?"

Elda's mind flashed to many a cold Russian winter evening in Moscow, laughing, sipping vodka, and eating blinis and caviar with Korinna. Korinna worked as a translator at the Kremlin, and she and Elda had become fast friends during Elda's time in Moscow. Korinna was of Scandinavian heritage, standing over six feet tall. She had a stylish flair and insisted on wearing a bright red coat. When they trudged over the snowy Moscow sidewalks, Elda, at five foot, four inches, decked out in gray and looking rather round in a padded coat, blended in with the Russians shuffling by. She had even perfected the Russian flatfooted way of walking on the icy sidewalks. But Korinna could never blend in with her height, and the coat just accented that fact.

"*Da*," Elda replied. "*Ya pomnyu*—uh. Yes, I remember Korinna. We were good friends."

"She's in trouble and needs to be extracted to the States, but she will only deal with you."

Elda sighed. She could see through the railing uprisers the meticulously decorated Christmas tree and Dawn reading a book, with the dog lying on her feet. Elda so wanted just to spend these holidays at home with them. She listened to Ed describing Korinna's situation, absorbing the facts as she wandered toward the bedroom door, only to be caught short and pulled backward by the phone cord. From her new vantage point, she could see that Dawn had lit a fire in the fireplace and was heading toward the stairs, into the bedroom to change out of her work-out clothes. After their many years of living together, Dawn was familiar with what that phone ringing meant. Elda turned and stepped back into the bedroom to relieve the stress on the cord.

While listening to Ed, Elda shrugged and rotated her neck. The stiffness and crackling were more pronounced these days and certainly weren't there when she'd last seen Korinna. She hoped this operation wouldn't require much agility and wished even more that it would be a quick in-and-out mission, so she could be back home before Christmas. *The Cold War never ended.*

She felt Dawn come up behind her, gently placing her hands on her neck, massaging the tension there.

After hanging up, Elda followed Dawn to the living room and snuggled with her on the couch.

"You promised," Dawn snipped through gritted teeth.

"I know. This is the last one. I *promise*." Elda looked beseechingly at Dawn.

Dawn sat up straight and faced Elda. "What makes this promise different from the last ten?"

Elda added her predictable refrain to the all-too-familiar argument, "I don't know. I'll just stop."

"Then stop now," Dawn insisted.

"You know I can't do that."

"When do you leave?" Dawn asked, sighing heavily. The argument had reached the same conclusion as it had many times before.

"Tomorrow."

Dawn sighed again. She asked flatly, "Should I worry?"

Elda shrugged her shoulders. Any mission was dangerous, but she didn't want to say that. Smiling to deflect the seriousness of her job, she quipped, "No more than usual."

Dawn rolled her eyes and finished out her side of the script, "How long will you be gone?"

And predictably, Elda gave her rote answer: "I don't know."

Chapter Four

28 November, 2018

Aurelio snorted a line of cocaine and then danced around the bedroom, throwing clothing into a small bag for his trip to Moscow. He was leaving before Christmas on a short trip to get together with a group of expats. He stopped, drew a line of cocaine on Natasha's makeup mirror, and snorted it in one smooth motion.

Natasha strolled into the bedroom. He admired the way her blond hair draped over her shoulders and the way she glided on her long legs. She had maintained her shape nicely. He briefly toyed with the idea of forcing her into bed with him, but let that idea go when he remembered the shame of trying to bed her yesterday.

"*Pozhaluysta, voz'mite eto s soboy*," Natasha requested.

"Speak English, damnit," Aurelio retorted. "You know how sick I am of your Russian."

"Please take this with you," Natasha repeated in English as she placed a small, rectangular wrapped gift into his suitcase. "It is a present for my cousin, Tanya. She will meet you at the hotel tonight before you go out."

Aurelio sighed. Again he was transporting presents for Tanya. It seemed that every trip he made to Moscow, Natasha had him carry something there for her. Well, at least it saved on the hassle of trying to mail it there. He nodded and placed a folded shirt over the box.

Aurelio threw in the book his half-sister had written. How could she do so much, when he was clearly superior to her? She had a master's degree and had published books, and he was saddled supporting his lazy wife, who was not even good in bed anymore. He would get his half-sister, he promised himself. He would pick through the book and throw her words back at her. She would see how clever he was.

He popped two antacids and threw the rest of the bottle into the suitcase. His stomach felt so acidic lately. He'd go see the doctor when he returned home, but all that quack kept telling him was to stop drinking. Aurelio believed it was something Natasha was slipping into his food. *I should insist on being tested for poisons.*

He had stopped eating out when he'd visited his brother, Carlo, last year. He'd told Carlo that others were trying to poison him. Carlo had laughed. In fact, he'd turned against Aurelio, and Carlo had thrown him out of his apartment after only two weeks. Aurelio could not see how Carlo could be happy in his life. He had no money to speak of. Certainly nothing compared to the millions Aurelio had made. How could he achieve happiness when Aurelio felt so angry and miserable every day? It must have been part of the mind control games his siblings were playing on him.

"Natasha, get me my driver. I'm leaving now."

No response.

Aurelio scowled and stomped into the living room to find his cell phone and call his driver. On the coffee table lay a note from Natasha, saying she had gone out with Yuri. Aurelio tipped over the coffee table in a rage. He sat and poured himself a large scotch, downing it before calling the driver.

***

Sighing heavily, Elda regrettably placed her locked box with her pistol in it into the bedside table.

Dawn glowered at her, requesting, "Can't you find a different place for that thing?"

Not understanding why Dawn objected to its placement, Elda explained for the umpteenth time, "It's safely in my bedside table. You won't have to worry about it. And it's readily accessible if you need it."

Snorting, Dawn stormed out of the bedroom.

Vee jumped on and off the small stack of clothing next to Elda's leather carry-on, staring at her reproachfully.

"Vee, not you too. Please sit. Wait. Good girl."

Elda quickly shoved the clothing in and zipped the bag shut. She felt insecure leaving her weapons behind. Hopefully she could request a revolver and other tools of the trade once she had cleared Sheremetyevo International Airport in Moscow.

"Honey, I remember the day you gave me this bag."

Dawn peeked her head into the bedroom. "Ah yes, and I remember the fights we had about the mysterious trips you went on so often. You would take off with little-to-no notice. And you're still doing it."

Uncertain why Dawn's tone was so angry when Elda felt full of love when she looked at the bag, Elda explained, "But that day you gave me the bag was special. It was our first anniversary. This bag is a symbol of all the years we've been together. It's like I'm bringing part of you and our relationship with me."

"Look how tattered and worn that bag is now." Dawn's eyes filled with tears.

Elda rushed over to hug her, then glimpsed the time on her watch. She dropped her arms and pivoted to kneel at the bedroom closet to get money and passports out of the floor safe.

Elda stood and spotted Dawn silently watching her. "What?"

Dawn shook her head and wiped tears from the corners of her eyes. "I can't believe you are going on another mission. I thought you were done with them."

Elda blurted out, "I *have* to go, honey. I thought you understood." She glanced up at Dawn in surprise.

Dawn stamped her foot and shouted, "Why? You promised me you would quit these missions."

She continued in a gentler voice, "And it's clear that you're scared of something there."

Elda turned her head away so Dawn couldn't see her eyes. She agreed, "Yes, there's a lot of history for me there, but I have to save my friend."

"Last night you were dreaming, and you mumbled the word *Tosh*. What is that?" Dawn demanded.

Elda sighed and bowed her head. "I can't tell you."

"You never can," Dawn mumbled, shaking her head and turning her back on Elda. She bent over Elda's carry-on to insert a small brown stuffed dog, Sobaka. It was a ritual Dawn had started on Elda's first trip. Sobaka had a smooshed appearance from having been in so many carry-ons, and his fur was wearing off on the side of his head where Elda kissed him every night she was away, as a proxy for Dawn.

Elda loved that Korinna had told her that her husband, Egor, also packed Privet, a small white bear with big black eyes, for Korinna. And like Sobaka, Privet, when she had last seen him four years ago, was rather dingy and worse for wear.

Vee observed intently from her bed. Her head lay on her paws, her eyes sad. She was also familiar with her mother leaving her for long trips. It tore at Elda's heart to see Vee's sad brown eyes and little downturned mouth.

"I love you, Vee. I will miss you so much."

She turned and saw Dawn with her hands on either side of her head and such an exaggerated sad look in her blue eyes that Elda burst out laughing, and Dawn did the same.

"Aw, honey, I love you and will miss you too."

Elda hugged her, squared her shoulders, picked up her bag, and marched out the door. She whirled to wave goodbye before she slid into her car. There, side by side, staring out the window, were Dawn and Vee. Elda waved and blew a kiss. Dawn picked up Vee and helped her wave, then turned away.

***

Elda scanned the crowds at Terminal E at Logan Airport, wondering if she was being followed yet. She delayed boarding so she could view the other passengers on her flight. As she settled into her first-class seat, a well-built young man rushed on and settled into the seat behind her. *Damn.* She needed to find out who he was. Dashing onto a plane or train at the last minute was a common spy trick to ensure you were alone. No one sat next to her, so she rose and ambled her way to the restroom. On her way back, she stopped, took a good look at the young man, and tapped him on the arm to get his attention. "Excuse me, sir."

He looked up politely. "Yes, ma'am?"

Elda tapped her watch on her arm and stated, "I'm not sure my watch is correct. Can you please tell me what time you have?"

He glanced at his own watch and told her, "Nineteen-thirty."

"Thank you," Elda said. "Are you in the military?"

Proudly, he answered, "Yes, ma'am. I'm on leave and going to London to visit some friends."

Elda smiled at him and commented, "You almost missed making the plane, hey?"

He looked at her with a sheepdog expression on his face and rubbed his close-cut hair. "Shucks, I've never been good at being on time. I've been written up for being AWOL just for oversleeping."

"Have fun, and thank you for your service."
Satisfied, Elda returned to her seat. When he'd
answered her question in military time, Elda had
assumed he was probably an American serviceman.
Her questions were to check her instincts. Even
though it had been years since Elda had left the
military, she still set her watch and the clocks in the
house to military time. It had driven Dawn crazy at
first, but she'd become so used to it that she now set
her own watch to display military time.

"I wonder if there are other things I've forced
on Dawn because of my lifestyle? She seems upset.
We'll have to have a good talk when I get back. If I
get back." Elda realized she was talking to herself
and checked to see if anyone had heard her musings,
but no one appeared to be paying any attention.

She told the steward that she would like to
sleep as much as possible on the flight, but not to
touch her food. She didn't care if it was cold when
she woke up.

"It's not like being hot will improve the taste,"
she muttered.

With that, she drank some water, put on her
eyeshades and neck pillow, and fell promptly asleep.
She woke up because of turbulence, ate the roll and

the yogurt from her food tray, and then let the turbulence rock her back to sleep.

She dreamed she was standing in a snowbank, surrounded by Russians.

They were all waiting for a taxi. Suddenly, an unmarked black sedan pulled up. Elda glanced around to see whose car it was and was astonished to find that everyone had vanished.

She traipsed up to the car on shaky legs. The windows were tinted, and she could not see who was driving. The car was too clean to be a normal Moscow car. It appeared recently polished. Even the tires were new and inflated. The Russians in Moscow often let air out of their tires to get better traction on the slippery, unplowed roads.

The passenger-side window silently rolled down as Elda neared.

"Dobryy vecher," Elda offered.

"Good evening," the driver replied. "Please allow me to give you a ride."

She pointed at where she had been standing "No, thank you. I am waiting for a taxi."

"Yes," the driver said, "but it is cold outside, and you never know when an accident might occur. It would be much safer if I gave you a ride to your hotel."

Elda's feet were freezing from lack of movement. Siberia could not be much colder than this. She opened the door and slid into the car, jostling to get her bulky coat around her.

The driver smiled at her and made a U-turn, driving away from the hotel. Ah crap, that couldn't be good. Elda forced a smile back at him and offered him a cigarette. They sat smoking in silence while they sped over the near-deserted Moscow streets.

Elda analyzed the driver. Nothing distinguished in his looks. He was probably in his thirties or forties, with a slender, almost skinny, but athletic build. He had long, muscular hands. Probably able to strangle someone with them. She stubbed out her cigarette in the nearly full ashtray, cleared her throat to check that her voice came out strong, and asked, "So what do you do?"

"I'm a student at the university," he answered. "What do you do?"

"I'm a teacher. We probably have a lot in common."

He chuckled a throaty laugh. "Touché."

Elda lit two more cigarettes and passed one over to him as she watched the landscape speed by. It was devoid of color, except for the occasional red, Russian hammer and sickle.

She glimpsed two stooped ladies cleaning debris in a park near the entrance to the metro station. There was no sense trying to figure out where they were going. She would find out soon enough.

"So, what do you do?" he asked again.

"I'm a teacher. I teach mathematics," she answered and then asked again in return, "And what do you do?"

"I'm a student at the university," he answered.

It was Elda's turn to laugh this time. "Touché." She handed him another cigarette.

She woke up with a start, covered in a cold sweat.

***

Elda deplaned, and the sounds and smells transported her back to the last time she had been here. Grateful to have a driver waiting for her, she maneuvered over to the taxi stands after immigration. She smiled, remembering how puzzled the Russian immigration officer had been at her *Winnie the Pooh* book. She always carried it with her into Russia, just to see the look on their faces as they flipped through the book, wondering if there was some sort of code or secret message hidden in it. Elda got a kick out of playing harmless mind games.

"Pozhaluysta, otvezite menya v otel', Crowne Center." Elda climbed into the backseat of the taxi. She always stayed at the Crowne Center Hotel when in Moscow. Elda was a creature of habit, which was dangerous for an operative. She constantly had to remind herself to take different routes and stay at different places. This trip, however, she wanted those who would be tailing her to watch on her terms.

After checking into the hotel, Elda filled a shopping bag and hopped aboard the metro. Walking into Gorky Park a few minutes later, she stopped to get her bearings. Something was different. The park seemed larger, brighter, and cleaner than she remembered. She wandered along a path, hoping that the quaint, old fairy-tale carousel, with its bright, whimsical colors and that small horse rearing on its back legs on the ball atop the canopy, was still there. It had looked like it had been transported from another era. She missed the dark, almost sinister atmosphere the park formerly boasted. It was now too open and clean. It had been a favorite area for spies to pass information to each other. Today, it appeared to be a family amusement park.

She passed the skaters on the central skating rink and took a right to weave her way to the river. She periodically stopped to look down at her phone and adjust the large shopping bag on her arm. When she stopped the third time, a large, well-built man wearing a black leather jacket over a tight sweater ran straight into her and knocked her down, spilling the contents of her bag.

"Izvinite menya! Mne ochen' zhal'!" the man apologized, as he scrambled to pick up the scattered souvenirs and return them to her shopping bag.

Elda slowly stood and brushed herself off. She had to smile at how apologetic the man was.

"What's the rush?" she asked, and then switched to ask it again in Russian. *"Chto za speshka?"*

"Excuse me," he said again in English. "I meet my girlfriend here, and I am late!"

He handed Elda her bag and asked if she was all right. Elda nodded and thanked him for picking up her things. He gave a half bow and ran off.

Another man materialized from Elda's left. He was well dressed, with impeccable posture, and cut a distinguished figure in his long wool greatcoat.

"Are you okay?" he asked in unaccented English as he adjusted his round wire rims on his nose with his index finger.

"Yes. These young men in love should slow down," she said.

The man pointed at her bag. "Did you check to see if everything was there?"

"There isn't anything I'd mind him stealing, but he seemed like an earnest young man." She opened the bag and allowed him to see what she was doing as she rummaged through the contents. "Yes, yes, it appears to all be here."

"*Khorosho*," he said with a sigh.

"Yes, it is good," Elda said as she walked back toward the park exit. When she glanced over her shoulder, the man was still standing there and staring.

Interesting. They were watching her already.

****

Elda paced quickly away toward Oktyabrskaya station to ride the metro back to the Crowne Center Hotel. She switched through two stations so she could identify anyone shadowing her. The Moscow metro stations were lavish, and the lines moved neatly East–West and North–South, with an inner ring to move between them, making the stations easy to navigate.

Elda's favorite was the Novokuznetskaya, with the colored marble punctuated by octagonal ceiling mosaics, bas-reliefs, and cast bronze depictions of Red Army and Russian war heroes, floor lamps, and large, ornate benches. It was opulent but simplified by the muted colors of the marble and the stained glass. She didn't like much the more modern stations. If she were here as a tourist, and if she didn't detest the steep escalators leading down to the stations, she might tour all of them. Perhaps someday.

As she made her way to the Crown Center, she counted one tail behind her and one in front of her.

***

Elda spotted Sobaka sitting on the bed in her hotel room, reading a map. Her support team had left something for her in the room. Elda reached under the mattress to remove a small computer. She then took a small Russian nesting doll out of her shopping bag. Inside the first doll was a smaller doll, and inside that doll was another whose head came off to reveal a USB stick. She logged in to a secure VPN, bounced the signal through several IP addresses, and uploaded the contents of the stick to a secure CIA server. She then wiped the computer clean and replaced it under the mattress for retrieval while she went for supper. She took the stick, crushed it, and flushed it down the toilet.

She thought silently, *Thank you, Yuri.* The information from Natasha, who slept with so many expats with loose lips, was of interest to the CIA. Elda rubbed her hip ruefully. There would be a bruise there, though. Perhaps they could find a gentler way to exchange information next time.

She sighed and stared longingly at the bed. The trip had taken twenty-two hours from her home to Moscow, with a stop in Heathrow. She found it hard to believe that she used to travel to Moscow from the United States almost every week. Ignoring her fatigue, she stretched, threw water on her face, and changed her clothes to head out to savor blinis with caviar with Korinna at the Café Pushkin. Too bad they wouldn't be eating at the Czarskaya Okhota restaurant. It was probably no longer open, since Korinna had requested they meet at the Café Pushkin.

Elda would miss the atmosphere at the old Czarskaya Okhota. It had been dark and dismal, as a Russian restaurant should be. She remembered darting in there to lose a tail when she was in Moscow on a mission years ago. She had been compromised and forced to flee the city quickly, and she'd needed to meet a contact for new papers.

The inside had been decorated with dark mahogany wood with macabre touches of wolfskins, cannons, bearskin rugs, busts of Russian emperors, mounted reindeer heads, stuffed partridges hanging from wall sconces, and even an indoor water mill and a curved, wooden bridge. She had been so disorientated. It had felt like a different world in there—like she could be lost for days. And the sinister feel had made her wonder if she were the hunter or the hunted.

She had turned a corner in the restaurant and found herself in a dark hallway where the lights were either broken or turned off. Just in time, she had caught the flash of a knife as an attacker lunged at her. She'd sidestepped the woman at the last moment, and turning, brought both fists locked together into the middle of the attacker's back, causing her to stumble forward. Elda had stuck out her foot and caught the woman's leg, helping her crash down onto the animal-skin rug. Then, she'd leaped on top of the woman but felt that she wasn't moving. The lance from a nearby statue had impaled her through the neck during her forward fall. Elda had rolled her off of the lance and under a nearby bench, thrown the rug on top of the body, and then ran down the hallway to the door at the end. With relief she'd found herself outside in the alley. She'd had to force herself to walk calmly away to not attract attention.

She missed that old restaurant. It represented Moscow, which in turn represented the true feeling of being a spy: never trusting, never knowing when the next attack would come.

She wondered what had happened that Korinna needed to leave Russia. Korinna, as a translator for the Kremlin, was a trusted confidant to many powerful men and knew many state secrets. What had she learned that was worth killing her for?

Elda didn't know anything about Korinna's job directly but had learned a bit through MI6's deep asset in the Kremlin. Elda and Korinna had placed boundaries on their conversations, never venturing into details about the other's job, out of respect for their friendship. They'd talked of their mutual love of animals, especially their dogs; reviewed their favorite books and movies; discussed the art they admired; shared self-care advice through exercise, massage, and yoga; and even analyzed the patterns on the hotel rugs and the algorithms behind the elevators in the hotel lobby.

As road warriors having traveled through their jobs for long periods, they also shared stories of jet lag, time-zone changes, and stale sandwiches while sitting on the edge of a bed in a strange hotel room. Elda had often traveled to global scientific and educational conferences as part of her cover story, and on occasion she'd been surprised and delighted to see Korinna translating for diplomats.

What danger was Korinna fleeing from? And how much danger was Elda in?

***

A slender ghost of a man took his interoffice mail out of the mailbox and stepped quietly into his office. Sitting at his desk, he opened the brown envelope and withdrew the single page of orders. He sighed and nodded a few times as he absorbed their significance. He would make sure his operatives observed her movements while he devised a plan for her elimination. He read through the original orders again. Korinna's husband, too? They were covering all their bases. He swung his chair around and reached into his file cabinet. *Yes. He will fit the bill for this job.* He placed the folder in his desk. The tab was labeled, ANATOLY.

***

Elda stepped outside the hotel and was assaulted by the fierce wind and sharp cold. She tightened the strap on her dark-brown fur hat, wrapped her scarf around her face, and walked briskly on the ice, heading to the metro station.

Three men kept an eye on her now, two in the back and one in the front. *Oh, crap.* They were really covering her. She needed to ditch these tails in order to see Korinna alone. Should she hop on the Purple Line, change to Brown at Taganskaya Station, and catch the Blue Line at Kurskaya, and then continue on the Blue to the Partizanskaya Station? There were some stations she'd love to see, but this was not a vacation. She'd take the route with the most changes. *Sharpen up. Snap to it. Be an operative again.*

After chastising herself, Elda switched into operative mode. She dashed onto the Purple Line train just before the car door closed. No one appeared to follow. Ensuring her followers were gone, she changed trains a number of times. She delayed getting off until the last minute, pretending that she hadn't been paying attention. There. She had definitely lost all three.

Were there others?

***

"Shit! What are the chances of this happening?" Elda cursed as she recognized the man who was staring at her from across the street. From the way his head snapped up and his eyes bore into hers, she knew he had identified her as the woman who was leaving the apartment building the day his twin brother died.

It was years ago on a mission in Moscow. Elda had been sent in to turn or eliminate a traitor to the United States. Both brothers were expats living in Russia. One had been a US government agent, and his brother had started a high-tech start-up in Moscow and was living high off the hog on the investor's money. Elda had gone to the agent's apartment to reason with him, and when he wouldn't listen, slipped into his drink a non-traceable chemical that mimicked a heart attack. She had watched him fall to the ground, clutch his chest, convulse, and die. Satisfied that she had left no trace of being there, she had quickly slipped out of the apartment. Exiting the stairway, she had passed by the twin brother. The brother's death had been attributed to natural causes, but Elda had heard that his twin never believed that and had devoted himself to finding his killer.

"I really do not have time for this," Elda muttered. She flagged down a cab that was heading away from the Izmailovsky Market. Miraculously, it skidded to a stop, and she jumped in. She looked behind her and saw the brother had also managed to snag a cab. She snorted in frustration, "What on earth is the probability of that happening?"

The driver looked into his rearview mirror and inquired, "*Proshu proshcheniya?*"

"*Izvinite,*" Elda apologized, "That wasn't for you." She took out a stack of American dollars and asked, "Can you please lose the cab that is following us?"

The cab driver's face lit up. He reached back for the bills as he slammed his foot down on the accelerator. Elda dropped them into the front seat as the velocity threw her backwards. She looked back, and the other cab had also picked up speed. Elda's driver turned his wheel sharply and skidded into a 180-degree turn down a side street. Recognizing where she was, Elda shouted directions to the driver, who zigged and zagged through the streets. Horns blared as they barely missed the other cars. Elda instructed him to speed up to the next alleyway, stop suddenly for enough time for her to get out, and fly away again. She tossed more bills into the front seat. Approaching the alleyway, he started to slow, and Elda opened her back door, dropping and rolling into the alley and behind a dumpster. She heard the second cab speed by after the first one.

Dusting herself off, Elda muttered, "This mission is not starting well." She checked for any damage to herself and then set off to the main street to find a taxi to take her back to the market.

***

Glad that she had built in a buffer time for her meeting, Elda arrived at the Izmailovsky Market. She wandered past booths crowded in concentric rings, stopping to admire the craftwork while checking to see if she had picked up another follower. The market was so large that she could not see one end from the other. As Elda's boots crunched on the hard-packed snow, she noticed it had melted to bare ground behind the tables where the vendors had set up makeshift stoves with fires to keep warm. She looked longingly at the fires. The cold penetrated her boots. *Damn, they were supposed to be rated to ten below zero! I paid enough for them to be warmer than this!*

At one booth she found little inlaid pictures made entirely of wood, by a man whose muscular, large, but stubby fingers seemed incongruous with his beautifully detailed artwork. The craftsman drank vodka to stay warm and had a small fire in a portable stove behind him.

"*Vashi podelki prekrasny,*" Elda said, admiring his work.

"*Spasibo.*" His craggy face broke into a smile as he inquired, "*Ty otkuda?*"

"*Amerika.*"

"*Amerikantsy khoroshi!*" He gave her a thumbs up. The arctic air whipped around the stalls, and she shivered and stamped her frozen feet. Having given his approval about Elda's citizenship, the man motioned for her to join him and warm up.

"*Spasibo.*" Elda quickly moved to the back of the table to warm her hands, giving her an opportunity to scan the area. Good. No tails. No sign of the expat either.

She bought two of the vendor's pictures depicting Russian peasant life and, thanking him again, headed back out to catch the metro to the restaurant where she was meeting Korinna. She again wove her way across the stations and various lines and arrived at Café Pushkin.

Elda surveyed the space, and then she was escorted to her seat in the library room. The tall, built-in bookcases, dark wood, old telescopes, and ancient globe maps lent an air of mystery to the café. She grinned when she caught sight of Korinna, already seated at a table in the back corner next to a window. Since it was early, there were not many people there yet. From that viewpoint, Elda would be able to see if anyone else came in.

Korinna stood up, a friendly smile on her slender face.

Elda greeting her warmly, "It is so good to see you again, Korinna."

Korinna replied sincerely, "As is it to see you, Elda."

As Korinna looked about to say more, Elda held up her hand to silence her. "Let's order before we start talking."

Korinna's eyes crinkled and her lips trembled.

Unsure of how to handle Korinna's tears, Elda asked, "What's wrong, my friend? Please don't cry."

Korinna breathed deeply and smiled through her tears. "For the first time in a long time, I feel hopeful just at having you here, being you. I love that you need to order food, no matter what is going on around you. I know well your need to eat frequently and on schedule."

Elda reached across the table and patted Korinna's hand. She explained, "It helps me think. And it will get the waiter out of the way so we can talk."

Elda ordered a goat cheese salad and Beluga caviar blinis. Korinna ordered a Russian salad and a lamb pie. They both asked for vodkas since neither cared if they picked up a tail on the way back. Elda also ordered tea to warm herself up.

While they waited for the food, Korinna, nervously looked around and then, in her soft voice, asked, "Elda, can you help me get out of Russia?"

Elda replied in a voice just over a whisper, "I can, Korinna. What's going on?"

Trembling, Korinna answered, "A friend within the Kremlin has told me that the Russian government is eliminating loose ends and assassinating anyone familiar with the details of the dossier on the Russia and America scandal."

Nodding, Elda knowingly responded, "Ah yes, I have heard that a former KGB general was found dead in the back of his car in Moscow, a former media czar to the Russian president had been bludgeoned to death, and a former Russian agent was poisoned with a nerve agent in Salisbury, England. But what does that have to do with you, moy drug?"

Korinna looked around again and then whispered, "All of these men had had internal knowledge of the relationship between the Russian and the American presidents and helped compile the dossier on the American president. The original author and his family went into hiding until he was sure of his own protection through MI5."

Confused, Elda replied, "Yes, and even so, Russia has been proving that it could reach into the UK and murder those it wanted to. No one is safe. But what do those men have to do with you?"

Korinna snapped, "I am a translator for the Kremlin, Elda."

Still not connecting the dots, Elda asked, "Are you involved with these men, Korinna? How much danger are you in here?"

Korinna shook her finger at Elda. She said breathily, "I cannot tell you any details of the information I know. Suffice it to say that I know all the players. I have translated many top-secret meetings and have intimate knowledge of how Russia has worked to assassinate traitors across the globe and to manipulate other governments."

Elda showed her understanding and probed for more from Korinna, "Yes, I have heard that Russia has blackmailed the United States president."

Korinna's eyes darted around. She held a finger to her mouth. "I cannot say, but my information could incriminate the American president and cause his removal. Russia is not ready to lose their pawn yet."

Wanting to understand the depth of this danger, Elda peppered Korinna with questions: "So, this information also shows how Russia operates behind the scenes to manipulate countries? Does it also show how Britain and other countries have helped cover up the assassinations on their soil in order to not anger Russia? Is there a wide conspiracy with Russia in the background pulling the strings?"

Korinna shook her head and stated emphatically, "Again, I cannot tell you. It would put you in danger, and it would betray my country.

Exposing the truth to a wider audience could cause panic and could even cause major volatility in the stock market. They want me silenced. I am loyal and would never give out the information. But they have no guarantee of that."

Elda peered around the restaurant. She lowered her voice even further. "What do you need?"

"I need to leave Russia quickly, but I have no one I can trust, except you. I know you are in education, but I have also been taught that all Westerners know CIA members or are part of the CIA. I am hoping you know someone and can reach out and help me escape."

"There are people I can contact." Elda's mind raced, calculating the ways to save her friend. She motioned to their full plates. "Enjoy your meal, Korinna. There is no guarantee we will be eating this well in the days to come."

They worked their way through the generous portions of food, topping it all off with chocolate cake and Irish coffee. By then, Elda had figured out the next steps for the problem at hand.

"How long do we have, my friend?" Elda asked.

"I think it's a matter of weeks," Korinna answered. "They are watching me closely, and I am no longer able to travel out of the country. They claim it's a paperwork issue, but I know my papers are in order."

"Okay. Meet me tomorrow in the Novodevichy Cemetery. It's okay if you are watched. We will want them to overhear part of our conversation. Just follow my lead. Bring your passport and money, just in case," Elda instructed. "I'm not sure how quickly I can get plans to extract you in place, but do carry those on you at all times now, in case we have to move quickly. In the meantime, do you remember how we used to talk about others at the conferences without them knowing we were making fun of them? We will need to use that same way of talking to distract attention when we are being observed."

Korinna flagged down the waiter. *"Prover'te, pozhaluysta."*

"Spasibo, Korinna." Elda thanked Korinna as she paid for the two of them. Elda was always struck by how kind and generous her friend was. *"Vy khoroshiy drug."*

"You are a good friend too, Elda. Thank you."

As Elda and Korinna walked out of the café, Elda was taken aback at the sight of Aurelio sliding out of a Yandex Taxi black car. She had been informed he was in Moscow, but she was surprised to see how old he'd become. She would always think of him as the annoying younger brother who photobombed himself into every picture and talked incessantly about himself. A wave of sadness came over her at what a pitiful specimen he had become, when he'd had so much potential as a child. She dismissed the emotion. He had no compassion for others, and she'd considered him dead to her when he'd lost his ability to relate to the real world. He was off to the left and muttering to himself, intently paying the driver, who seemed nervous and anxious to move on.

"Korinna. Quick. Let's turn away from here. That's my half-brother Aurelio."

***

Aurelio was the first to arrive at the Café Pushkin. He was angry at the driver, who didn't get his sense of humor. Aurelio thought himself quite charming and could never understand when someone didn't take to him right away. That driver, obviously, was stupid and too full of himself to hear well.

Natasha had told him that finding fault in others was his pattern. That Aurelio projected his insecurity and self-obsession on others and that he put others down to make himself feel good. He believed that she was wrong and just projecting her own issues onto him.

Aurelio checked his watch. Olav was late again. He muttered to himself, "Lazy bastard no longer has a job, but he has enough money to live the good life in Russia. He'll never be important like I am." Although, it was harder to be an important man in Russia than when Aurelio arrived. These days, more people had money, and the expats were being pushed out.

His hands shook, and he wished he had more cocaine on him, or perhaps weed. His friends would have some, however, and they would be here soon.

Aurelio stopped in the bathroom on his way in and caught sight of his pasty face in the mirror. He admired his reflection and told it, "What a handsome man you are." His yellowing teeth were framed by his pale, pink lips. When he was younger, his face was almost pretty, but it was no longer pretty or young. Sweat ran down his armpits and back, and he wondered why the café was so hot.

He exited the men's room and was immediately seated at his table. After surveying his surroundings, he flagged down the waiter and ordered a scotch. Drinking scotch made him feel important. It was as if he could embody his father just by drinking the same drink. Life was all about making money, and Aurelio couldn't fathom why people did things that didn't make them much money. His drug use had stripped away any sense of charity, human kindness, and connection, true, but he figured he hadn't had any help in his life, so he had no reason to help others.

"Olav! William! Over here!" Aurelio waved at them, spilling his scotch onto the green tablecloth.

A waiter appeared and changed the tablecloth as Aurelio stood to shake Olav and William's hands. The three had worked together at a multinational company headquartered in Oslo and had handled the sales region that included Russia. When Olav's marriage had failed, he'd taken Aurelio's advice to become an expat and live the life of booze, women, and money; after his divorce, he'd moved to Moscow. William still worked for the Oslo company. He was in Moscow on business, which was the excuse for them to get together and party, as in the old days. Aurelio hoped that Olav had arranged a night of drugs and prostitutes, as he often had in the past.

"Aurelio! Here, man, take this."

Aurelio's hands shook as he accepted from Olav a small vial of white powder passed under the table.

"Thanks, man." Aurelio excused himself to go back to the bathroom. Now the night had begun. In a stall, he laid out two lines on top of the toilet tank and quickly snorted them up. That familiar rush and power and invincibility returned as the cocaine hit the back of his nose. He wet a finger and slid it across the top of the toilet and then sucked his finger clean to get all the powder. He returned to the table to start the celebration of debauchery and old friendship.

***

On the walk from the metro to her hotel, Elda stopped at a bench in the park and took off her boot. While replacing her footwear, she shoved a white Kleenex in between the slat and the back of the bench. Once back in her hotel room, she called for room service to bring up a bottle of Georgian red wine. Although she was expecting it, the knock on the door startled her. She peeked out the spyhole and viewed a large, fit waiter with a gold chain around his neck.

"*Tvoya vinnaya*, madam?" He stepped into the room and closed the door.

Elda grimaced and rubbed her sore hip in an exaggerated gesture.

Yuri shrugged and mouthed, "*I'm sorry.*"

Elda nodded and grinned and asked to see the wine. As she grasped the bottle, she slipped a note into Yuri's hand. Elda approved the wine and reached into her wallet to hand him some rubles.

"*Spasibo. Vot vash chayevyye.*" She thanked him and handed him his tip.

"*Spasibo*, madam. Go with God," Yuri replied.

Chapter Five

30 November, 2018

The next morning, after a breakfast of buttery scrambled eggs, toast, and a delicious pot of tea, Elda went for a brisk walk by the river. The air was cold, yet clear. She could see the clouds moving in, however; the forecast had called for more snow. She periodically stopped to adjust her scarf and turn slightly so she could check on anyone following her. They were trying to be discreetly obvious, ensuring she knew they were observing her. However, these were the watchers she could easily see. Was that all there were, or just all they wanted her to know about?

When she returned to her room, Sobaka was propped up on the pillows, reading a map. She reached under the mattress and found a rail schedule and map of the railway lines and a shipping schedule from the port of Riga to Hamburg, Germany, as well as a shipping order for containers, gas turbines, and cars.

So, she would be smuggling Korinna via train to the border. There, Korinna would cross over into

Latvia and continue to Riga, where the train's shipment would transfer to a cargo ship on the Samskip line toward Hamburg. The trip at sea would take four days and six hours, weather permitting. The train ride from Moscow to Riga would take an additional sixteen hours. The Russian rail lines, RXhD, were state owned and tightly monitored. The cargo container would leave the Rizhsky railway station located at Rizhskaya Square. It would have to cross the border from Russia, so the paperwork for the cargo needed to be impeccable.

There was little time to pull this all together. The timing needed to be just right too, so that those looking for Korinna would look in the wrong direction. Korinna's husband, Egor, and their two little Troodle dogs, Dasha and Sasha, also needed to be brought to safety.

How in the world would she pull this operation off?

Egor would be easy to keep safe, since he was currently in Canada on a music tour. Egor played violin for the Russian Philharmonic Moscow City Symphony, and he would be overseas for another three weeks. There would have to be some planning, but removing him was easier to stage than if he were in Russia.

Elda memorized the schedules and other information. The ashtray in the room was rather small for burning all that paper, so she burned it, slowly, piece by piece, in the sink, keeping the smoke to a minimum. She ran the water and cleaned all traces. She calculated time and logistics and slipped an encrypted note of requests under the mattress.

She then bundled up in her long, black, wool coat, sheepskin gloves, and her favorite fur hat, which was reversible, with long flaps that pulled down over her ears and clipped together at the chin. She'd purchased it many years ago on her first trip to Russia, when she'd discovered a wool watch cap did not effectively cut the Moscow wind.

The wind whipped around her legs as she plodded flatfooted over the packed snow to the metro, on her way to Novodevichy Cemetery.

The front tail was missing. So there were only the two accompanying her. She needed to make sure she didn't lose them. They probably noted how ineffective they were yesterday when she lost them, and, hopefully, would pay more attention. She wanted them to see her meet with Korinna today, so that having dinner with Korinna tonight would be seen as a natural outcome of their accidental meeting.

Korinna often came to the Novodevichy Cemetery to lay flowers on the graves of some important men she had supported as a translator, so her being there today would not be seen as unusual.

***

Elda left the metro at the Sportivnaya station and ensured that she still had her tails behind her. She passed the three towers of the Novodevichy Convent, with the central gold tower sparkling in the sun. The two blue towers bookended the gold one, and their colors went well with the reddish brown and white of the building they grew out of. The plainness of the white structure with the aqua roof next to the red brick building accented the glory of the towers and their pointed tops and crosses. It was so wonderfully Russian in appearance. She wished she had time to explore the grounds and view the frescoes inside.

She entered the cemetery.

The gravestones there were more like monuments to the departed. The first time Elda had seen them, she was struck by how many cosmonauts had died in the Russian push to be the first in space. The cemetery held statues dressed in detailed space suits, commemorating those who hadn't made it into space or home from space. She hoped someday to see a stone for Laika, a heroic little dog sent into space during the Sputnik 2 mission. It was a one-way trip, but he deserved a stone too. The dog's sacrifice should be commemorated, along with the human ones!

Elda's favorite gravestone was a large hand that reached up out of the earth, holding a painter's palette. She would love to have that on her own gravesite, but unfortunately her Maine town regulations limited her to a small stone marker. Her other favorite was the black-and-white tower that supported a marble head that was the spitting image of Khrushchev. The name in Russian on the pedestal confirmed, sure enough, that was where he was buried.

Khrushchev and Kennedy were two larger-than-life figures from the news reports during Elda's childhood. Khrushchev declared in 1956, "*My vas pokhoronim*!" These words, "We will bury you," had sent chills down Elda's spine when her parents had mentioned the Communist threat coming from Russia and China. It was during these formative years of her life that the importance of keeping America strong in the face of Russian aggression and manipulation was instilled into Elda.

The cosmonauts were over to the right, but if she went straight on, she would be at the palette; farther on from that was Khrushchev's grave. She had arranged to bump into Korinna near the hand with the palette. She recognized Korinna one row over, bending down and setting flowers on a grave. When she straightened, there was no mistaking her long red coat and blond hair. Elda had tried to get Korinna to wear a hat, but she insisted that the Moscow cold didn't bother her. Well, it certainly made Elda feel colder to see Korinna's reddened ears.

"*Korinna, eto ty?*" Elda called out.

Korinna turned around and laughed at seeing her old friend. "Yes, it is I. My friend, Elda! What on Earth brings you to Russia?"

Elda ran up and hugged her. As they wandered around the cemetery, looking at and admiring the various gravestones, Korinna loudly told Elda about the background behind some of the famous men buried there. Elda answered her in a loud voice, while whispering to fill Korinna in on details about how she would be extracted from Russia. Korinna nodded and smiled, and occasionally they laughed, ostensibly sharing a joke.

As they parted, Elda called out, "*Do vstrechi v restorane otelya*!"

"Yes, my dear friend." Korinna replied, "Dinner at your hotel tonight, and we can catch up there!"

Elda returned to the metro with as much of a bounce in her step as the ice would allow. It was genuinely good to see Korinna, and she was hopeful this plan would work. She had only one pursuer remaining and figured the other one was trailing Korinna. Good! They would be confused for a while and then conclude that neither of them was a threat. She hoped.

She'd requested additional logistics and funds, since this operation was going to be a complex one with misdirection and plan changes. The most important thing was to get Korinna to the States and reunited with Egor, Sasha, and Dasha. But it was equally important that Elda get out of Russia and back to the States safely too.

She wished she had some backup on this mission, but she didn't want to spook Korinna, who was adamant that she would only deal with Elda. For a brief moment Elda wondered if she was being set up, and then she quickly dismissed that thought. Korinna would never do that to her. But Elda desperately needed more knowledge about who would be sent to eliminate Korinna. Anyone from

Elda's early days in Russia would no longer operate at that level and would more likely have a desk job.

But… could Tosh be involved? That thought scared her, and not much rattled Elda.

Toshchiy Chelovek, or "The Skinny Man," was a master at his craft. He was silent and deadly; a legend in the spy world. Although rumored to possess a rather underdeveloped muscular system, he was also said to be extremely strong. Elda had nicknamed him "The Amazing No-Muscles man," or "*Ne Muskulistyy*," and combined his names in her mind as Mr. Nemusk Tosh. Making up stories about these threats and giving them names was her way to deflect fearful lines of thinking.

***

30 November, 2018

Aurelio raised his head up off the pillow and then slowly lowered it as the light from the window beat through his eyeballs and pounded the top of his head. He groaned, reached for the glass of scotch on the coffee table, and took a large gulp from it. He saw the lipstick stains on the glass and briefly wondered whose glass it was. He checked his watch to see what day it was: Friday, the 30th. He gently rose to a sitting position on the couch and looked around to see if anyone else was stirring. He foggily remembered being in the hotel lobby where he, Olav, and William had selected prostitutes to come up to the men's room to have a ménage à trois—or rather, a ménage à six.

He and the other two men had sat in the hotel room waiting for the women. Olav had laid out some lines of coke, and Aurelio called room service for a large bottle of scotch while he raided the minibar. By the time the prostitutes arrived, Aurelio had been well lubricated with scotch. Again, he'd selected a brunette but instead found he was paired off with a blonde who disturbingly resembled Natasha. He'd drunk more to make the image go away; the rest of the night had disappeared from his memory.

He gingerly wandered toward the kitchenette to get something with caffeine in it. As he passed the bedroom door, he saw Olav sprawled out on the floor and William passed out on the bed. Olav's jacket was tossed by the bedroom door, and Aurelio rummaged through the pockets for some coke. Finding a small bottle of a white, powdery substance, he turned back to the living room, laid the powder out on the mirror, and snorted a couple of lines before returning to the kitchen to start the coffeepot. The rush cleared his head, but he still had no memory of the night's activities.

Returning to the living room, he plunked down his coffee cup and placed his laptop beside it. He went into the bathroom to pee and splash water on his face, finding his pants on the rug near the bathroom door. When he tugged them on, he checked his wallet to discover that a large amount of money was missing. He assumed the blonde had taken it for payment.

Well, I must have been really good to her, he told himself, angry that he had no memory of the night. He was sure he gave the blonde a good time. How could he not remember? It must be the mind manipulation that his brother and half-sister were doing on him. They obviously had techniques they'd learned as spies for the US government. He sat down at his computer to strike back at the two of them. His rambling insanity flowed from his brain through his fingers into emails that he rapidly sent.

Olav wandered from the bedroom into the bathroom.

Aurelio shoved his laptop to one side. "Hey, Olav, want me to order some breakfast?"

Olav grunted in reply, which Aurelio took for an affirmation, so he picked up the phone and ordered room service. Olav came out of the bathroom, picked up the small bottle by the mirror, and laid out more lines for the two of them.

"Great night, hey, Aurelio?"

"Fantastic! That blonde was great!"

"She sure was! After she must have finished with you, she came and joined us."

Aurelio forced a smile. "I was worn out after her!"

Olav slapped him on the back and gave him a thumbs-up. Inside, Aurelio seethed at his memory loss.

Chapter Six

1 December, 2018

Elda arrived early for breakfast at the hotel restaurant. The hostess, a stocky, pallid Russian, greeted her warmly and assigned Elda her favorite table, away from the kitchen doors. The violinist wandered around, already tuning up and checking the layout for his nightly serenade. After Korinna arrived for dinner, he would come over and play "Moscow Nights" for them. They had learned from past dinners there that if they requested this one song and tipped him handsomely, then he would leave them alone for the rest of the night. He played well but loudly.

Elda had already been in Moscow two days but still didn't have her plan ready to execute. Her requests to the CIA might take a couple of days to fulfill. Damn red tape. This was all taking too long. If there was already an order to kill Korinna, then every passing day raised the risk for both Elda and Korinna. She caught herself biting the dead skin from the sides of her fingertips and quickly pulled her hand away from her mouth. She commanded herself to relax. *Tonight will be a night for two longtime friends to kick back, appreciate each other's company and some good vodka.* The hotel was bugged in many places, and their words would be recorded and dissected, so they would not discuss the plans for Korinna's escape, but they could set the stage for additional meetings.

After breakfast, Elda again went for a snowy trek by the river, to see who was assigned to her. The wind whipped the snow sideways. Elda wrapped her scarf more firmly around the lower part of her face and snugged her fur hat around her chin, ensuring the built-in earmuffs landed securely over her ears. She loved the warmth of this fur hat, but it would be frowned upon if she wore it in some places in the United States, especially Cambridge, Massachusetts. She did not want to have paint thrown at her for wearing real fur, but it was the warmest hat she owned, and in Russia she fit right in.

With only one operative in front of her and another behind, they must be feeling secure that she was sticking to her morning routine, so they had not assigned the second rear tail. By now, she recognized their faces and had given them names: Timur was the big, burly one; Grisha was the nervous with the darting eyes and twitchy demeanor; and Konstantin was the one who stuck around all the time. Konstantin, with his erect posture, round glasses, and long greatcoat, was clearly the leader. It amused her to make up stories about her watchers. Timur was ex-FSB and the muscle of the team, Grisha was newly assigned and terrified of messing up, and Konstantin was the brains. It was handy how consistent and predictable Russians could be. She warned herself not to let that lull her into complacency. Anyone could be reporting on her movements.

As she strode along, she continued to flesh out the plan and routes for Korinna's extraction. She wished she could get another agent to sanity-check her plans, but she was on her own for this one, at least until Korinna trusted the plan enough to accept another agent. There should be more support from the consulate once she reached Germany.

The bitter cold made her pick up her pace, and Grisha struggled to keep up with her, but Konstantin kept a good distance in front. He would occasionally turn, appearing to admire the river view, but he was gauging the distance between them while trying to appear that he was just out for a stroll, much as Elda was. Elda amused herself with the image of stopping him and asking if he wanted to walk with her in the mornings.

When Elda neared the hotel, she took off her gloves and blew her nose. In the process, she dropped a glove. Bending to pick it up, she tucked the Kleenex into the snow by a granite column that connected the railings beside the river. She stood, and after making a show of brushing off the glove and putting it back on, she continued to her hotel.

There. Hopefully, Yuri would see the signal. Back in the hotel room, she set her watch alarm and paced back and forth. She kept stopping and holding her fingers to her forehead as she puzzled out the details of Korinna's and her canine companions' extractions.

Her watch alarm rang, and she called room service for lunch. Not long afterward, someone knocked on the door. Elda peeked through the spyhole; the large waiter stood outside with a tray on the cart.

"Dobryy den'."

"Dobryy den'. Here is your lunch, madam."

"Spasibo."

Elda closed the door behind him and motioned for him to place the tray on the desk, where she'd left a sheet of paper with instructions. He would memorize the instructions before placing the tray on top of them.

"Sobaki? Ya lyublyu sobak!" Yuri seemed to realize he had spoken out loud, glancing at Elda with

wide eyes and a puzzled look as to how to correct his error.

"*Ya tozhe lyublyu sobak. Eto foto moyego shchenka doma*!" Elda said as she, with a deft hand, picked up a picture of Vee from the desk and showing it to Yuri. She had quickly removed it from her wallet while looking for money for the tip.

"*Ona milaya,*" Yuri said, picking up the conversation and chuckling to himself.

"Spasibo." Elda handed him a sizeable tip and placed the picture back into her wallet.

"*Spasibo,*" Yuri said with real relief and gratitude. He pocketed the wad of cash and, pushing the tray, opened the door and headed to the elevators.

Elda shut the door behind him, smiling, since she'd observed that the two "sobaki" would be in a dog lover's hands. Korinna would be pleased.

***

After a dinner of blinis and caviar, Korinna and Elda sat in the hotel bar and amused themselves with the antics of the men and the prostitutes and the elevators. They had determined that the elevators were programmed so that there was always one at the lobby level and always one at the balcony level. The third one was free to move to any floor for the other hotel guests.

Korinna and Elda toasted their friendship with shots of vodka followed by large glasses of water. They talked about their "jobs" in vague terms and mused where the future would take them as they moved toward retirement in their respective countries. Both agreed that they would like to focus on self-care and exercise, as well as pursue creative endeavors in the future. Near the end of the evening, Elda and Korinna arranged an outing to Izmailovsky Market so that Elda could pick up more souvenirs. It would be easy to talk more freely in the open-air of the market.

Elda caught sight of, through the glass of the third elevator, Aurelio stepping on with two others, so she delayed leaving and let them go first. Aurelio was disheveled. His face was pallid, and he had huge, dark circles under his eyes. Frankly, he did not look well at all.

"Honestly, I have no sympathy for him," Elda said. "He chose his life; he did it all to himself. And there's no way to help him, even if I could."

"*Da, ya znayu.* I agree there is nothing you can do, my friend."

"Yes, but… it's unfortunate." He'd seen her suggestions to get help through a paranoid lens, assuming she meant to undermine him. It only drove him further away. Her role now was to ensure he did no more damage to the United States through his manic rage and paranoia.

Elda walked out the doors with Korinna and down the steps of the hotel. Korinna and Elda hugged their goodbyes once outside the hotel. Elda whispered into Korinna's ear, "All is being arranged. Trust what I tell you. Egor and the troodles will be safe. More tomorrow."

Korinna sauntered off with her red coattails sailing in the strong breeze.

***

Korinna climbed the narrow, cluttered stairs to her apartment, dodging spare toys and small pieces of furniture. Because of Egor and Korinna's elite status, their apartment was slightly larger than the others and had a small balcony off the living room. Jutting out from the corner of the top floor, it had more windows and light than the interior apartments. Since it stuck out from the rest of the building, there was no noise through the thin walls from the other tenants.

The two deadbolts clicked open as she unlocked them. She questioned if these locks would keep an assassin out. Perhaps tonight she would jam a chair under the doorknob.

Dasha and Sasha jumped up on her legs. Korinna nervously checked the narrow hallway past the bedroom/study, the bathroom on the right, and the living/dining room on the left of the kitchen.

She and Egor had added additional cabinets for storage in their small kitchen. It had an electric stove left over from the Soviet era, which still worked well, and a small refrigerator. The cadence of the dogs' nails hitting the linoleum floor made her pulse race. She needed to get them groomed and clip their nails. Careful not to alert the bugs in the walls, she silently calmed herself. *Get a cup of tea and relax. There's nothing you can do if someone comes after you.*

She inhaled deeply to calm her heart rate, put on the kettle for tea, and spooned some food into the dogs' dishes. Then she sat at the tiny kitchen table to wait for the kettle to boil. She examined her small, homey kitchen with a fond smile. She had painted their cupboards a warm off-white, and Egor had hung hooks on the walls for their pans. It was a cozy spot where they could spend their mornings together before going to work, then return to in the evenings to decompress over a cup of tea. A wave of melancholy rolled over her. Where would home be for them in the future?

Korinna jumped when the teakettle whistled shrilly. *Silly goose. It is only the kettle. Breathe!* As she poured her cup of tea, she felt that as long as she, Egor, and the pups were together, she would be all right. She sat in the kitchen with Dasha on her lap and Sasha on her feet, keeping them warm. She was careful not to speak any of her thoughts out loud, since the walls had ears—or, as Elda liked to say, they "crawled with bugs."

Korinna stepped down the hall, carrying her cup of tea, while her dogs pranced around her feet all the way to the bedroom. As she passed the double bed she and Egor shared, she straightened out her grandmother's knitted throws, continuing on to the desk where her computer sat. Nothing of interest was stored on her computer. She reached under the desk and triggered a hidden compartment that popped open. She reached in and found her Russian passport and one that listed her as Scandinavian, as well as a significant number of American dollars. She would be in dire trouble if these IDs were discovered. She reached farther in and found a Scandinavian passport for Egor also. She vowed to carry them in a hidden wallet inside her clothing at all times, since she was unsure of the timing of her extraction. She speculated on how they would smuggle out the dogs.

Korinna began the nightly struggle to get the harnesses, coats, and leashes on each twirling little dog. They gently nipped at her fingers as she fastened the metal clasps. Her long fingers felt stiff with the onset of arthritis, and she wondered if the dogs were taking advantage of that and teasing her. She laughed at how silly it was that two little dogs had so much control over their human.

Finally they were ready. Korinna buttoned up her own coat, and the three of them maneuvered through the hallway and across the street to the park. Korinna checked her pocket for her doggie bags. Sasha liked to be expansive in where she left her droppings. One bag never sufficed. Korinna sighed, missing Egor even more, since the two of them had much laughter over Sasha's and Dasha's habits.

Leaving the park, she spotted a candy wrapper and picked it up. *This trash would never have been allowed in the past.* Although politically some things had stayed the same, there were cracks in the totality of governance that she didn't agree with. And then her mind jumped to the fact that this regime was trying to eliminate her and a number of other people.

Some things had not changed much since the Stalin era. *The treatment of human life has degraded throughout the world. Is there any country left that truly respects individuals and treats them with dignity and respect?* Sighing, she pocketed the wrapper and turned toward her apartment. She nervously glanced around. The night shadows ominously danced across the street.

Chapter Seven

2 December, 2018

Anatoly sat at his kitchen table and methodically arranged the tools of his trade. On the right side of the table, he placed his 9mm PYa beside his Makarov pistol, flanked on the other side by his MP-412 REX .357 Magnum revolver. He fondly stroked the .357 Magnum, his favorite, as he laid it on the table. He added to the collection his MSS Vul silent pistol and NRS-2 survival knife, with a single-shot pistol round hidden in the hilt. And then he placed his VSS Vintorez silent sniper rifle across the top of the table. He prided himself in keeping these weapons in tip-top condition, but he rarely used them, since he more often preferred the close-contact stealth killing he had learned as a SPETSNAZ operative. He touched each gun, moving each a fraction of a centimeter to check that they lined up. He lifted onto the table a worn but well-maintained black leather satchel that resembled a large photographer's bag with many pockets.

Anatoly reached into a pocket and extracted a number of implements that could be used for choking a victim. He particularly liked the wire noose that slipped easily over his victim's head and quickly cut off the airway without applying much pressure. He also liked the variant that was hidden inside a tie, allowing Anatoly to slip his tie off and over a victim's head, then tie it back on his own neck, ensuring he left no evidence at the crime scene. He smiled as he remembered how useful these implements had been.

He carefully searched the interior pocket and drew out a zipped, black leather case. Inside, on the right side, were vials of poisons that had different effects on those injected with them. One mimicked the effects of a heart attack; another caused a stroke; a third caused a diabetic coma; a fourth caused a catastrophic asthma attack; and the last—well, that one caused instant paralysis. On the left side of the case were ways to administer these poisons, including a ring, which could be popped open to inject someone discreetly. Some of the technology in front of Anatoly had been in use since the Cold War. He liked the tried and true.

Anatoly reached into the bag again and drew out a collection of knives, from switchblades to skinny stilettos. He sat at the table and methodically sharpened each one. He confirmed the mechanisms that opened them worked, along with the throwing mechanisms of those that could be fired from a hidden arm holster. He then moved on to his collection of guns and carefully cleaned each one.

After he stowed his equipment, he checked the bag for his fake IDs and assorted currencies. He never knew where the Kremlin would send him with only a few moments' notification. Though a freelance assassin, he worked exclusively for the Russian government. He hoped that the security of a steady job was not making him soft, but he liked the predictability of the jobs the government assigned him. Most were quick in-and-out hits. The efficiency and routine satisfied him.

Anatoly's last check was to pull out the monitoring equipment and validate that the receivers still worked. Anatoly routinely did these checks every few months, but he sensed unrest; his services might be needed sooner rather than later. He stretched and strolled into his kitchen to make some food. As he passed the open door of his bathroom, he caught a glimpse of his reflection in the mirror and paused to take in the view.

Anatoly was a large, solidly built, muscular man. As he flexed his biceps, his shirt strained to contain the bulges. His collar was left unbuttoned to accommodate his thick neck. The soft silk was stretched tight over his pectoral muscles and smoothly tucked into his pants, where his belt cinched around his flat abdomen. Although he could not see below the beltline in the mirror, he looked down at his powerful thighs in his black slacks and firmly planted feet in steel-capped shoes. Anatoly was a killing machine. He did not always need weapons and had successfully snapped necks with his bare hands.

Anatoly had grown up in the Communist regime of the Soviet Union. Early on, his emotional tests showed he had almost no empathy for others, and he bullied smaller children in the schoolyard to get what he wanted. His muscle-to-weight ratio destined him to develop into a powerful man. The system funneled him into a program that trained KGB agents as well as assassins. Often the two overlapped, as they had for Anatoly. When they'd sent him out to do his first hit, he'd done so quickly and efficiently, and it was clear he enjoyed it.

Anatoly's love for order and routine made him the perfect soldier, and his lack of need for sex from either men or women, combined with his distaste for drink or drugs, made him hard to corrupt. His perfect record on missions soon brought him to the attention of the handlers in the Kremlin, who recruited him as one of their elite force and global assassins. He was trained to think in and speak many languages, and his hand-to-hand combat skills were refined during that time.

It's a good life, Anatoly thought, smiling at himself in the mirror.

He'd recently felt the buildup of internal pressure and near anxiety that came to him when he paused too long between jobs. They saved him for special operations, but he really wished his handler at the Kremlin would call him soon. He respected his handler, who had been a superior operative himself.

One day I will ask you, to learn from you, Anatoly spoke in his head to his handler. *Skoro, soon,* he added, aware that his handler was aging and that there weren't that many more years that he would be around, and probably not that many more years that Anatoly himself would be an operative in the field.

***

Elda ran down the stairs to the gym—these operations were always an adrenaline rush. She threw herself into her usual vigorous morning workout routine: forty push-ups, thirty crunches, twenty one-legged squats per leg, ten full circuits of bear crawling around the room, followed by a three-minute plank, after which she transitioned up into Downward Dog and stood fully upright into Tree Pose.

The empty gym had only one way in or out. Elda kept one eye on the door as she performed her routine. Her muscles tightened up too much from having to be alert, so the exercises weren't as effective as when she was more relaxed. She quickly finished and jogged back upstairs.

While toweling off her short, brown hair, she jumped ahead to the day's logistics. She would take her morning walk after breakfast and then catch the metro to Izmailovsky Market. Transferring information with Korinna would be tricky, since like yesterday, she wasn't planning to lose her tails today. She wanted them to overhear select pieces of her conversation with Korinna.

She dressed quickly in her Moscow-style, drab-colored long sleeve T-shirt, overlaid by a long-sleeved flannel shirt that she tucked into her long underwear and black jeans. She cinched the jeans tight at her waist. She was lucky she had inherited a flat stomach from both parents, and her daily workouts gave her a six-pack on top of that. She pulled on her warm UGG boots and laid out her long wool coat, scarf, and fur hat to be worn after breakfast.

***

Tosh gathered the pictures and information on the women. The woman with the brown hair was familiar to him. She would not still be an operative, however. That was many, many years ago. He took out a magnifying glass to see the passport picture more clearly. Silently, he cursed being old and not being able to see as well as he used to.

Tosh scrolled through his mental pictorial Rolodex of contacts from his missions. *Aga! That's it!* He recalled being in Moscow and doing a simplistic shakedown of a possible American spy, while others searched her room. The woman had called her contact at the embassy and arranged to go over to her apartment for dinner. They were already keeping an eye on all tourists, but that action had flagged her for more follow-up. Although he had only been in operations for a few years, he had shown an acute ability to evaluate who was a threat and who wasn't.

He'd found the woman waiting for a taxi and offered her a ride to her hotel. He could see her weighing whether she could say no. She correctly assessed the situation and slid into the car. That showed that she had a certain level of awareness that many tourists lacked. He'd sensed her size him up and take his measure. He could tell from their discussion that he would not get any information out of her easily. When enough time had passed for her room to have been thoroughly searched, he turned the car around and dropped her off at her hotel.

At the time, he'd guessed that she was about ten years younger than he was, in her early twenties, military or ex-military, possibly CIA. He liked her and thought that when she matured, with more experience, she might be a force to be reckoned with, but he'd never had the opportunity to deal with her again.

He frowned as he scrutinized her picture. "And here you are again . . ." He continued talking to the picture, perhaps hoping to get some answers. "But why are you here? Are you on an operation? Or are you, as you are pretending, just reliving memories with an old friend? I find that hard to believe. The timing of your visit is suspicious."

He sighed. No response was forthcoming. He rubbed his furrowed brow and reflected on how to get more answers.

"I cannot let you interfere with this operation."

***

She sat facing Tosh, her eyes alight with anticipation. Her hands nervously tied and untied her long brown ponytail as she listened to his instructions.

91

He spoke tersely and quickly. "You will take one of the black cars and go to the hotel and pick her up as she heads out to the metro."

She nodded, agreeing. "*Da dyadya.*"

"You will drive her around and make small talk for a while."

"*Da dyadya.*"

Tosh's grey eyes bore into her, and he shook his finger, instructing her further. "Now, the next part is vital to get right. You will say, 'So, what do you do?' You will use exactly those words and that tone. *Ponimayu?*"

"Yes, I understand."

"And if she asks you what you do, you will reply with the words, 'I am a student at the university.'"

"*Da, ya ponimayu.*"

Tosh waved his hand at his office door and commanded, "Go now before you miss her."

Tosh sat back and gave a satisfied smirk at the closing door. That would rattle her.

But that woman was strong. He would send a second volley. He reached into his file cabinet and pulled out two folders. No, he would save him for later. Brute strength was needed here. Yaromir would do. That would send a clear message. And it would be interesting to see how she reacted. It would help Tosh measure her as an opponent... if she survived.

***

Where were her tails? The one day she needed those three to overhear her and Korinna's conversations, they were missing. She stood on the hotel stairs, biting her fingers and pondering her next move, when an unmarked black car pulled up and the driver beckoned to her. *Oh no, not again.* She moved, seemingly through concrete, toward the car. The passenger-side window slid downward. The driver motioned for Elda to get in.

Elda hesitated, "You must be mistaken. I am on my way to the metro."

"I'll take you there."

"It's a short walk."

"I will take you there. Get in," the driver commanded.

93

Curious, Elda acceded, "Ah, well, if it's no bother."

Elda slipped into the front seat and wished that she hadn't given up smoking.

They took off toward the metro.

Elda thought it was at least a good sign that they were heading where she wanted to go. She inquired, "So, may I have your name?"

"No."

"Hum, how about, what is your occupation?"

"I am a student at the university."

Elda's eyesight blurred, and her head felt like it might explode. It was all she could do to retain her composure and ask, "Really?"

"Yes, and what do you do?"

Elda played out the script. "I'm a teacher. I teach mathematics."

"Really?"

"Yes." Regaining her composure, Elda probed, "Do you come from Moscow?"

"Yes."

"Have you lived here long?"

"All of my life."

"You remind me of someone," Elda commented, tapping her fingers on her knee.

"Really?"

"Yes."

They pulled up in front of the metro. Konstantin and Timur were positioned near the entrance.

Elda jumped out and leaned back in through the open window, "Thanks for the lift. The ride was informative."

"I'm sure we'll meet again."

***

Korinna froze in place. She was being pulled in two different directions. Dasha was trying to chase a squirrel, while Sasha was wagging her tail at an approaching stranger.

"*Izvinite*," he said as he approached her. "*Ya zametil, chto u tebya dve sobaki.*"

"Da u menya dve sobaki..." Korinna cautiously replied, thinking it strange to be talking about her having two dogs.

He handed her a business card and let her know that he groomed dogs and would give her a first-time customer discount if she wanted to use his services. Strange coincidence. She had been thinking of having the dogs groomed, but she hadn't told anyone or even said it out loud. She inspected his card and asked if he had any recent customers he could use as references. There were many scams in Russia, and if he wasn't reputable, she could lose both money and her dogs.

"Da, Elda moya rekomendatsiya," he answered in a low tone.

She almost shouted, "Elda is your reference?" back at him but kept her face impassive. *"Ya pozvonyu vam."* She promised to call him.

He nodded and marched away. She considered it a good sign that the dogs hadn't barked at him, but then saw that they had found, and inhaled, a piece of bread on the ground. They'd left mere traces of crumbs and had guilty looks on their little faces. Two pairs of remorseful brown eyes peered up at her from under their shaggy brows.

Korinna reentered her apartment and left the card on the kitchen table, then cut herself a big slab of brown bread and slathered it with butter and jam. It would be cold out, and she would use up a lot of energy.

She grabbed her long red coat, placed a warm scarf around her head, and drew on her black leather gloves. On the way out, she patted the dogs and told them to be good. The next-door neighbor would be in to walk the dogs again around noon.

With her long-legged strides, Korinna moved at a fast pace to the metro. Behind her was a slender, nervous-looking young man she hadn't noticed before. Korinna didn't mind. She was often followed and considered it part of her job. Elda had told her that it was okay to have the surveillance today. The wind had picked up, and gusts of snow circled around her. *Oh, it* will *be cold at the market.*

She realized she had thought that in English and not Russian, and she laughed at herself. One of the side effects of being a translator was thinking in different languages. On a trip she'd made to Spain, in which she had traveled to three different countries just before, her brain had been so foggy that she'd ordered her meal in French and hadn't realized it until she'd seen the puzzled look on the waiter's face.

Talking with Elda again had brought her mastery of English forward.

Would she ever see Russia again? Most of all, would she be able to flee Russia?

***

Elda and Korinna met at the entrance of the market and hugged warmly. They wandered around the outer edge of the market, pausing to view each artist's work and look at the various antiques and musical instruments for sale. Each time they stopped, Elda took note of the positions of the tails and looked for additional ones. Whenever she and Korinna were out of listening range of them and of the vendors, Elda filled her in on the plans in a low voice, while adding in a louder tone bits and pieces of a joke. Korinna periodically laughed out loud, and Elda waved her hands in large gestures to emphasize her stories.

Once back in hearing range of the tails, Elda asked Korinna, "Can you get a couple of days off and go to St. Petersburg with me before I go home? I would love to see it, especially since you've told me so much about its history."

"When will that be?" Korinna asked.

"I don't yet know, but I'll let you know in a few days—probably toward the end of the month."

Korinna nodded. "*Da*. I can get a few days holiday to tour St. Petersburg with you."

When out of earshot, Korinna said she needed to have the dogs groomed and that a nice man approached her in the park this morning, and amazingly he was a dog groomer.

"*Kak chudesno*! What a nice coincidence! Perhaps you can have them groomed while we are in St. Petersburg? Can your neighbor handle that?" Elda asked.

"*Da*."

"*Khorosho*." Elda winked subtly at Korinna, who laughed loudly in return.

Back in earshot, Elda asked if Korinna wanted to do dinner again, in a coded way that meant Korinna should answer *not tonight*. Having dinner together too often would raise suspicions.

"*Nyet. Ne segodnya*."

"Perhaps toward the end of the week then."

"*Da*."

"I have to find the artist who does those wonderful wooden paintings. Will you come see them with me?"

"Yes!"

Elda briefly filled Korinna in on the plans for Egor and Sasha and Dasha. Korinna, although usually pale from the long Russian winters, turned white as she listened to what would happen with Egor.

"Not to worry." Elda patted Korinna on the back and said loudly, "Look! There are the wooden paintings I like so much. I have to buy more to take home with me!"

The two friends explored the crafts for a few more minutes, until Elda felt her toes would fall off from the cold wind and from standing so long in the snow.

"Let's go get some lunch," Elda said, "and I can tell you my story of the violin I once bought at this market."

***

Leaving the restaurant, Elda counted three tails again, with Grisha focused on Korinna.

Aha, that's where he went. It was a good sign they were reusing the same three for both Elda and Korinna—they could not yet be suspicious of Korinna's impending defection. Sure enough, when Korinna and Elda parted ways, Konstantin and Timur fell in behind Elda, while Grisha continued with Korinna.

Striding toward the Metro, Elda felt the hair on the nape of her neck bristle. She glanced back. Konstantin and Timur had fallen off and were walking away. That couldn't be good. She looked ahead. A large man stalked in her direction. *Oh crap.* Elda wheeled around and took off in a sprint. She flagged down a taxi and slid in as the large man reached into an idling car and pulled the driver out and jumped in.

Crap.

"Head north, *pozhaluysta.*"

"*Kuda?*"

"The Vodnok Sea Club, and fast." She threw a large number of rubles into the front seat.

The taxi shot into traffic. Elda glanced out the back window. The other car was keeping pace with them. They blasted through the National Park, and the second car moved in to tailgate position. Closer and closer.

"Faster, *pozhaluysta*!"

"*Nyet*. This is it."

The car behind them tapped the taxi's back bumper.

"*Der'mo*!"

"I will pay for repairs. Lose him." Elda threw more money into the front seat. Traffic had picked up. The driver wove in and out of traffic, passing cars at a dizzying pace. The large man had fallen back slightly but was still on their tail. Elda made a quick phone call. Satisfied that her arrangements were in place, she started praying that she would live long enough to evade her pursuer.

The taxi screeched into the Sea Club parking lot, and before it stopped, Elda had hopped out and hightailed it to the piers on the Moscow Canal. She cut through a tent, wove her way around a wedding reception, and dashed out the other side. Behind her she heard screams and tables crashing over—the thug must still be on her six.

Elda reached her waiting jet ski, hopped on, and headed out of the inlet and north into the

Klyazma River. She heard the distinctive noise of a second jet ski pursuing her. *Damn it, Elda, do you even know where you're going?* She opened her throttle but knew she was losing ground. She turned sharply to take a run at him with her jet ski.

The brute continued full bore in a direct line at Elda, and when she turned suddenly at the last second, he sharply turned his watercraft into hers. The impact threw her into the water. He took a sweeping turn and aimed straight for her. She took a deep breath and dove. The wake of the ski drove her down deeper in the water. She bobbed up to the top gasping for air only to see the attacker's jet ski zooming toward her a second time. She inhaled and dove again, kicking toward the shore. When she came up for air, she saw the bastard turning to run her over a third time. Again, she filled her lungs as he came at her, and then dove. This time she came up near a dock and pulled herself to hide under it. She watched through the dock legs as he circled in search of her. After what seemed an eternity, he chugged South.

Elda waited under the dock for several minutes, shivering from the cold water and the shock. Composing herself, she swung up and onto the dock to start her trek back to the hotel, stopping at the Admiral Marine Club to grab a towel. Anger set in as she wrapped the towel around her shoulders. They were trying to scare her off, but they would have to do better than that.

***

Back at the hotel, Aurelio staggered out as she walked in. She was certain he didn't have a clue who she was. She wanted to avoid him and the drama he brought with him. Upstairs in the room, Sobaka was arranged as reading Elda's Moscow tourist manual, opened to Gorky Park, with Sobaka's paw on the skating rink. She picked up the pad of hotel notepaper and peeled off the first sheet. She held it up to the light. The impression of the number ten shone faintly on the paper. So, she would find out more tomorrow morning at ten, in Gorky Park, by the skating rink.

Khorosho. Her Russian was certainly coming back to her! *Good, good, good...* she repeated in her head.

She threw off her wet clothes and took a hot shower, then turned on the TV and dialed in BBC to fill the room with English and stave off the loneliness that flooded her at night when traveling. She missed Dawn and Vee, though there was so much unresolved with Dawn right now. And she missed the familiarity of the people, food, and culture of the

States. Most of all, she wanted to relax. She sighed again. She couldn't wait to get home.

Being home will be a while from now, so get rid of those ideas. She needed to be tough for the rest of this mission.

***

Aurelio stepped out of the hotel door to meet Olav and William, who had been out souvenir shopping. Aurelio was unable to muster enough energy to join them. Plus, he had no one back home he wanted to give presents to. Natasha had enough of his money and things already.

He caught a glimpse of a woman in a brown fur cap climbing up the hotel stairs, and he foggily questioned where he had seen her before. He shrugged. She was too old for his tastes anyway. He patted his pocket to affirm he had his drugs with him and flagged down a taxi to take him to the restaurant. He could do a line in the back of the cab, on the way there.

Aurelio's mind wandered to his brother and his half-sister again. *How could Carlo and Elda accuse me of mental illness? They told me he needed a drug rehab program! Me! They've gone insane! They must have been projecting their insecurities*

The gray Moscow scenery, punctuated by lights of various restaurants, flew by. Before he even had time to snort a line of coke, they arrived at the restaurant.

Aurelio absentmindedly paid his driver and wandered into the restaurant, stopping at the bathroom. He pulled out his coke. He would miss the free drugs his friends always shared. Back home in St. Petersburg, he usually ended up having to pay Yuri for his drugs. He decided to not offer what he had to Olav and William but to see if they would offer him more for tonight's activities. He was not looking forward to returning home to Natasha's constant nagging and their high-volume arguments. It was a good thing they lived in the penthouse apartment—that way they were not disturbing their neighbors with their almost daily fights.

He was sick of Natasha again, but as long as he stayed married to her, she would not kill him. She and Yuri both plotted against him. But Aurelio had made sure Natasha knew he did not carry any life insurance, so he was worth more to her alive than dead. He'd signed the apartment over to her. That was a mistake, but she did not have the codes to his offshore Cayman Island accounts, and he planned on keeping it that way.

Aurelio eyed his reflection in the mirror and jumped, thinking that someone was there trying to attack him. He relaxed when he realized it was only a reflection. These days, he often startled at phantom movements that were only artifacts of his decaying brain. He shook it off, and he brightened as he felt strength from the coke flowing through his system. He entered the dining room and saw his friends at the table. *Yes! I'm ready for another night of fun!*

***

"Dead?" Tosh fixed his steely gray eyes on Yaromir, who shrugged. "Perhaps, perhaps not. I didn't see a body float up, but if alive, she should be very worried. Well done, Yaromir. We will see if she shows up for her morning walk tomorrow. You are dismissed."

Something told him she would show. If so, he'd know more about her mettle, and they could play this out further. It should be amusing.

Chapter Eight

3 December, 2018

Drat, where are they? Elda flinched as a black sedan drove by. She peered through watery eyes and tried to focus while her head pounded from the freezing wind. She almost missed spotting that good ole Nervous Nelly, Grisha. She worried that they might have switched out the others. Perhaps they were so used to this routine that they felt only one tail was needed. It would be easy to lose Grisha and meet Yuri at Gorky Park. She had a feeling, however, that someone else was watching. Another black sedan drove by. Was that a different one or the same one? *I can't read the license plates with this wind bothering my eyesight. If I'm wrong, I could compromise Yuri and the whole mission. Gotta be extra cautious.*

Elda returned to the hotel and flagged down a taxi. Inside, she replaced her hat with a colorful scarf and turned her coat inside out so that she now wore a brown coat. Exiting the cab, she stooped over and shuffled onward. She saw another cab drive by her, with Grisha in the backseat, scanning the roadway, speeding after the first cab. Suddenly, a black car sped by. She was right—someone else was in the game.

Once Grisha's taxi was out of sight, Elda veered to the metro station and changed trains a few times to prove she had no other tail. At the park, Elda found the skating rink and sat on a bench, watching the skaters. By the shift of the bench, Elda sensed a large man sat down next to her.

"*Dobroye utro*," Yuri said.

"*Dobroye utro*."

"*Pozhaluysta, prosti menya.* I'm the person who ran you down the other day," Yuri apologized.

"*Ty proshchen.*" Elda shrugged, accepting his apology again for having run into her the last time she was in the park.

Yuri went on to explain he was a dog walker and handed her his card. She accepted it, grasping it with two hands and studying it as Yuri kept watch.

"Tomorrow you will take Korinna to the Rizhsky railway station," Elda said in a low tone. "It is located at Rizhskaya Square, at the crossing of Mira Avenue and Sushchyovsky Val. The station is served by Rizhskaya Metro station."

Yuri nodded.

"There, she will be met and taken to a cargo container. She will be hidden within the container for a long train ride to Latvia. At the port of Latvia, the container will be loaded onto a ship for Hamburg, Germany. I will meet her there."

Yuri nodded again.

"You will take Dasha and Sasha to London. I will meet you at the Montague Hotel in London and pick up Dasha and Sasha from you there. You can pick up the paperwork for Korinna's cargo container and any last-minute changes in instructions, as well as the necessary paperwork for the dogs at the normal drop box later today."

Yuri nodded a third time and then walked away.

Elda viewed the skaters for a few more minutes. Depending on the schedule for loading the ship and the weather, it should take Korinna about a week to arrive in Hamburg. She had plenty of time to get Dasha and Sasha safely to the United States from London. She breathed deeply and then switched her coat around and took off the kerchief, replacing it with her brown fur hat. On her return route to the hotel, she would stop at Skazka on Arbat Street and then the GUM store for some typical Russian souvenirs.

She arrived back at the hotel with bags that contained a few nesting dolls, colorful scarves, lacquer boxes, and an amber necklace. As she wove around busloads of tourists in the lobby, she caught sight of Konstantin, who immediately picked up his cell phone to report that he'd spotted her. Elda made sure he could see the GUM bag at her side as she moved toward the elevators.

Using the hotel phone, Elda bought a single ticket for herself and a return for Korinna to travel by train to St. Petersburg the day after. This way the Kremlin and the operatives would all know where they were going, in case they had missed the conversation at the market. She also called and booked her flight on British Airways from St. Petersburg to London four days from then. For good measure, she also called Korinna and asked if she could get a few days off and take the train to St. Petersburg tomorrow. They arranged to meet that night for dinner at the hotel to plan their outing.

Elda glanced at the date on her Garmin watch. *I need to move this along faster!*

***

As Elda sat in the hotel restaurant waiting for Korinna, Aurelio and his two buddies staggered off the elevator and out the door. She idly considered how long his liver would take the abuse he had subjected it to. She then returned to her game of checking the algorithm for the three elevators and seeing which prostitute would accept the man they motioned up and which would reject. She wondered what the basis of rejection was.

Could it be just about the money? Deep in thought, she almost missed the flash of Korinna's red coat as she entered the hotel. Elda let go of the breath that she had unconsciously been holding. Korinna and Elda hugged, and Korinna took off her coat and sat down. Elda gestured to the waiter, who came over with a small tray with shots of vodka and water chasers.

They both shook their heads in dismay.

"We've had too many dinners here," Elda said.

"*Da. Na zdorov'ye!*"

"To health!" Elda returned Korinna's toast.

They both drank their shots. Korinna signaled for two more as they drank their water chasers. Elda spied the violin player warming up on the other side of the room and gave him a nod, which he returned.

"Might as well get this part over with," she said.

Korinna smiled thinly as the violinist came over while playing the beginning of "Moscow Nights."

"I'm excited about our trip to St. Petersburg," Elda said. "I have your ticket here and am leaving on the train at thirteen-thirty tomorrow. Will you be able to make that one?" She handed Korinna her ticket.

"Da, the groomer is picking up the dogs and then returning them to the neighbors. If I am late, I will just catch the sixteen-forty and meet you at the hotel. Where are we staying?"

"At the Radisson Royal Hotel on Nevsky Avenue, forty-nine two. It has a free breakfast and is a five-star hotel."

Elda and Korinna motioned the waiter over for their usual blinis and caviar, along with a vodka and tall glass of water for each of them. For the observers, they would make this a night of celebration of their continual friendship and pending road trip. For each other, it would be a bittersweet recognition of the friendship and dinners that they had shared, since they didn't know when, or even if, they would see each other again. However, after the third vodka, they decided they had enough celebration, as tomorrow would be a busy day for each of them. It was an unusually large amount for the two of them to drink, but they needed to show their watchers and listeners that they were relaxed and in vacation mode.

"Prover'te, pozhaluysta," Elda said, raising her hand and asking for the check.

After they left the restaurant, Elda watched from the hotel door as Korinna went down the stairs with her long red wool coat flowing in the wind with Grisha pacing behind. *Travel safely, my friend.*

***

4 December, 2018

Egor lovingly wiped off his violin and placed it gently into its case.

"Spokoynoy nochi, moya skripka. Spasibo," he whispered to it as he closed the top of the case.

Each time Egor played the symphony, he envisioned the story behind the music and imagined it being painted in his mind. He enjoyed traveling abroad, but he was happiest when he was home with his wife and their two little dogs. Korinna and he worked hard at making their marriage work, with the two of them traveling so often, and they had successfully completed thirty-five wonderful years together.

Both Korinna and Egor had grown up when Russia was still Communist. Egor's talent for music and Korinna's for languages were discovered when they were young children, and they were each slotted into a special school to develop their talents. Egor and Korinna agreed that they were grateful for the training and the opportunities the government had given them. Egor was creative and loved to compose his own music. According to Korinna, it was this creativity and gentleness, combined with his masculinity and ability to navigate life so well, that had attracted her to Egor in the first place.

Egor stood and stretched. He was a tall and lanky man, with a full head of gray hair cut short and a hint of a mustache. He liked to keep clean shaven for Korinna when he was home. As he scrutinized the auditorium, he observed that the guards who usually traveled with them were not there and that new ones had taken their place. Having lived so long in the Soviet Union, now Russia, and being an observant man at his core, Egor was attuned to changes in his environment, and usually, change was for the worse.

"Eto ne khorosho," he muttered to himself.

It was best not to draw attention to the fact that he noticed the change, so he finished packing his gear and left to catch one of the buses that would take them to the hotel in the next town or city on the tour.

A bus driver motioned him over to his bus, which had no line. Egor smiled at his good luck and stepped onto the bus. The driver was also not one of their regulars, but that was not unusual since they traveled such long distances, often with tricky roads that required a local driver. They were, after all, in an area with mountainous roads, twists and turns, and icy conditions.

The driver reached out and shook his hand. "Wonderful performance."

"Spasibo."

Egor palmed the piece of paper placed into his hand. As he squeezed down the aisle, he glanced back, and the driver motioned him to go farther. He sat near the middle of the bus because there was equipment and luggage stowed on the seats behind him. He peeked at the note.

It was written in Russian and English, and in both languages, it read: *Egor, buckle your seat belt and stay on the bus until the driver tells you by name*

A few more individuals from the concert hall entered and sat in the front seats, per the driver's encouragement. Egor strapped himself in and buckled his violin case into the seat next to him. He looked up and saw the driver nod at him in the mirror. There were more buses than usual to cart the players and crew, so his was sparsely populated. One of the new guards sat between Egor and the rest. Egor formed his brows into large V over his long nose. The driver grinned at him in the mirror and laughingly massaged his own brow between his eyes. Egor relaxed slightly.

The bus took off on the winding roads, the last in line. The driver rolled forward slowly, since it was snowing, and the roads were icy. Egor reached down and ensured that his seat belt was tightly fastened, then checked that the strap around his violin was secure. As he glanced back up, a huge truck on the other side on the road came up out of the snow squalls. It lost control, sideswiping Egor's bus. Luggage crashed off the seats in the back. The other passengers fell forward, some even out of their seats, but Egor, Egor's violin, the driver, and the guard were safely strapped in.

The driver managed to control the skid and stop the bus inches from going off the cliff on the other side of the road. He threw open the door. "Everyone off the bus."

Egor unbuckled his seat belt and started standing up, when the driver, while herding others toward the door, made a slight motion for Egor to stay back. Egor unbuckled his violin and held it close as he moved to the aisle. The guard took the rest of the passengers over across the street, where they could no longer see the bus through the falling snow.

The driver came back and grabbed Egor's arm. "Egor, go quickly to the truck that just hit us. Keep on this side of the road so the others cannot see you. Your life depends on this."

Egor huddled against the vehicle as he moved along the side of the bus and toward the lights of the truck.

The truck driver opened the passenger-side door and pulled him up and into the cab. He pointed to the back. "Quick. Go back there and hide under the blankets in the back of the cab."

Egor crawled under, still holding his violin. Luckily, it was a large space—after all, there was a lot of Egor to hide. The driver closed the passenger door, adjusted the blankets over Egor, and then started the truck. Soon the passenger-side door opened, and the bus driver climbed in. As he shut the door, a crash and an explosion vibrated the truck. The driver drove off in the opposite direction as quickly as the ice would allow.

***

Thuds and groans of tearing metal filled the air as the bus rolled down the mountain, hitting boulders along the way. The guard huddled with the remaining passengers across the street from the bus. He couldn't see the large vehicle through the veil of snow, but he gaped at the glow of flames shooting up as the broken bus descended the mountainside. He could smell the burning rubber from the tires. He tried to call another bus, but reception was unavailable.

He counted the passengers. *"U nas bylo yeshche dva."*

The others confirmed that two were missing, Egor and the driver.

"Oni mertvy," one passenger said.

The guard agreed that Egor and the driver were dead and suggested that the group go down the mountain single file, holding onto the person in front of them and hugging the mountainside, staying away from the cliff face.

"Nas kto-nibud' spaset," he said, assuring them that they would be rescued.

A white Jeep Renegade Trailhawk emerged from the snow gusts, sliding directly toward the remaining group that was lined up, hugging the side of the road and ready to shuffle down the mountain. Screaming, they scattered in different directions, some nearly running into the skidding vehicle. It bounced off the mountainside, swirled around, and finally stopped. Another guard jumped out of the driver's seat.

"How did you know to come back?" the first guard asked the other.

"We were at a rest area, and your bus didn't show up, so I borrowed this vehicle to come see what had happened."

"I hope you gave a security deposit." The guard turned to the huddled group. "Everyone, get into the Jeep now!"

The group piled two men into the front and squished the remaining into the back. It was not going to be a comfortable ride, but they were not going far. They opened the windows to make more space and drove with limbs hanging out. The rear passengers told the other guard about how the bus had rolled off the cliff and exploded in a burst of flames, with the driver and Egor still on board. The Jeep took off, skidding and sliding back down the mountain.

In the front seat, the guard nodded to the driver and acknowledged the success to himself. *Just as planned.* They had their story prearranged and their escape route planned. After they safely returned this group of passengers to the other buses, there would be no need for any extra guards, and they could just silently disappear. If there was any inquiry by the Russian government into details or a request for Egor's remains, they had a detailed report of the incident ready to send to Russia. They even had a copy of Egor's dental records, so if needed they could always doctor up a corpse from the morgue to be him. However, it would be much easier to say it was far too costly a mission and logistically impossible to get down the mountain to retrieve any portions of his remains, which were probably charred and scattered about with the bus parts.

The guard noted how skilled that bus driver must have been to stop the bus just inches from the side of the cliff. His partner was having difficulty controlling the Jeep on this snow and ice. He hoped that they would all make it back safely. It was bitterly cold in the Jeep with the windows rolled down, and he wished it could go faster. He turned the heat up to its highest point.

The group rode back to the rest stop in silence out of respect for the loss of Egor and the bus driver and because they were too cold to think of much to say. The guard breathed a sigh of relief as they drove into the rest area. One bus had waited for their return, while the other had moved on to the next hotel.

The guard considered how they would phrase the leak to the Russian press. The more publicized Egor's death was, the better. The guards would tell the Russian government about the loss before the Canadian government could. He would send an encrypted email to the proper Canadian officials as soon as he was within cell range again. He sat back in the bus seat and closed his eyes. For now, his part was done.

***

No, no, no. This cannot be. Nothing was there! Elda bent over again and double-checked the drop box under the bench. She did not have her final instructions on how to rescue Korinna in Hamburg. The chill of the blustery wind penetrated her forehead, making it hard to think. *I hate Moscow for so many reasons.* She needed the instructions, but she also needed to leave immediately to stay on schedule. She adjusted her sock and straightened up. *Okay.* She'd just have to wing it.

Walking over the crusty snow, she noted that she had only two tails. Grisha must have been assigned to Korinna, but where was that black sedan, and who was in it? Was it the same driver who'd given her a lift?

Elda caught herself grinning as she witnessed Konstantin and Timur struggle to keep pace with her. She sadistically picked up her pace on the way back to the hotel. *It would serve me right to fall on my ass.*

On her return, she shoved everything in her bag and shouldered her backpack. She had arranged to have the hotel staff transport her bag to the hotel in St. Petersburg, so she wouldn't have to drag it behind her. She dropped it off with the front desk and checked out.

She wanted one last look at the beauty of the metro stations before she left Moscow. Elda strolled this time, ensuring her tails stuck with her. The black car inched by her. She resisted flagging it down for a lift. Yes, that was the same car. They were trying to intimidate her.

The closest station to the Crowne Plaza Hotel was Vystavochnaya, on a branch of the Pale-Blue Line. But more convenient for connections was Krasnopresnenskaya, about a fifteen-minute walk from the hotel, on the Purple Line, to an interchange on the Brown Line. Elda chose to take the Brown Line to Komsomolskaya, where she could pick up the train at the Leningradsky station.

The exterior of the historic Leningradsky station recalled the lavish days of the czars. The interior, however, had no charm and was stark and sterile, like a laboratory. She was over an hour early, which would give her plenty of time to observe the comings and goings. She picked up a copy of the *Moscow Times* and the Russian tabloid *Zhizn* to help her hide. *Ah, there are Konstantin and Timur.* The two were talking with each other, but they both had their phones up to their ears, probably asking for more instructions. She refrained from waving as they strode out of the station.

Crap. That means someone else is following me to St. Petersburg.

***

Anatoly threw himself into his 5:00 a.m. morning exercise routine: push-ups with claps in between, alternating with one-armed push-ups, squats, bicep curls, tricep kickbacks to offset the bicep exercise, and a fast run so he would get back in time to report in. He returned sweating and panting. Checking his watch, he was pleased with his eight-minute mile. He ran fast, considering his bulk.

He congratulated himself: *Ochen khorosho. Neplokho dlya 45!* He didn't know how many more years he would be effective at his job or what they would do with him once he couldn't do it anymore. He had many false identities and escape routes saved for that time.

The phone rang as Anatoly came out of the shower, toweling his cropped blond hair. He tied the towel around his muscular waist and padded over to answer the phone.

"Da . . . Da . . . Da . . . Khorosho . . . Spasibo," he said as he listened to his instructions.

He hung up and packed his to-go bag for the trip to St. Petersburg. A tall, blonde woman in a long, red coat with a kerchief on her head should be easy to spot.

His superiors at the Kremlin had told him this woman should not return to Moscow from St. Petersburg. It was up to him to figure out the best way for her to have an "accident" while vacationing.

Anatoly booted up his laptop and checked the train schedules, then researched St. Petersburg. He was familiar with the city, but he wanted to know it inside and out and have a few plans for where this woman would meet her end. She would be wandering around the city playing tour guide to her American friend, so he memorized the metro stations around the different tourist attractions. He hoped the canals weren't completely frozen over, since they would be a convenient place to stage an accident.

He checked his watch and saw that it was only 09:00. His marks were scheduled for the 13:30 train from the Leningradsky station. "*Ya priyedu v 13:20,*" he decided. Arriving ten minutes before the train left would allow him to board without being noticed, since the others should have boarded by then. Satisfied that his plan was solid, he rechecked the weapons in his to-go bag. He might return to Moscow in two days, three tops.

Dve zhenshchiny. He laughed, hoping that he would get to kill two women, and not just the one. *That would be fun! Dve zhenshchiny, ne odna zhenshchina,* he thought with a chuckle.

As an ex-FSB agent, Anatoly was fluent in English, French, and German, and often thought in these languages, as well as Russian.

Anatoly checked his stainless-steel Rolex, a present to himself that was accurate and still in almost new condition after all that he had put it through. He felt successful every time he glanced down at his wrist and glimpsed the brand name.

***

A knock on the door sent Korinna's heart rate soaring as the dogs flung themselves into a spurt of dancing and frantic barking. She jumped and tossed her hairbrush onto the counter. She threw on the rest of her clothes and peeked through the spyhole. In the hallway was the dog groomer; a second man, who could have been his twin; and a third man, who was tall and slender and wore a long coat and a hat.

"*Odna minuta!*" She buckled the dogs' jackets and opened the door.

Yuri held his finger to his mouth as he entered the apartment. The dogs, obviously recognizing Yuri from the park and excited to see so many people, jumped up and down against Yuri's legs. Korinna was amused to see that Yuri didn't budge, whereas when the two of them jumped at her like that, she had to widen her stance to keep from falling over.

Closing the door, the third man, whom Yuri called Padma, took off his hat and coat and handed them to Korinna—she promptly donned them. He smiled at Korinna and motioned that she was to go with Yuri's "twin," Pavel. Padma then struck out to the kitchen and sat next to the landline to wait for Elda's phone call from the station.

The whistling of the teakettle put Korinna on edge. Her stomach lurched at the thought that her journey had begun. She wanted to scream, *No, no, let's forget about this*, but her life was in danger.

Then Korinna straightened, squared her shoulders, and nodded that she was ready to go. Pavel, picked up Korinna's bag and inserted it into a bag he had carried in with him. Korinna and Pavel would leave the apartment together. Yuri would head out shortly thereafter with Dasha and Sasha.

Korinna bent down and hugged Dasha and Sasha tightly, and they licked her face. "*Poka-poka*, girls. Be good." She feared she might never see them again.

***

Aurelio felt the imprint and grit of the carpet on his cheek, combined with a dampness from where he had been drooling. He could smell the mold from the carpet and bathroom tiles. He remembered that he'd made it into the room and had shut the door

128

before passing out in the bathroom doorway. He checked in with his body. His head pounded, his mouth was dry, and his breath was rancid. He glanced at his watch to see what day it was. December third.

He crawled into the bathroom and pulled himself up to his knees, then reached over and grabbed the counter to pull himself upright. The image in the mirror scared him. He appeared old and sick. He quickly turned away and peeled off his clothes and padded to the shower to try and steam himself back to normal. Again, he had no memory of the night before.

Ya dolzhen idti domoy, he thought. *Speak English!* he yelled to himself. *Yes, I should go home*, he translated. *I have such a beautiful wife, the lovely Natasha. I miss her! I don't know why I left her to hang out with these guys. She loves me, and we have a fantastic life together. Ya yeye lyublyu. Speak English, damn it!*

Aurelio left the shower and tiptoed to the phone to book himself a first-class compartment on the train to St. Petersburg.

"*Da*, thirteen-thirty. *Da, da.*" He hung up the phone. His vision seemed blurry. He shook his head to clear it. That movement made his head pound, and he had to sit down on the edge of the bed. He tiptoed back into the bathroom to check his bag for painkillers. He found a lint-covered codeine-aspirin pill at the bottom of his shaving kit bag and swallowed that with a water chaser.

Aurelio dressed quickly so he would have time to eat before leaving for the train. He snapped his Rolex on his wrist and smiled thinly. He was a rich, important man here in Russia. That thought, combined with the codeine, made him feel confident. He continued to throw clothing into his bag. He would have the hotel deliver it to the train for him. As he pranced into the living room, he spied traces of cocaine left over in the crumbs of food on the table. He licked his finger and swept up the remaining coke and crumbs and rubbed it into his gums. Feelings of omnipotence and well-being filled him.

Aurelio slid his computer into his larger bag and added a small brick of hash he had lifted from Olav, hiding some money he had taken from his friends in the bag, too. He could buy the hash, and he had enough money, but he got a secret thrill from screwing over his friends. He wished he had taken more coke from Olav but figured Yuri could get him some when he was back home.

Aurelio tagged his bag with his last name, Ainsworth, and left it at the front desk to be delivered to the train. He liked his last name, as it spoke of his father's English heritage. *Probably descended from royalty.* He puffed his narrow chest out more. His mother used to say he was the spitting image of his father. He only remembered his father as having gray hair, but he remembered being told that his father's hair was originally brown, as were his eyes. Aurelio had blonde hair and blue eyes. He shook his head to clear out that sneaking suspicion.

The smell of the food at the restaurant turned his stomach, but he managed to get a cup of tea and a thick slice of black bread inside to settle it down. He patted his stomach. *I really do need to lose weight*, he thought as he took in the feel of the flab of his thickening waist through his palm. But didn't all successful men eat well? Look at the president of the United States. His body screamed success. He beamed, thinking how much he was like that man: successful, rich on Russian money, married to a beautiful, blonde wife.

He returned to his room and took one last look around to ensure he hadn't missed any drugs. He guzzled the half-glass of scotch on the coffee table, then grabbed a handful of drinks from the minibar and slid them into his outside coat pocket. He briefly considered giving a tip to the maid but figured she'd probably stolen from him, so he wouldn't. At the desk, he asked the hotel clerk to call him a taxi for the Leningradsky station.

Standing inside the hotel doors, waiting for the taxi, Aurelio envisioned Natasha opening the door, taking his hand, and leading him into the bedroom. He would show that bitch what a man he was. He would climb on top and pound her for hours until she screamed for him to stop. She'd scream what a good lover he was. He also fantasized about mastering Yuri and having Natasha watch. That would show her who the better man was. Yuri would cry like a little bitch. Aurelio was beaming by the time the taxi arrived.

***

Elda made a big show of checking her watch, a Garmin GPS she used for tracking her exercise. At 13:15, she took out her phone and called Korinna to tell her to meet her in St. Petersburg. *"Privet, Korinna."*

"Privet," Korinna answered. She apologized, saying the dog groomer had been late picking up the dogs, but she was leaving now and catching the next train out to St. Petersburg, so she should be at the hotel around 23:00.

"*Spasibo. Poka.*" Elda swiped her phone to end the call.

She folded her newspapers, grabbed her backpack, and ran to hop onto the train just before it pulled out of the station. She spotted a large, blonde man with a mustache carrying a small bag jumping onto another car right after her. Konstantin and Timur had not returned. Was this new man their substitute? He could have been doing a last-minute boarding to avoid detection. She wandered to an economy-class car near the middle of the train and settled in for the four-hour ride.

***

Back in Korinna's apartment, Padma switched off the recorder and hung up the phone. He rinsed his teacup and left it in the sink. Donning Korinna's long, red coat and tying a bright kerchief around his head, he took leave of the apartment. Focusing on keeping his walk as much like Korinna's as possible, he set off at a good pace to the metro station. Pasha, the tail Elda dubbed Grisha, fell into place about twenty feet behind him.

***

Grisha, aka Pasha, reached for his phone to call his superiors and let them know Korinna was on the move, but his hand came up empty.

Ya budu v bede. Sweat flowed down his back as he thought of just how much trouble he would be in. This was the fourth phone he had lost while on a mission. "*Eto ne moya vina. Oni slishkom malen'kiye,*" he said to no one in particular, holding himself blameless because the phones were just too small and easy to lose. He hoped this would not be another black mark on his record. He would call his superiors from the train station. Hopefully, they wouldn't notice the delay in his communication.

***

4 December, 2018, 13:25

After boarding, Anatoly stopped to catch his breath and check that his bag was still securely on his shoulder. "*Ya stareyu,*" he said under his breath. *Nyet. I am not getting old.* He might not be able to do everything at the same pace as he could in his twenties, but his expertise and training compensated for that. However, he vowed to get more serious about his cardiovascular training when he returned to Moscow.

He headed back toward the car the American woman had entered, to see if she was joining his target. He wished he could just shove them both under the wheels of the train at a stop. It would be so easy to fake that accident. But his superiors had been clear that the woman in the red coat was his target, and she needed to be taken care of in St. Petersburg. However, they didn't care if the other woman became collateral damage.

***

Coughing and out of breath from running to catch the train, Aurelio boarded the train and settled into his first-class cabin. He rummaged through his bag in vain, looking for something to get him high. He took out his wallet and searched its compartments for pills of any kind. In disgust, he threw it on his table. He'd find a drink and see if he could score drugs from any of the passengers in economy class. He stopped in the bar car on his way to coach and purchased a scotch on the rocks. He didn't care for ice in his drinks, since it watered the alcohol down and delayed the buzz, but it made him look more sophisticated.

Aurelio strutted through the economy cars. *Ah, the poor souls who can't afford to live the way I do.* He looked at each person as if they were dirt, but then he spied a woman staring out the window, who

135

was rather familiar. He couldn't quite place her. His mind vaguely registered a large, blonde man striding in from the opposite direction. Then it dawned on him who that woman was. Anger overwhelmed him, and he rushed at her, screaming loudly in his hatred of himself, projected onto his half-sister.

***

Anatoly wandered down the aisle in the direction of where the woman sat, wondering where his target was. A man screamed and rushed toward him, and Anatoly automatically flipped the blade out from its sheaf inside his sleeve, reached out, and stabbed the man, who was clearly intending to attack him. Blood spurted from the wound, and the man fell forward—Anatoly jumped over him and sprinted through the dining car to first class to escape as the screaming passengers in the economy car ran in circles.

The woman he'd had his eye on, in the flurry of screaming and jostling passengers, grabbed her backpack. She raced from the commotion to the end of the car and jumped off the train. Anatoly scanned for his own escape route.

He twisted his large body around a few frightened passengers huddled together, blocking the others from following him. By then, the train picked up speed again, and there was no chance to chase after the woman.

The mark was the woman in the red coat anyway. The sooner he killed her, the better. This job did not feel right. Already, people he had not been briefed about were attacking him. Who was the elderly man he'd stabbed, and why had that man attacked him? *I need to disappear quickly.*

Anatoly tugged on a thin pair of black gloves and ducked into a first-class compartment. He reached into a pocket of his carry-on bag and pulled out a razor and hair dye. He shaved off his mustache into a towel, which he folded over the hair and stuffed into his bag. He dyed his blonde hair brown, washed the sink out thoroughly, and put in brown contact lenses to disguise his deep-blue eyes. He added a thick pair of glasses, buttoned up his jacket, and pulled on a sweater, so he appeared fatter. He finished by inserting lifts to his shoes, for added height.

Scanning the car to inspect that he had left no trace, he picked up a thick wallet from the table, and while removing bills from it, an ID spilled onto the table. He examined the picture—it belonged to the man he'd stabbed.

"Mr. Aurelio Ainsworth," he read aloud, memorizing the name. He stuffed the money into his pocket, and after peering out to vouch that the coast was clear, he stepped out of the compartment, removed his gloves, and shut the door behind him. Returning to the dining car, he ordered a cup of black tea and a sochnik.

Anatoly stretched out in the seat, propped his feet up on the opposite bench, sipped his steaming hot tea, and bit into the crisp pastry. He let his tongue savor the taste of the creamy dairy filling. *Zhizn' khorosha.* He chuckled at the thought of a "Life Is Good" T-shirt with a picture of sochniki on it.

He would find and kill his target, so he was not worried about the woman who'd jumped off the train. She probably hadn't survived that fall anyway.

The conductor entered the car. Anatoly flagged him down and asked, with a concerned look on his face, "*Chto zdes' proiskhodit?*"

"A huge monster of a man stabbed a passenger. There was blood everywhere. I doubt he will make it. An eyewitness observed the attacker jump off the train."

"*Spasibo.*"

Anatoly finished his sochnik and tea. He briefly thought of cleaning the cream off the plate with his finger. That pastry was a weakness of his, so he strongly resisted the desire. Instead, he stood up and roamed through the cars, looking for the woman in the red coat. He would not be concerned if he didn't find her. His superiors had let him know she might not make this train but would take the next one. They also had given him the name of her hotel, so if she wasn't on this train, he would wait for her there.

Anatoly was stopped when he approached the car where Aurelio had been stabbed. Someone was working on the body in the aisle, and most everyone else had been directed to other cars. The conductor politely told him that he had to return to the dining car and ride the rest of the way from there. If he had any luggage, the conductor would bring it to him.

"*Spasibo, ya ponimayu*," Anatoly said in compliance, and he returned to sit in the dining car again. He was disappointed, since he'd wanted to burn off the first pastry and would have to resist the temptation of ordering another. Frustrated at the delay and inaction, he longed to get off the train.

He glanced out the window and saw a tall, blonde woman in a red coat walking away from the train. He jumped up and dashed to the door, where he was stopped by a policeman holding a semiautomatic weapon.

"I'm sorry, sir. You cannot leave the train."

He gnashed his teeth in frustration.

***

4 December, 2018, 13:30

Korinna and Pavel left the metro at Rizhsky station. Although not a busy station, its connection to Latvia was Moscow's sole route and was mostly used for that purpose. Pavel and Korinna ducked into a nearby Holiday Inn, where they changed into uniforms in a bathroom off the lobby, to allow them access to the cargo container area.

The two uniformed inspectors stepped through the snow, weaving their way among the multicolored, stacked containers until they reached a red one on the bottom. "Eto ono," Pavel said, pointing to the red container.

He took out a set of keys and unlocked it. They maneuvered past the heavy equipment loaded in the front, to the back, where Pavel pushed a hidden button to reveal a keypad. He pressed the buttons and selected ENTER. A door slid back to reveal a three-and-a-half-foot-deep room, with a mattress at the far right, wool blankets folded at the end of it, and a pillow at the top. A basket of food and two cases of water were stacked on a side wall, with a number of large, covered buckets at the other end of the room.

Korinna's heart sank when she viewed her home for the next week. The train would leave that evening to go overnight for the sixteen-hour trip to Riga. There, the container would be loaded onto a ship to Hamburg. Once the ship sailed, the 614-nautical-mile trip would take about three days.

Pavel explained she would have no light and requested she hand him her phone. They could not risk her being tracked, and no light could lead out from that end of the container. Pavel handed her a new flip phone, to be used only in an emergency once she reached Hamburg. Elda's number had been preprogrammed for her. She sighed as she entered the compartment.

She settled down on the mattress, and the door slid closed with a soft, metallic sound. She heard his steps clatter down the length of the compartment, then heard the clang of the main compartment door shutting and the exterior lock being set. She crawled in the darkness to grab one of the blankets, rolled herself in it, and settled in for the long, lonely, dark trip. Tears rolled down her cheeks as she reflected if she would ever see Egor or Dasha and Sasha again.

***

Pavel marched away from the container and changed out of his uniform at the hotel. He pocketed Korinna's phone in his outside coat pocket, then left the hotel and meandered toward the metro. Near the station, he was bumped into by a short, nondescript man who slipped on the packed icy snow.

"*Izvinite menya,*" the man said.

"*Khorosho,*" Pavel responded. He strutted toward the metro and smiled as he patted his empty pocket.

***

Elda climbed out of the pile of hay, bruised and shaken up. She patted herself down, shook her arms and legs, and verified that nothing was broken. *I sure wish I had used the toilet before this all happened.* She hoped that she would find a place to relieve herself soon. Heading down the dirt road, she picked hay out of her clothing and hair and brushed the dust off of herself. After ten minutes, she spied a farmer in a tractor pulling a cart, heading up the road toward her. She flagged him down. With an exchange of money and a handshake, he let her climb into the cart. The bottom of the cart was covered with hay and smelled suspiciously like farm animals.

Having grown up in the city, Elda couldn't readily identify the origin, but she didn't feel any urgency to find out what had been on the hay before her.

The cart jostled down the dirt road heading for the nearest town, where the farmer had told her he was picking up some feed for his animals. Elda now had more hay and what appeared to be chicken feathers on her clothing. *Ah, the glamorous life of a spy.* A smile came to her lips. There was a long way to go, however, before she could relax enough to see the full humor in her situation. And there was not enough hay in the cart, or fat on her body, to successfully buffer her from the bumps in the road.

The cart stopped. The wide dirt road went by a number of wooden shacks with a four-foot-tall wooden fence running along the side of them. Laundry was hung out in the cold, frozen on the line. In front of her, on the right side of the road, was a scenic, wooden church. On the left was a general store. Elda hoped someone in this town had a car they did not need for a few days. She hopped off the cart and jogged into the store.

"U tebya yest' mashina? Avtomobil'?" Elda asked of the man behind the counter.

"Da." He pointed out the window.

Elda looked to where he was pointing and saw an older AvtoVAZ model, a bit beat up but seemingly in reasonable shape. She negotiated to buy the car from him for cash—far more than it was worth—and to park it when she was through in the parking lot near the Church of the Spilled Blood in St. Petersburg. Since he had a spare set of keys, she would lock it with the keys under the front seat, in case he wished to reclaim it.

Elda bought some food for her journey, used the toilet, and set off back along the dirt roads toward St. Petersburg. She tried to avoid the ruts, as clearly the shocks on the car had long ago worn out from the beating the roads gave. She pulled over by the side of the road, folded her coat in fourths, and placed it under her already battered butt. She started the car again, and black smoke filled the air from the exhaust pipe. She realized why there was a spare can of oil on the passenger-side floor.

***

Padma stopped and picked up a *butterbrot* of rye bread and ham and another of rye bread and butter to eat on the ride to St. Petersburg. He had plenty of time to make the 16:40 from Leningradsky. He traveled slowly, focusing on walking more like Korinna, so as to not lose Pasha-Grisha. He kept his scarf tight around his neck and lower face, and he carried a small case of Korinna's. Inside, however, were his own clothes. Once on the train, he would ditch the scarf and red coat and put on his workman's coat, hat, and gloves. Anyone waiting for Korinna in St. Petersburg would be disappointed when she didn't leave the train or show up at the hotel.

At Leningradsky station, Padma bought a newspaper and took a seat, opening the paper so that his face was completely hidden.

After boarding the train, he settled into an economy coach seat. Pasha had settled into a seat in a car behind him. Padma spread out his newspaper and opened up the rye bread and butter sandwich and placed that beside the newspaper. Padma raised his hand and flagged down a conductor, asking loudly in a breathless, high-pitched voice, *"Gde tualet?"*

The conductor pointed back at Pasha's car and forward to another car. Padma rose and stepped to the car away from Pasha. Inside the bathroom, he changed back into a typical, male, Russian workman. Walking back between cars, he surreptitiously threw the case with the Korinna disguise clothing off the train. He passed Pasha and sat down two rows behind him. Satisfied, he elevated his feet up on the seat across from him and opened the ham and rye *butterbrot* and took a large bite.

After twenty minutes, Pasha was visibly nervous.

***

Pasha checked his watch every minute. Finally, forty minutes into the ride, he stumbled toward Korinna's car. Her paper and sandwich were just where she'd left them. He glanced around the car and saw no signs of her, so he walked to the toilet in the next car, which was occupied. After waiting for five minutes outside the door, he finally knocked.

"Khorosho, khorosho! Ya idu!"

Pasha recoiled from the sound of the angry male voice coming from within the toilet. There wasn't room for two people in there, so he frantically checked the economy cars in that direction, then the first-class cars, receiving more angry retorts as he knocked on their doors. She was nowhere to be found.

Pasha returned to his seat, shaking and sweating. He chewed at the insides of his mouth as his mind vainly tried to solve the puzzle of where Korinna went to. If he didn't find her by the time the train reached St. Petersburg, his career—and possibly his life—would be over. He dropped his head into his hands and wept silently.

***

Anatoly finished his second chai and sochnik and delicately licked the crumbs off his fingers. As he wiped his hands with his napkin, his phone rang. It was his superiors, letting him know that Korinna had missed the 13:30 but was definitely on the 16:40 train. He hung up and sat back, closing his eyes and visualizing St. Petersburg from the map he had memorized. There was no convenient place to do the job near the train station. He would follow her tomorrow and find a better place to get rid of her. He really did want to throw someone into the canal. He wondered if she would stay more than a day when her friend failed to show up. *Ya budu bystrym,* he thought. *Da, Ya budu oche' bystrym. Yes, very quick. Her service to the Kremlin deserved a quick death anyway.* He would wander the streets tonight and pick a few alternative locations for her death.

***

Back in Moscow in Korinna's apartment, the phone rang again and again. Clearly, someone was trying to reach her. Anna, her neighbor, having returned from a full morning of shopping, took Korinna's keys off the hook in her apartment and went across the hall to let herself into Korinna's apartment. She reached the phone on the last ring.

147

"*Privet.*" As she listened, her hand went to her mouth. "*Kak uzhasno!*" she exclaimed, expressing her dismay and horror at the story. Egor had died in a tragic accident in Canada! Korinna would be bereft! And poor Sasha and Dasha. She glanced at her watch. The dogs should be home momentarily.

***

The 13:30 train slowed as it came into the Moskovsky Vokzal station in St. Petersburg. A disembodied voice came over the intercom system, instructing the riders to stay in their seats: "*Ostavaytes' na svoikh mestakh!*" An ambulance stretcher and a company of police officers stood on the platform. Anatoly sighed, since it meant a slight delay in starting his exploration of the city. He stared out the window as a body was carried off the train. From his viewpoint, he couldn't tell if it was alive or dead.

The police swarmed onto the train, interrogating the passengers. Anatoly briefly thought of showing his credentials to cut through the wait, but he didn't want to blow his new cover. And they might associate the blonde man on his credentials with the man who had done the stabbing. So, he sat patiently, waiting his turn. The police had started with the first-class passengers, and he was next in the dining car. When the police finally came his way, Anatoly answered all their questions.

"*Nyet. Ya nichego ne videl.*" He denied seeing anything. His description of his wonderful sochniki in the dining car brought a smile to his interrogator's lips, and Anatoly was released from the train. He picked up his gadget bag and wandered into St. Petersburg.

*****

Dense, blue-gray smoke permeated he car. Coughing, Elda pulled off to the side of the road and reached for the oil can. She lifted the hood and checked the level. Almost empty. She poured the oil in. She was almost to St. Petersburg. Hopefully, one can would do the trick.

She took out a folding cane and a gray wig from her backpack. Reversing her coat to the gray side and turning her hat inside out to the black lining helped amplify the washed-out, elderly look. She inserted contacts that turned her eyes a faded pale blue and replaced her glasses with hornrims. She shoved filler into her cheeks, then rolled up her pants and pulled on thick stockings that she rolled down around her calves. She then added an ankle-length, colorful wraparound skirt and wrapped a gray shawl around her shoulders before putting her coat back on.

She placed her backpack into an old beat-up backpack. She substituted her current ID with a fresh one and then drove toward the city with a final puff of black smoke. Despite the persnickety car, she had made good time, on track to arrive at the hotel only an hour later than planned.

Elda left the car off at the Church of the Spilled Blood parking lot and wrapped the keys in a few additional bills with a note that read *Dlya mazut*, but she was hoping the owner would just get a new car instead of retrieving this oil burner.

She then embarked on the twenty-three-minute walk past the Mikhailovsky theater and Italian bridge to Nevesky Prospect over the historic Anichkov Bridge to the Radisson Hotel. It had been many years since she had been in St. Petersburg. She had, of course, memorized the city map, but there was nothing like seeing it on foot. She figured with her disguise, the walk would actually take her closer to forty minutes, but that would help with spotting tails. She unfolded her cane and started out with a hunched-over gait, affecting a slight limp on her right side.

When Elda reached the hotel, she discreetly surveyed the lobby. A large man with brown hair sat off to one side, reading a newspaper. He seemed familiar, with features similar to the man who had stabbed Aurelio. She limped to the front desk, hunched over from age and the weight of the backpack. She gave her new name and handed her backpack to the young bellhop, who showed her to Room 608. Succumbing to his flattery and aid, she overtipped him, as any grandmotherly woman would. After she shut the door behind him, she reached into her backpack, pulled out a scanner, and searched the room for bugs. She figured the phone was bugged at the central switch for the hotel. Finding no bugs in the room itself, she placed her backpack on the bed and took out her lockpick set.

Elda placed her ear to the door that connected to the next guest room. Hearing nothing, she slipped on a pair of thin gloves and picked the lock, entering the room that she, as Elda Ainsworth, would have occupied. There on the bed was her bag, and next to it, another bag, both labeled with her last name. She was surprised to see the second bag. She opened hers and took extra money and IDs from a hidden compartment, leaving the clothing. She carefully arranged the contents, with pieces of hair and touches of lint in strategic places, so she'd be able to tell if anyone else searched the bag after her. She then picked the lock on the other bag and found IDs and money in the lining, as well as a brick of hash in the main compartment, all of which she removed. *Aha— Aurelio, I will relieve you of these items.* Aurelio's computer was sitting on top of his clothing. She downloaded the contents of his computer and installed spyware that would send every keystroke back to the FBI. She locked the bag back up and silently returned to her room, locking the connecting door behind her.

Elda went through her IDs and money. *Good. Nothing is missing. What to do with Aurelio's IDs and the hash? I guess I can bundle up the hash and get it to Yuri. He would be able to figure out what to do with it.* She double wrapped the brick in newspaper and taped a note on the outside. She then picked up her phone and called a friend of Yuri's, who lived in St. Petersburg, to meet her at the Fontan U Admiralteystava the next day. She figured he could take it to Moscow and give it to Yuri. If he unwrapped and kept it, so much the better. The IDs were easy enough to take with her, and the money might be useful on this trip.

Elda sat on the edge of the bed. The last time she had been in St. Petersburg, she'd been attending her half-brother's wedding with the rest of the family and had been activated by Ed to investigate a killing that had happened in the city. The man who had been killed was a double agent who had been a reasonably good source of small but significant tidbits of information. His loss was not huge, since a double agent could never totally be trusted, but the US could not figure out how or why he'd been killed.

In between wedding events, Elda had met with her contacts to see if she could get more information. She'd managed to obtain the autopsy report, which was also inconclusive. The double agent had been stabbed with a round, sharp object, probably about a foot long, but there was no weapon found at the scene and no tracks around the body. It appeared to be a robbery, but there had been rumor that the Kremlin had sent an assassin. Elda had dug around and heard the additional rumor that the assassin had been a man called Tosh. If that was the case, her chances of finding the killer were zero. Tosh was like a ghost. He slipped in, did his job cleanly, and slipped back out. She'd also heard that the Kremlin had tried to turn the agent again so that they could control the information he passed to the United States.

Elda had felt disappointed that she'd had no real facts to come back with from this job. And the wedding was a boring, self-indulgent display of her half-brother seeking approval from his family. Little did he know what his mother was saying behind his back and how his siblings were joking about his peasant in-laws. Elda had been glad to get back on the plane to the United States. Russia was fascinating, but sinister and dangerous.

Tosh. That name keeps coming up. Where is he now?

Chapter Nine

4 December, 2018

Through a blur, Aurelio saw a woman in white. He wondered if he was in heaven. Then, he spied her nurse's cap and instead hoped he was role-playing with a prostitute. "What happened?" he asked, but no sound came out. He attempted to move but was immediately shocked into stillness by a sharp pain in his gut. The woman put a hand on his shoulder, and he passed back into blackness.

***

The nurse turned and nodded at Natasha, who sat in a chair next to Aurelio's bed. Natasha frowned. It was disappointing that Aurelio might live through his accident. During one of his periods of semiconsciousness, she had guided his arm through his signature on a new will that left everything to her. She would send Yuri to officially file it when she was with him next. Even if Aurelio had passed, Yuri would be able to get it backdated on record. *Gde, Yuri?* she puzzled. She hadn't seen him in days. She missed having him to talk with, and the side benefits were pretty good, too. Yuri was much better in bed than Aurelio ever was.

Natasha surveyed the private room Aurelio had in the Amerikanskaya Klinika and nodded her approval. It was good he had money and was not crammed into a room with other sick people. Frankly, weakness and sickness disgusted her. She had clawed her way out of poverty and made a good life for herself. If it weren't for the fact that she had to suffer through being with Aurelio, her life would be nearly perfect.

The nurse, apparently seeing the emotions playing across Natasha's face, assumed she was worried about her husband. "*Tam, tam*," she said reassuringly, patting Natasha on the arm and then returning to check the speed of the morphine drip through Aurelio's IV.

Natasha hated the nurse's reassurance. She admitted that, after so many years together, she was sometimes fond of Aurelio, especially when they role-played mommy and son. That brought out her maternal instinct and made her feel slightly protective of him. But the rest of the time, not much that bonded them. They had no common interests, nor similar backgrounds. They even thought in different languages. But, being an expat, he had all his teeth and didn't smell the way many Russian men did, so that was a plus.

Aurelio groaned. Natasha regarded his face with disgust. Her hand played with the plastic line running from the IV bag into his hand as she thought how easy it would be to turn up the morphine drip and let him drift into death. She smiled pleasantly at the nurse adjusting his covers, grabbed her handbag, and left the room before she gave in to the impulse to overdose Aurelio. *I have better things to do than look at Aurelio all night.*

***

Pasha's train rolled into the station. As he disembarked, he wondered why so many police were on the opposite platform. He reluctantly found a pay phone and, with a shaking hand, dialed the number for his superiors. From the phone he watched as the 16:40's passengers cleared the platform. Korinna was nowhere to be seen. His heart sank. He told his superiors the bad news and was shocked that they did not fire him. Instead, they gave him a new assignment.

Pasha carefully listened to his contact. He didn't want to make another mistake. They told him to go to Griboyedov Channel Embankment near the

Mickey & Monkeys restaurant and wait for instructions.

He scuffed along slowly through the dark to the nearest metro and took a train to Spasskaya station. Alighting from the car, he trudged along the canal to the meeting spot. He'd had little to eat that day and hoped they would be going to dinner while he received his orders for his next job.

Pasha paced back and forth. He was not adequately dressed for the cold and hoped that his contact would show up soon. He wished he had asked for a description, since he had no idea if he was meeting a man or a woman.

His mind meandered through the different scenarios. They might be downgrading him to a clerk in Siberia. Or perhaps they would fire him, and he would work in some low-level civilian job. He'd never been good at manual labor, so he hoped it would not involve working with his hands. He sighed loudly. His career was not off to a good start.

***

Watching the guests check in at the hotel, Anatoly picked up his phone. It was unusual for his superiors to call him once, let alone twice, when he was on a mission. While he listened, his eye caught an old lady limping across the hotel lobby. He idly thought she might want to upgrade that cane to a walker. His attention sharpened when a tall blonde walked in on the arm of a handsome man. As the voice on the other end rattled off instructions, he stood up and wandered closer to the desk to overhear their room number, then returned to his seat.

"*Da, poka*," he acknowledged and hung up.

Anatoly left the hotel and took the Blue Line from Nevsky Prospect to Spasskaya. He jogged in the dark toward Mickey & Monkeys. He slowed his pace. Highlighted by the nearby lights was the outline of a slender, nervous man pacing by the canal, as expected. Anatoly staggered by him, seemingly drunk, and fell into him. As Anatoly grabbed the man's arm to right himself, Anatoly kicked him in the shin.

"*Izvinite menya*," he said in a slurred voice.

The man, Pasha, attempted to say "*Oy*," but no words came out.

Anatoly deftly flipped Pasha over the railing onto the thin ice of the canal, and the now-paralyzed Pasha sank through the ice, which slowly re-formed over the hole he'd made. Anatoly looked down to verify the needle had retracted into the sole of his shoe, and he jogged away.

Hopping back onto the metro, Anatoly returned to the hotel. His superiors had given him Korinna's and Elda's names and had told him that Korinna had not been on the 16:40 train. He would find out what rooms she and her friend had and what information he could glean from searching them. Anatoly approached the desk and explained to the clerk that he was meeting these two women for dinner, but they had not shown up yet. He asked if they had checked in.

The clerk checked his computer. "*Nyet, yeshche nyet.*"

Anatoly asked for a pad of paper and wrote notes for both of them and handed each note to the clerk. The clerk turned and placed the notes into the room key slots: 606 and 607. The keys were in the slots, confirming the women had not checked in yet. "*Spasibo,*" Anatoly said. When he was certain the clerk was distracted by another customer, he slipped into the elevator.

At Room 606, he took a master key card out of his bag and swiped it. He did a quick check of the room. No one was there. Two bags left on the bed caught his attention. He checked the tags. Ainsworth!

What a coincidence. The name of the man he had stabbed. Or was it a coincidence? Was that man part of this mission somehow? He checked the cases. One had women's clothing in it, and the other had men's. "*Interesno,*" he said as his mind struggled to put the puzzle pieces together.

Finding nothing else of interest, he left and crossed the hallway to Room 607 and let himself in. No luggage. The bed covers were turned down, with an animal sculpted out of towels propped on the pillows, so clearly a guest was expected. He guessed from the size of the clothing in the other room that this room was for the taller woman, Korinna. Apparently, she had not made it here. *What happened between her boarding the train and it arriving at St. Petersburg? Did she transfer at an earlier stop to throw any tails off?* He wished he had interrogated the nervous man before eliminating him, but it was too late for that.

Anatoly returned to the lobby and obtained Room 609. He asked the desk to notify him of any calls in or out of either woman's room, and sat back down in the corner of the lobby to view the incoming guests. He called his superiors to let them know that the nervous man had met his end.

He checked with the local hospitals to see if Ainsworth was in any of them. With that wound, if he survived, he would not be going anywhere soon.

Having found Aurelio in the American clinic, Anatoly popped over to pay him a visit.

***

Elda sat stiffly to attention, stifling her reaction. Her heart pounded. *There's someone in there.* She'd been focused on detailing her plans in her head when she'd heard a sound from the adjoining room. She softly crept out of her chair and across the floor to the connecting door. *Yes!* Again, a faint sound came from in there. Breathing quickly and shallowly, she kept an eye on the doorknob, hoping it wouldn't turn. She heard the click of the corridor door being closed and let out a sigh of relief.

I really need to get a weapon.

***

Aurelio woke up in a sweat. He opened his eyes and saw, looming over him, a large man in nurses' scrubs, with a pillow in his hands.

"Who are you?" Aurelio asked in a hoarse voice.

162

"Who are you?" the nurse replied. "And who is she? What are you to her? Why did you attack me?"

Aurelio's addled brain tried to parse what the large man was asking, and he struggled with all the pronouns, wondering who *he* was and who *she* was.

The man stepped toward him with the pillow held out. Aurelio screamed a high-pitched crackling sound and frantically rang the buzzer for the real nurse. *It must be the man in the black truck*, he thought. *He has finally caught up with me!*

As the nurses ran in, the man puffed up the pillow, tossed it onto the chair, and shrugged his shoulders, making a circling sign near his head to imply that Aurelio was not right in his mind.

How dare he! I am sane! "Someone help me," Aurelio croaked. Another nurse rushed in as the man slipped out of the room. Aurelio thrashed about frantically, crying and babbling about a black truck and the FBI, CIA, and DEA. The nurse gave him a shot, which sent him back into peaceful blackness.

***

Korinna unsuccessfully tried to hold on as she rolled from the middle of the mattress. She crashed hard into the wall and cried out in pain. She now understood why the row of covered buckets were strapped to the other wall and why ropes were tied to each wall near the mattress at every half meter. She could see nothing in the inky blackness, but she had the sensation of being lifted.

The container bucked and pitched as it was lifted up and over onto the train. It was hard to keep silent as she struggled to hold on to a rope. She finally tied the rope around her waist and crawled in the dark, fumbling for the one on the opposite wall to counterbalance her and keep her from crashing into the sides. She tied herself in and covered herself again with a blanket. She had no idea where her pillow had gone, but she would wait until the container had stopped moving to find it. She didn't know what time or day it was or how long she had been in the container waiting in the railroad yard. She needed to visit one of the buckets, but that would have to wait until she was no longer being thrown around!

The container was dropped with a jarring clang, and she guessed it settled on top of a similar container. She heard more clangs as other containers were loaded. She didn't know how long she had before the train left, but she wanted to take advantage of the stillness and find the food basket, the buckets, and her pillow. She crawled in circles around the mattress until she located two more wool blankets and her pillow. She dropped them at the top of the mattress, where hopefully she could find them again. It was cold in the container, even though they had insulated this end of it to deafen any sounds.

She crawled toward the middle and found the basket of food tied to the wall with cases of water secured with straps. She reached in the basket and found it was filled with food boxes. As she reached in deeper, her hand touched something soft, and she screamed and recoiled. The feel was familiar though. She reached in again, and her hand closed around the soft, cuddly, well-traveled Privet! Ah, so like Elda to remember. Taking a food box and a water bottle out of the plastic that held the case together, she crawled back to the mattress. She briefly asked herself how clean the floor was and if there were any insects or small animals in there too, then shuddered.

Dropping her goodies next to her pillow, she crawled to the foot of the mattress, past the food and water, and located the buckets. She would work from left to right. The train ride would be sixteen hours from Moscow to Riga, and combined with the travel time for the ship from Latvia to Hamburg, the total trip could take close to a week. She crawled along the width of the compartment and counted the buckets by touching the top of each one. There were three across the end of the compartment, with another five tied in the back, making an L shape. She calculated that she had about a bucket per day of journey but would probably only need half of that, especially if she limited her intake. So, she would use a bucket for two days. She didn't want to have any of them overflow, nor did she want to check in the dark to see how full each one was. She used bucket "number one" and covered it, checking it twice to make certain it was securely closed.

She crept back along the floor to her pillow, wrapped up in two blankets, and tied herself in. In the dark she opened the cardboard box and took out what felt like a sandwich. She placed it on her lap and reached in again. There was a round object that felt like it was probably an apple. She placed the box with the apple in it between her knees so it wouldn't go anywhere and unwrapped the sandwich.

She took a bite. "*T'fu!*" She nearly spit out the *butterbrot* of rye bread and cold butter. She managed to keep it in her mouth and slowly chew it. She would have to eat what they had given her to keep her strength up. She shook her head in disgust at the awful Russian lunch sandwich. The only thing worse was the British buttie, which had tasteless white bread and butter. At least they often gave it some flavor by adding jam. She finished her sandwich, drank sparingly of the water, and then crammed the water bottle into the box with the apple and tied it with a rope so she could find it again when she was hungry.

She checked her ropes so she wouldn't roll too far the next time the container was lifted and curled into a ball to keep warm. *I wish Dasha and Sasha were here to keep my feet warm,* she thought as she hugged Privet.

Her journey had begun.

Chapter Ten

5 December, 2018

"You cannot be in that lane, sir."

Sighing, Yuri switched lanes for the third time. "*Chert*. Why can't they label these things right?"

"What is your business in the UK?"

"I am on holiday there."

"Please stand over to one side, sir. We need to validate your paperwork."

Yuri moved to the new area, and the officer closed his station and jogged over to talk with another. A third official joined them. They were looking at an iPad screen and back at Yuri. His stomach churned. Had his drug running finally caught up with him?

Finally, the officer returned.

"My apologies for the delay. You are free to go."

Shaken, Yuri left immigration and customs and caught a taxi to the Montague on the Gardens Hotel at 15 Montague Street in London, England. He was to wait there for additional instructions. He had changed his route several times and hadn't detected anyone following him.

"Don't worry, little doggies. *Ya lyublya tebya.* I'll keep you safe."

He peeked into the complimentary treat bags and found a squeaky hamburger in one and a squeaky hotdog and a gun for Anatoly in the other. He hoped they weren't particular about who received which toy. He poured water for them in one of the stainless-steel raised bowls, and kibbles in the other, and then reviewed the room service menu for himself. He took off his coat and shoes, placed his gun under a pillow on the bed, and flopped onto the bed to wait for room service. *Nitstsa, I could get used to this type of assignment*, he thought as he lay there with his hands folded beneath his head, resting next to the gun.

***

Are they dead? Could someone be holding the dogs for ransom? Korinna's neighbor, Anna, frantically paced the floor in her apartment, trying to figure out what to do. She had repeatedly called the number on the dog groomer's card, but no one answered, and now she was getting the message *"Chislo nedostupen."*

Why would the number not be available? Anna had guessed that Korinna had an important but secretive job. *Egor is dead. The dogs are missing.* She gasped and clutched at her chest. She shook her head and flung her hands in the air to wave her thoughts away. Whatever it was, she didn't want to be part of it.

Anna burned the card in her sink and washed the ashes down the drain. Korinna could handle finding the dogs when she returned. Until then, Anna would act as if nothing had happened. It was better to say nothing and keep a low profile.

Anna crossed the hall and checked Korinna's apartment one last time. *Strange.* Korinna had left a teacup in the sink. Anna picked up the cup and washed it, dried it, and returned it to the cupboard.

The silence in the apartment was rather overwhelming and a bit scary. Usually, the two tiny dogs filled the space with their energy and barking. Anna quickly left the apartment, locked the door, and scurried across the hall to lock herself in her own apartment. *Ya nichego ne vizhu. Ya nichego ne znayu,* she said to herself as she clicked the locks. *I see nothing. I know nothing.*

***

A crash from the kitchen was followed by loud swearing. *Is the assassin here?* In answer to her question, a waiter rushed out of the kitchen, knocking down another waiter coming into the kitchen with a tray of dishes. A man with a double-buttoned, long-sleeved jacket ran out waving a frying pan.

"*Ty uvolen*! And don't expect your last paycheck. It will barely cover this mess."

Well, he's obviously not the assassin. To help stifle her reaction to the scene, Elda charted the layout of the restaurant and its patrons. The large man with brown hair looked through her to a tall blonde with a handsome man, who were fawning over each other, not caring who was watching. *Almost as if they're acting out a scene.* Elda made a mental note to keep an eye on that couple. *They could have sent more than one assassin.*

She sighed as the waiter placed her breakfast plate in front of her. The eggs were surrounded by a liquid moat of butter, with pockets of melted butter scattered across the top. *Egad. Did this chef go to*

cooking school with the previous chef in Moscow?
She sighed again, and with an elderly tremble
brought a forkful of eggs from the plate to her mouth.
She then coughed and spit into a napkin.

A look of disgust crossed the large man's face
as he averted his eyes and rose to step from the room.

***

Anatoly took a long look at the amorous
couple as he passed their table. He was suspicious of
two lovebirds who were up and out of bed this early.
He intended to follow them wherever they went. He
had the room numbers for the two women, so he
could check if they were in yet on his return to the
hotel.

***

Elda sopped up the rest of the grease from her
plate with a hunk of dry brown bread. She nodded to
herself as the rest of her plan fell into place and her
mind ran through it one more time. She finished her
tea and shakily pushed herself up and out of her
chair. The waiter rushed over and handed her the
cane from the back of her chair.

"*Spasibo.*" She smiled weakly at him and
tottered shakily away with a hint of a limp.

172

Once in her room, Elda took out her blue contacts and added them to the backpack's contents, along with her disguise. She added the package for Yuri and then took the original backpack out of the well-used one covering it.

Elda peered out the peephole and then slipped out of her room and went to the door leading into the staff-only stairwell. She ran down the stairs and out the side door. Elda walked around to the front and through the doors into the lobby. She was not surprised to see the large man sitting in a lobby chair, where he could observe all the comings and goings. She did not turn toward him or glance at him, but she marched up to the desk to let them know she was checking in, apologizing for the delay.

The man sat up a bit straighter as Elda walked through the lobby, then settled back into his chair.

In the elevator, Elda unfolded the note, only to find a blank piece of paper. *Interesting...* She concluded the note must have been a ploy by someone to determine what room she was in. She bet that Korinna's room key slot also had a note in it. *Was it the large man in the lobby?*

Elda hopped off the elevator to check that she wasn't followed, spun around, and quickly reentered the elevator. It jarred to a stop at the third floor, and the amorous couple entered.

"*Dobroye utro*," Elda said, wondering if they spoke Russian.

"*Dobroye utro*," they replied.

"Are you off to see the sights?"

"*Da*, we wish to see the Hermitage."

"Are you from here?" Elda asked, trying to place their accents.

"*Nyet*. We are from Nizhny Novgorod."

Elda's eyes narrowed slightly. Their accents did not add up to that area east of Moscow.

The doors opened to the lobby, and Elda motioned for the couple to leave the elevator in front of her. She fell into step with them while walking through the lobby.

The large man almost snapped to attention in his chair in the lobby.

"I bet you are newlyweds," Elda said to the couple.

"We are!" They grinned and held the other's hand more firmly. "We are on our honeymoon. Moscow was our first stop, and now St. Petersburg. We have not had the chance to explore much of Russia before now."

"And you have always lived in Nizhny Novgorod?" Elda was still trying to place their accents.

"Yes. We have an apartment in the Moskovsky district of Nizhny Novgorod and both work there at the Sokol Aircraft Plant."

"Have you ever traveled outside of Russia? I would think that you might have wanted to take your honeymoon in a different place—perhaps, say, England or Canada?"

The couple glanced at each other, and the blonde said, "*Nyet*. We do not trust the Westerners. And the British are so bland. We love Mother Russia. Plus, it's much more affordable to travel within Russia."

Elda asked them a variety of questions about their city. Either they were well briefed, or they were who they said they were.

"You ask a lot of questions."

"Russia fascinates me. I am delighted to find out more about it, especially an area outside of St. Petersburg or Moscow. I don't mean to pry."

They walked in silence for the rest of the way to the metro. Elda put on her therapist hat to analyze the truthfulness of their answers, and she could not find anything that rang a warning bell. *Perhaps a cigar is just a cigar, but my instinct is usually correct. I don't totally trust that they are who they are. There's really no one to trust in this occupation. Anyone could be the enemy.*

They descended into the station and paraded onto the blue line toward Spasskaya station. Elda had sensed the large man's presence behind them, and at one point, she turned toward the couple and caught sight of him out of the corner of her eye. *Good! Hopefully, this will confuse him.* She found a seat behind the couple and settled back for the short jaunt to Varota. If the couple was really going to the Hermitage, then they would get off at the next stop, Sennaya Plochard, to switch to the Purple Line.

The large man strolled by and plopped down in a seat facing both Elda and the couple. He stared directly at Elda, who looked unflinchingly back at him.

The train slowed down, and the couple departed, as Elda had anticipated. The large man had a split second to decide if he was getting off or not. He jumped up and off just before the doors closed and the train moved on. Elda wiped her brow. *Who and where is the assassin? What if it isn't him?*

***

Elda whirled around as someone brushed against her. She distrusted crowds and wanted to get out of the station as quickly as possible. Another man bumped her from the right side. *Is this an intimidation ploy? Would they target me without Korinna nearby?*

Elda dodged in and out of stores and restaurants, trying to identify any familiar faces. She hurried back to the Ploshchad Vosstaniya station and continued on the Red Line to Pushkinskaya station, where she jumped over to the Purple Line.

After leaving the train, she saw the couple, with the large man to one side of them, waiting to take a train in the opposite direction. The couple were deeply absorbed in each other. The man narrowed his eyes as he spied her, and he scanned the area as if looking for a way to get over to her side of the tracks.

She sighed in relief as she turned around and headed to the escalator. It was so obvious that he was conflicted about who to follow. Now she could put a face to the person spying on her and perhaps, even, the assassin. *I'm not being paranoid about that one!*

She soon wasn't feeling relief as she held onto the handrail in panic and focused on the back of the legs of the person in front of her. *Here I go! Funny what things I can face, but heights freak me out. I need to get over this.*

She repeated over and over under her breath, "Do not fall backward… Do not fall backward… Do not fall backward…" *All it would take is a gentle shove, and I would be easily eliminated.*

When she reached the top of the first escalator, she stepped to one side and paused to catch her breath and calm her heart rate. *I can't do this. I should just head right back down! Snap out of it, Elda. It's time you conquered this fear!* She took a deep breath and headed onto the second escalator. When she hit the fresh air at the top, she was shaking but ecstatic. *I did it!* She went around to the fountain at Admiralteystava and regained her bearings. *Damn I was so rattled by the escalator that I didn't check who was around me.* She did a slow, 360-degree turn to assure herself that no one had tracked her here. Feeling confident again, she marched off. She identified Yuri's friend a few feet away. As she passed him, she dropped the package at his feet. He quickly picked it up and strode away.

Elda returned to the Admiralteyskaya Metro station, took a deep breath, and started her trek down to the trains. She visually selected a mole on the back of the neck of a man in front of her to focus on. She was elated at her conquest when she reached the stable ground. She looked around and was surprised to view the large man waiting on the station platform.

***

Elda forced herself to travel slowly and calmly. The large man had followed her back to the hotel and then left as she walked into the lobby. *Well, that was certainly pointed.*

In the hallway she made sure no one was around and went into the old lady's room, 608, instead of her own room. She figured that since she was in the adjoining room, she would be able to hear if he tried to enter room 606.

If you try to kill me tonight, I won't be there.

***

5 December, 2018

Elda picked up the hotel room phone and dialed Korinna's cell phone number.

Korinna's voice answered, *"Da?"*

Elda quickly gave instructions for Korinna to meet her at the State Hermitage Museum at 13:10 today.

"Khorosho," Korinna responded, acknowledging the meet.

Elda hung up, hoping her hunch about there being a tap on the hotel was correct.

***

A short, nondescript man took the battery out of Korinna's phone and threw the tape recorder with Korinna's voice on it, her phone, and battery into the canal.

***

Anatoly prowled around the city to find the right spot to eliminate the two women. His phone rang.

"There has been a call from Room 606. They are meeting at the Hermitage this afternoon at 13:10."

"*Spasibo.*"

Otlichnyye novosti, he thought. *Such excellent news!* He would get there early and wait for them. And that would give him the morning stalking the lovebirds, if they left their room at all during that time. *There is something not right about that couple. No one is that consistently affectionate in public. Even newlyweds have spats.*

What is that man doing over there? A man dug under the front seat of a car, and Anatoly wondered if he was stealing it. The man stood up and was holding keys in one hand and money and a note in the other.

I have my assignment. Let that go. Anatoly quickly punched in a number on his phone and asked his superiors to trace the number that Elda had called. An hour later, he received a message that the phone his target had called was the tall woman's phone, but there was no trace of it at this time.

Anatoly loped back to his room to select the right equipment for this afternoon. He had liked watching yesterday's victim sink into the canal and thought that might be a good method to off these two also. Careful not to touch any liquid, he refilled the paralytic agent in the shoe needle. The special toxin disappeared after a few hours, so it was virtually untraceable in the body. It was also so rare that it was not part of the toxicology screen normally done on corpses. These women had just been lucky. They were no match for him. He would separate them and handle them one at a time.

"Perhaps the tall one should be first to go, since she is my priority, and since the shorter one would probably return directly to the hotel," he pondered aloud. He checked the knife that had been used on Mr. Ainsworth, to reassure himself he had cleaned it enough and there was nothing to impede its smooth slide into a body. He then placed a noose into his right pocket and the knife into the sleeve holder.

Anatoly left the Radisson Hotel to catch the metro to the Winter Palace. From the station at Nevskiy Prospekt, he took the Blue Line to Spasskaya, to switch to the Purple Line for Admiralteiskaya, by the Winter Palace, the main building of the Hermitage. *With two changes, I should be able to easily identify anyone who might be following me.*

***

Natasha showed up at the hospital later that afternoon, carrying some English magazines for Aurelio. She hoped he wouldn't be well enough to

182

read them. She turned the corner by the nurses' station and entered Aurelio's room. His bed was empty, and Aurelio was nowhere to be seen. Her heart leaped for joy. Had he died? Was she finally free of him? *Oh, I wish Yuri was there to share the good news! Gde, Yuri?*

Natasha set the magazines down on the side table. Aurelio was not there, but the room was still set up for a patient. She'd wait for a nurse to show up, to see if the good news was true. Just then a nurse entered, and Natasha turned to face her.

The nurse held up her hand. "*Pozhaluysta, podozhdite doktora,*" and she left to get the doctor.

Natasha anxiously waited. The doctor walked in, accompanied by a second doctor.

"*Privet*, Mrs. Ainsworth. I am the doktor in charge of your husband's care. I have asked for a consult from psychiatry to help assess Mr. Ainsworth's condition."

Natasha's heart sank. *O nyet, der'mo, he's alive.* But her face showed only concern and compassion. "*On zhiv?*"

"Yes, he is alive, but in critical condition."

"*Slave Bogu,*" she said with a forced smile, crossing herself.

She turned toward the second doctor with a quizzical expression.

"*Psikhiatriya?*" she asked.

"Your husband was hysterically thrashing and burst his stitches. We had to rush him back into surgery. He had been crying and screaming about a man with a black truck who had tried to kill him. It's obvious that Aurelio has had some sort of psychotic breakdown and is a paranoid schizophrenic."

She shook her head in disbelief.

"*On vsegda byl takim?*" asked the doctor.

Natasha considered how she should answer that question. If she said "Yes, he has always been that way," it might negate the will that was sitting signed in Natasha's purse.

"Could it be possible that this episode came on suddenly, Doktor?"

"*Da, da, vozmozhnyy,*" the doctor affirmed.

Natasha let out a sigh of relief and answered his original question, "*Nyet, on ne byl.*"

The psychiatric doctor nodded. "*Da*, this fits my theory. The paranoia and delusions had been triggered by the assault on the train."

Natasha sat down on the chair and leaned in to listen.

"We will stabilize Aurelio and move him down the road to the Psychiatric Hospital of St. Nicholas, where they will start him on psychiatric medications."

This could be the answer to everything, she thought as she listened to the doctor drone on about possible medications. As long as she retained control of Aurelio's care, she could live in their apartment until she found out where all Aurelio's money was, and then she could sell that horrid place and live somewhere more luxurious. Perhaps the hospital could help her get the rest of the information from Aurelio. Then, when she collected all his onshore and offshore assets, well... it was not uncommon for patients in a mental institution to meet their end at the hands of another patient, was it? They were all nuts in there, after all. She laughed at the thought and quickly covered it up with a cough that turned into crying.

"*Pozhaluysta izvinite menya*," she said, her blue eyes filling with tears.

"*Tam, tam.*" He patted her on her arm and told her there was no need for her to ask to be excused. It was, of course, a lot to take in all at once.

The doctor handed Natasha a handkerchief. "*Oh, Doktor, spasibo.*" She put her best smile on, blinked her eyes, and placed her hand on his for a few moments longer than necessary.

The doctor straightened his shoulders and puffed out his chest while sucking in his stomach. "*Ya dam tebe vremya podumat',*" he said, marching himself out the door.

Natasha covered her smirking mouth with the handkerchief. She didn't need the offered time to think if Aurelio should go to the mental institution, but she would play the part of the confused little woman who needed the strong doktor's help and advice.

Aurelio's money would soon be in her hands.

***

I hope the assassin shows up. Elda was worried. She had to eliminate the large man before he discovered where Korinna was, or worse, killed her! Drawing him out with this fake meet with Korinna at the Hermitage might give her an opportunity.

186

Elda spotted the large man standing outside the State Hermitage Museum as she approached. She passed him without a glance and went into the ticket booth inside the large green, white, and gold building. *Oh no, it is really crowded inside today. I need find another location to deal with him.*

Elda immediately headed for the Italian Renaissance paintings on the first floor. She was on a mission and had to get out of these crowds. She checked her watch frequently, as if she had somewhere to go. The Hermitage interior, with the gold on its furniture and fireplace mantels, was so lavish that it competed with the art for her attention. Sightseers jostled her as they swarmed from one attraction to the next. Claustrophobic, her chest tightened, and she took rapid, shallow, gasping breaths. She stopped and hung onto the wall while slowing her breathing down.

It would be hard to get back to the exit since tourists were strictly controlled, routed through the museum and out a door next to the entrance. Elda heard the confident echo of the man's footsteps on the marble floors behind her, stopping as she stopped and starting up again when she moved on. She walked quickly, but not in a way that might attract attention from the guards, who were stationed in every room and in all the hallways. In America that might make her feel safer, but here in Russia it made her nervous.

Elda finally made her way to the exit and departed the Hermitage Museum onto Nevsky Avenue for the Hermitage Theater. She checked her watch often and at one point said loudly, "Where is she?"

Stopping to tie her shoelace, she caught sight of the assassin still behind her. She took off at a fast jog and turned a sharp right onto the embankment river Moyka. The man sped up and kept pace with her. *Crap. For a large man, he's fast. I can't outrun him, so I need to distract him.* Elda did another right turn onto Gorokhovaya Street and ran into the KFC.

She stood in line and ordered two buckets of chicken. The assassin lurked outside the restaurant door. Leaving with her chicken, Elda held out a bucket to the man. "Here." Instinctively he took it, buying her the time to take off again.

She ran in a loop back down to the river embankment. While running, Elda threw pieces of chicken behind her, being rewarded by occasional exclamations of *"Chert!"* and *"Der'mo!"* Daring a glance behind, she was dismayed that she had gained only a slight bit of ground on the man, who was dodging chicken pieces. Regretting how much she'd had to litter already, she threw the empty bucket behind her. She stopped.

***

Anatoly stopped about thirty feet away from Elda. *Aga! There is no one around her. Khorosho. I will get rid of her and then find the other woman.* He palmed his knife and ran toward her.

***

Elda heard his footsteps and sensed him picking up his pace behind her. She calculated the distance. She heard him break into a run, but she did not move or turn around. Just as he leaped at her, she twisted sideways and bent, put her hip into him, and used his momentum to flip him into the canal. She observed as his heavy clothes dragged him down, and then she turned onto Nevsky Avenue.

***

A hand reached up out of the partially frozen hole where Anatoly had fallen into the canal. The fingers caught onto a metal ring on the side of the canal and pulled. Anatoly's head emerged, and he gasped for air. His other hand reached up and found leverage to pull himself out of the canal.

Icy and shivering, he searched for a cab. He had to change his clothes quickly, lest hypothermia set in. He stood with money displayed clearly in the clenched fist of his raised hand, and a cab driver going the opposite direction made a U-turn and picked him up, slipping and sliding across the hard-packed snow.

I will settle this score.

Anatoly's taxi approached the hotel as the old woman moved toward another taxi. It was like watching the ice form in the canal. She moved with that shuffling old-person's gait, with a slight limp, which was probably why she needed the cane. He was a patient man, but this ancient woman was so slow, it was irritating him. But more so he was angry at himself. How could the small, brown-haired woman have flipped him into the canal so easily?

Vozmozhno ya stareyu, he chastised himself, and then threw that thought of being too old for his job away with a physical shake of his head. *Old! Look at what old is*, he reminded himself as the old woman approached her cab. He was dripping wet, shivering, and cold to the bone. He had never had an assignment go so poorly.

Anatoly left a trail of puddles behind him on his way to his room, where he stripped off his wet clothes and threw himself into a hot shower. He stepped out of the shower, dressed in dry clothing, and checked the adjoining room. It was as untouched as when he'd first entered it. The stupid stuffed animal towel still lay on the bed, only this time, the maid had given it the *Ne Bespokoit'* card from the door. He went across to the other room, and it was also the same as when he'd last seen it. He returned to his room and sat in anger. He did not want to call his superiors and admit what had happened, but he had no alternative. He picked up his phone but found that it no longer worked after the dip in the frigid canal.

"*Der'mo*!" He reached over and used the room phone to call down to the front desk, asking for someone to pick up his phone and dry it out.

He heard movement across the hall and looked through the spyhole. A bellhop entered Room 606 and returned to the hallway with the luggage. He stepped out into the hallway and poked his head into the room, asking, "*Kuda eto idet*?" and pointing to the case the bellhop had picked up off the bed.

The bellhop frowned and stared at Anatoly, waiting to be compensated for his answer. Anatoly handed him some money.

The bellhop smirked. "The guest had checked out, and her luggage was to be sent on to the Hotel Brunelleschi in Florence, Italy."

"*Spasibo*." Anatoly helped load the other bag onto the cart, slipping a tracker into an outside pocket as he moved the bag.

He asked the front desk clerk, "Who gave the instructions to move the luggage from Room 606?"

"*Ya ne znayu*."

Anatoly pushed a number of bank notes across the counter. "Were they given in person or via phone?"

The clerk smoothly pocketed the money. "I received a phone call."

"Give me that number now."

The clerk checked back on caller ID and wrote the number down on a piece of paper. "*Vot*."

"*Spasibo*."

Anatoly tossed the paper into the trash bin. The instructions had come from an unknown caller. Probably a burner phone. He checked his watch. Good thing he had such a quality watch. All that water, and it still worked. *I will obey my orders to eliminate the tall blonde, but you, my little brunette, for you I will find a special ending.*

***

Elda backed out of the taxi at Pulkovo Airport, putting one leg out, holding onto the seat and the door and slowly rising to an upright position with the driver's assistance. After ensuring she was stable on her two feet, he handed her the cane and her backpack. She thanked him and tipped him generously and then hobbled into Terminal One.

Elda stopped inside the door and flagged down an attendant to get a wheelchair to ferry her through check-in, customs, and the gate. She would just catch the flight that left at 16:40 and arrived there at 17:20. With the time change, that would be a quick three-hour- and forty-minute flight. She breathed deeply to calm herself and then coughed into a handkerchief to keep in character. She rather enjoyed the ride in the wheelchair and had to restrain herself from grinning and saying "Whee!" She asked the attendant to grab her a few newspapers to read on the trip.

Relieved to have gotten rid of the threat, she sat back in her comfortable first-class seat and opened the papers. Buried inside the *Moscow Times* was a story about a busload of musicians from

193

Moscow that had rolled over and crashed on a windy snowy road in Canada. All but one had managed to escape the bus before it burst into flames. They had no hope to retrieve the charred remains of that last musician, nor of the driver, since the descent was so steep, and the bus had shattered into pieces on the way down.

Elda nodded. The plan was on track.

Chapter Eleven

6 December, 2018

Elda landed at Heathrow. Although she had dispatched the assassin, she felt tense: others could be sent after her. And there were cameras that could be hacked into at all the airports, so Elda would stay in character until she arrived at the hotel. She waited as the other passengers deplaned and an attendant brought her a wheelchair. Holding her backpack in her lap, she rolled her way to the taxi stand, wishing she could ask the attendant to go faster.

Heathrow and London were like home to her. She had been traveling to England since high school, and Heathrow hadn't changed that much over the years. It was a cluttered and confusing airport to those not used to it. But to Elda, it was like regaining a lost part of herself as she felt the cadence, listened to the sounds, and smelled the familiar scents. She maneuvered through customs and caught a taxi to the Montague on the Gardens Hotel. To her, the original black cabs were a symbol of England, much like the red double-decker buses were. The green double-decker tour buses just didn't belong.

The taxi driver had recently been to India. He was chatty about his experiences, even turning to show Elda pictures of his family back in India, a move that made Elda anxious as she kept an eye on the road for him. It was a bit unsettling to be driving on the left again. Years ago, when she had lived in the UK for over a year before returning to the States, she'd been driving down the road with her sister, who kept asking her to pull over into the right-hand lane. Finally, to shut her sister up, Elda complied, just as a car came whizzing toward them in the left-hand lane they had just vacated. It was amazing how the brain adapted and how one could be so convinced that they were correct and unaware of the adaptation. Where was the line between that form of adaptation and insane delusions that could have originated from adaptation?

The driver's chatter brought her back to the ride, and she nodded and smiled at his conversation. Despite his thick accent, Elda was relieved to hear English. Although she had spoken English with Korinna, it was almost necessary to think in Russian and as a Russian would, to survive in that country. She figured the driver had lived this long driving erratically and she could trust him to be wary of the traffic.

Tomorrow she would pick up the dogs and help them on the next leg of their journey. Then she would fly to Hamburg to meet Korinna's ship. Elda could only imagine how hard it was to sit in a hidden compartment in a container. But she had seen how strong Korinna was.

She had been watching the extended weather reports, for if the weather changed, it could result in Korinna being battered about in the container or, worse yet, the container being flooded. "I hope you are traveling safely and smoothly, my friend," she whispered as a prayer.

***

6 December, 2018

Korinna awoke a few times to eat and eliminate, and then plopped herself back on the mattress and forced herself to sleep through this ordeal. She awoke again as she felt the train slowing. *We must be at customs*. Her heart leaped in her chest. It was vital that she make no noise as the inspectors progressed in checking the inventory. There was no way they could see that the inside of the container was shorter than the outside, but it still worried her. She hoped that they had stacked the container up where they couldn't easily reach it. She started praying silently and hugged Privet tightly.

It seemed like hours before the train rolled slowly forward. Korinna cried from relief. She had one more hurdle to get through when the container was loaded onto the ship, but she had escaped from Russia! To celebrate, she crawled to the food and then back onto the mattress. The brown bread "jam buttie" tasted like a feast after the plainer rye bread *butterbrot*. She chewed the sandwich and envisioned it was a feast of steak and mashed potatoes and imagined that Egor was sharing it with her. She pictured him sitting there in the dark with her. She wondered if she was hallucinating from the loneliness and the dark but concluded that it was probably too soon for that.

***

Elda gasped for breath. The musty smell emanating from the carpet combined with the stale smell of cigars from the previous evening almost gagged her. The surrounding dark wood wainscoting suffocated Elda. She glared at the soggy cooked tomato on her plate and pushed it to one side, analyzing the rest of her breakfast. The eggs were sunny-side up with crispy edges. The toast was stiff and cold, and the rasher of bacon was much the same. She smiled. *A typical English breakfast!* She poured herself a cup of tea from the ceramic teapot and let the steam rise toward her nose. *What a luxury good English tea is.*

She finished her meal and then made her way to reception. "What room number is Yuri Kuznetsov in?"

She loped up the stairs to his floor. As she approached the door, she heard the yipping of two excited little dogs. Well, they weren't keeping well hidden, were they?

Yuri checked to see who was in the hall and then opened the door, letting the dogs rush at and jump all over Elda. She sat down in the middle of the room and let them bowl her over and lick her face.

"*Khoroshiye storozhevyye sobaki*," she said.

He laughed. "Yes, good watchdogs. They have you captured!"

Yuri closed the door and handed Elda the dogs' harnesses and leashes, as well as their bag of goodies and food and two soft-sided carry-on crates. She handed him an envelope that had a single piece of paper in it, with banking routing numbers typed on it. Yuri memorized the numbers and burned the flash paper in the bathroom sink. Elda clipped the harnesses and leashes on Dasha and Sasha and then shook Yuri's hand.

"*Spasibo*, Yuri."

"No problem, Elda. *Do svidaniya.*"

"*Poka, udachi.*"

"Good luck to you too. Until we meet again."

"*Da. Poka my ne vstretimsya snova.*"

Yuri hugged each dog, picked up his luggage, and started off on his trip back to St. Petersburg. The dogs sat and sadly stared at the closed door.

Elda patted each pup and gave them a treat, helping to distract them. She took them back to her room, called the airlines, and then grabbed her backpack and the dog gear and checked out of the hotel. She flagged a taxi for Heathrow airport. She would catch the 14:45 flight to JFK in NYC, hand off the dogs, and catch the 21:30 flight from JFK to Hamburg, and arrive there tomorrow afternoon in advance of Korinna's ship. Although she wouldn't get much sleep, she had managed to snag two first-class seats for the way out and one for herself for the way back. She made a phone call on the way to the airport to arrange the dog handoff.

Sasha and Dasha were a big hit as Elda proceeded slowly through immigration. People stopped to pet them, and they were spinning around on their hind legs, begging for treats.

An immigration official pulled Elda and the dogs to one side. "You're slowing everyone down and causing a commotion. Where are you arriving from?"

"I am so sorry, Officer. I am a United States citizen, and I am arriving from the United Kingdom."

"And whose dogs are these?"

"They are mine. I am bringing them home. Here are their papers."

The official examined her papers and left to consult with his superior. Elda patted the dogs until he returned, hoping that it wouldn't be noticeable that she had broken out in a layer of sweat.

"I'm sorry. You will have to come with me."

Elda looked up in surprise. The papers were supposed to flag the CIA to override any Homeland Security hassle and to let her in.

"Pardon?"

"Come with me."

Elda trailed behind the official to a small windowless room with a metal table, two chairs, and a bench. He motioned her in and closed the door behind her.

***

Biting the sides of her fingers, Elda sat in the small room talking to the dogs. "I don't know why that failed. I hope I can get a phone call. What will happen to you if I am imprisoned?" She breathed deeply to stave off her claustrophobia. Suddenly the door opened. Elda jumped up. A new official strolled in.

"Everything is in order. Welcome home." He led her out of the room and pointed her over to a kiosk.

After customs, she headed directly to the nearest restroom to freshen up and to let the dogs relieve themselves. There was a "wooftop" dog relief area over at Terminal Five, but it would be quicker and easier to take them into the handicap stall and have them use pee pads that she then disposed of in the trash.

"You have been such good dogs to hold it all that time," she told them as she scratched them behind their ears. Elda made sure their harnesses were secure and unclipped the leashes as she lured

202

them back into the crates, placing the leashes in the outside pocket of each soft crate.

Elda exited customs and felt a rush of love and relief when she spotted Dawn. She ran with the dogs over to her. Dawn stiffened but then relaxed as Elda held Dawn close and kissed her.

"Can we secure the dogs in the car and grab a quick bite before I catch the 21:30 flight back overseas?"

"You're flying back tonight?"

"I have to. The job is not finished."

"Why does it have to be you?"

"She trusts me."

"Is that more important than being with your family again?"

"No, of course not, but it's not an either-or situation. I have to go."

Dawn sighed heavily. "Promise me again that this is the very last time."

"I promise, Dawn. No more missions."

They each picked up a dog and walked to the garage. Elda so wanted to stay for a day or two, and she had time to do so, but if she did, it would be harder to get on a plane and she would lose her edge. She also wanted to arrange Korinna's next leg of the journey from Hamburg.

"I just can't explain it to you, honey."

"You never can."

After setting the dog crates into the backseat of the car, they returned to the terminal. There was nothing appealing to eat pre-security, and Elda hoped she could avoid conflict with Dawn.

They sat on a bench drinking water, and Elda leaned into Dawn.

Dawn pulled away and then leaned back in. She put her arm around Elda. "You know I wish you didn't have to go, and you know I understand that you have to go. And I know that you don't want to go."

Elda snugged in a bit closer for a few minutes. She let the warmth and security wash over her. Then she suddenly stood up and straightened into attention. "I have to go. This is too wonderful. I just want to stay more every minute I sit next to you. And if I stay much longer, we may have to find a dog-friendly hotel!"

Dawn wrapped her arms around Elda again and kissed her. Then, she squared her shoulders and walked away.

***

Anatoly studied the hotel security footage, playing the last two days over and over again. The woman entered the hotel, but she did not leave through the lobby. He cursed that the camera over the side exit wasn't working. There were not many guests staying at the hotel, and after hours of viewing the footage, he felt like he knew them all. He sat back in his chair, his eyes burning from staring at the small screen. He had no choice but to tell his superiors and to have them check the airports and train stations for any sightings of these two women. They would also be able to run their names and see if they had bought tickets for any type of transportation.

"*Der'mo*," he swore under his breath, and he picked up his phone to call the Kremlin. Thank goodness they had not only replaced his waterlogged phone with a new one but had also managed to transfer the contact information and other data from his old phone.

Anatoly disconnected the call. His handler was not available. The person on duty had assured him that his request for more information on the tall blonde and the airport and train station checks would be arranged. And they would gather details on where the tall blonde went on vacation, what stamps she had on her passport, who her friends were, what she liked to do for social activities, if she had a second home, if she had living relatives, and any other useful information to help him locate her.

Anatoly couldn't sit still anymore, and he packed up his go bag and checked out of the hotel.

"Pulkolvo Aeroport pozhaluysta."

He would look at the security footage at the airport himself. *"Der'mo, der'mo, der'mo."* He pounded his fist into his leg as he struggled to figure out where these two women were.

"Chto? Is there something wrong, sir?"

"Nyet. Vse khorosho."

On the way to the airport, he remembered the man in the hospital. Perhaps he knew something. The thought was like a lightbulb going off in his brain. He had a plan again. Anatoly leaned forward and spoke through the grate in the plexiglass.

"Votidel'."

The driver turned his head slightly. *"Da?"*

"Pozhaluysta, turn around and head to Amerikanskaya Klinika p., embankment river Moyka, 78."

The driver turned his wheel sharply in response, sending Anatoly across to the other side of the backseat. Anatoly growled, and the driver shrugged in apology.

As the driver slammed on his brakes and abruptly stopped in the parking lot, an ambulance raced out in front of them.

"Der'mo! How did you get your license?"

"What license?"

Anatoly threw money onto the driver's lap and slammed the back door. As he hastened to the hospital entrance, he briefly pondered where the ambulance was going. It wasn't in any hurry. *Perhaps they are picking a dead body out of the canal? No, it's too soon for the body to fill with gas and float to the surface.* He strode into the hospital and picked up a large bouquet of flowers at the gift shop. Big enough to hide his face from any security cameras.

***

6 December, 2018

Natasha leaned in toward the doctor so that they could speak over the rattling sounds of equipment in the metal boxes in the back of the ambulance.

"*Doktor*, what happens now?"

"We will have the psychiatric team work with Aurelio immediately. Hopefully, they can keep him calm and prevent any future hysterical outbursts so his wounds will heal."

Aurelio groaned as the ambulance turned a corner and shifted him on the bench. He was securely strapped in, but his injuries were painful. The stitches from the second operation were holding, however, and they had given him a tranquilizer, as well as pain medication, to keep him calm.

"Will his mind heal too, *Doktor*?"

"We don't have enough information yet. The team will need to assess him further." Over the noise of the ambulance wheels and the rattling sounds of equipment in the metal boxes, the doctor explained the plan of action for treating Aurelio.

"Aurelio is now severely paranoid and has invented stories to make himself feel safe and powerful. The Psychiatric Hospital of St. Nicholas just down the embankment river Moyka at number 126 is not far from the clinic. Aurelio is still in critical condition medically, so I will visit him daily. Once at the hospital, the team there can start him on psychiatric drugs and see if they can get the right combination. That will take some time, but hopefully that, combined with talk therapy, will enable Aurelio to return to a more stable state."

"How soon may I visit him, *Doktor*?"

"There is a risk that he may die from his wounds still or may not be able to recover from the breakdown. The hospital itself is violent, and fights break out, even with many guards there. It will probably be best to keep Aurelio in isolation, without visitors, until he is better."

"Not even his wife?" Natasha turned her tear-stained face to look into the doctor's eyes.

"I know how hard that will be, but it is for the best."

Natasha nodded and held the doctor's arm while he explained the next steps to her. "*Spasibo, Doktor. Spasibo.*" *This could work out well for me.*

Korinna woke again to the container bucking and rolling as the crane lifted it from the train bed, up over the pier to the cargo ship. She held on tightly to Privet and made sure her ropes were securely tied. She assumed that they were not storing the container in the shipyard but that the movement was up and onto the ship. The buckets sloshed, and she was thankful she had locked down each cover.

She examined the compartment, desperate to see some chink of light that would give her solace that the outside world was still there. She had to keep her mind busy so she didn't panic or hallucinate from the days of isolation and darkness. A detailed planner and organizer, she mentally designed the house she and Egor would live in once they were back together and settled.

Korinna was an excellent cook. Her perfect kitchen would have long, granite counters, a stainless-steel sink, and one of those wonderful islands in the middle, where she and Egor could sit and have breakfast each morning. And cabinets with plenty of space to fit dog food and treats. There should be a tall, skinny cabinet for the brooms and mops. She could picture it in 3D in her mind. Money was no problem. She and Egor had been skimming off extra money and hiding it in an offshore account in Cypress. They would tap into it and bring it incrementally over to an account at a bank near where they would be living. Perhaps, as part of the relocation they might receive a small sum of money to help with paying for decorating their new home?

She figured their apartment and the small amount of money in their Russian bank account would be confiscated. She was sad to think of losing her family photo album and the throws her grandmother had knitted. Tears ran down her cheeks at the lost history. She had many knickknacks her mother had handed down to her. Nothing worth a lot of money, but each one with a lot of sentimental value.

She wiped her nose and eyes on her sleeves and forced herself to think happier thoughts and stop crying. They were only things. *Egor, Dasha, Sasha, and I are family, and we will be together again. The memories will be forever in my heart.* She sniffed and stopped herself from crying, since she was running low on Kleenex tissues from her coat pockets. She didn't want to run out of tissue for the journey.

She noshed on the remains of a now stale *butterbrot* that was half-eaten, since she didn't feel like untying herself and crawling to the food basket. She wrapped her blankets tightly around herself to ward off the chill in the container and continued her daydreams of kitchen design. *Stainless-steel appliances and a gas stove is a must. Much better to cook on gas than electric.*

I fear I am losing my sense of reality.

***

As Anatoly came through the doorway of the crazy man's room, he noted that the bed had been stripped and was empty. He turned and flagged down a nurse.

"*Gde on?*" he asked.

"*Ya ne znayu,*" answered the nurse.

"*On umer?*" Anatoly asked. Was the man dead?

Again, the nurse answered "*Ya ne znayu*" with a shrug.

Anatoly felt his face turn red with anger and frustration at the nurse's lack of knowledge and lack of interest. He breathed deep to calm his breathing. The nurse scurried off before Anatoly could ask any more questions.

He left the hospital in frustration. He so wanted to kill someone.

***

Anatoly stormed up to the front desk. "I wish to check the security footage again."

The clerk jumped up nervously to help him. "Certainly, sir. Anything you desire."

Anatoly ran the footage backward and forward.

"I need a second monitor immediately."

The clerk grabbed one off his desk and brought it to Anatoly to hook up.

"What do you expect me to do with that?"

"You asked for it."

"Yes, I did. Hook it up for me. Now."

Hands shaking, the clerk kept dropping the connector as he tried to cobble the two monitors together.

"What is wrong with you? Give me that! *Der'mo*." Anatoly ripped the cable and connector from the clerk and plugged the monitor in. The clerk backed against the wall.

Anatoly took a screenshot of the old woman and another of Elda and compared them side by side. *The old woman is shorter than the other and has gray hair and blue eyes, but that could be faked. The cheeks look different. But the spacing of the features is about the same.* He wished he had the software with him to superimpose the faces. He printed out pictures of both.

"Thank you. We are done."

The clerk slid down the wall in clear relief.

***

"Stop!" Sitting in the security room at Pulkovo Airport, Anatoly was watching a DVR operator scroll through the day's footage.

"There!" The old woman was sitting in a wheelchair, being pushed across the terminal.

"Follow her." He trailed her progress through different cameras until she arrived at the British Airways desk.

"*Aga!*" She had purchased a ticket and was being pushed to a gate. "Give me the number for that BA desk."

The DVR operator dialed an extension on his phone and handed the receiver to Anatoly.

"I want your passenger list for any flights between 14:00 and 15:00."

Anatoly pounded the table, causing the DVR operator to jump.

"I don't have time to submit a form."

He slammed the receiver down.

"The BA attendant refused to give me the information. *Der'mo*!" He pounded his thigh.

"There was a BA flight that left Heathrow at 14:45 and went to JFK," mentioned the DVR operator.

Anatoly stopped and stared at the DVR operator. Finally he muttered, "*Spasibo*." At least he had a lead, but too bad he didn't have her name. He could ask his superiors to hack into the BA computer and get the passenger list, but without more information and something to compare it against, that would be useless.

"I will find her in London and shake Korinna's location out of her."

Chapter Twelve

7 December, 2018

Elda could smell his aftershave as he leaned closer to her, shaking her seat violently. She felt threatened by his closeness and his arms on either side of her. *Do not hit him.*

"I told you it's broken and won't straighten up."

"Ma'am, we have to have it upright for landing."

The plane landed with a jolt.

"Apparently we could land anyway."

The steward stomped forward to let the passengers off the plane.

Elda adjusted her creaky neck as she deplaned at Terminal Two and went to the taxi stand. She had booked two rooms at the Madison Hotel in Hamburg. Though a bit modern for her taste, it was close to a five-star hotel, had a pool, and was near the city center and the port. Perhaps Korinna would like some luxury—she might want to take a few laps in the pool after having been cramped up for so long? *I'm not sure how long we should stay here, though. We must keep moving and reach the American Embassy in London.*

On the way to the hotel, she spied a tail. *There!* "That blue car has followed us for blocks. *Bitte biegen Sie jetzt rechts ab.*"

The taxi driver took a sharp right as requested. The blue car continued onward. "*Ich war falsch.*" The driver acknowledged her confession with a shrug and turned back onto the main road again.

Elda leaned forward and asked the taxi driver, "*Wo kann ich Sonnenbrillen kaufen?*" Elda had the taxi stop along the way to the hotel so she could purchase a pair of sunglasses for Korinna.

Elda checked into her room, and on her bed was a suitcase with Korinna's clothing in it. Korinna's suitcase had been sent by Pavel to Florence, Italy, where the contents were removed and new clothing substituted. The original contents had been sent via courier to Hamburg. She carried the suitcase across the hall, let herself into Korinna's room, and placed it on the bed. She then went back to her room to plan the next stage of their journey.

They would do the trip to the US in a few legs in order to throw off any remaining operatives. Perhaps they could catch a ferry from Hamburg to Amsterdam. It was probably best to do that in disguise. The old-woman costume was too slow and probably burned by now, so she would have to come up with new ones for the two of them. Korinna would probably be satisfied with any mode of transport that didn't have her hidden in the cold and dark.

Elda caught a taxi over to the United States Consulate General, stopping on the way at a bakery to grab something to eat. She was torn between the Berliner jelly-filled donut and the *bienenstich* pastry, so she bought both the Berliner and the Bee Sting. In the cab, she separated the almond-caramel cake from the filling and bottom cake and ate each half separately. Licking her fingers, she placed the bag with the donut in her backpack for later.

Willl there even be a later? What if Korinna doesn't arrive?

***

"A ferry? How did you ever get this far in this intelligence game? Everyone knows our ferries are local and do not go to Amsterdam," opined the dumpy, discouraged-looking CIA station chief as he escorted her to his office.

Elda briefly considered pinning his pudgy hand to the table with her knife. "Then how would you propose we get there?"

"Not by ferry. You're the smart spy. You tell me."

The station chief and Elda heatedly discussed different routes and means of travel and settled on the train. Elda stopped arguing with him and dictated what she would need for papers and disguises. "I'll need this no later than tomorrow morning."

"You'll be lucky if we can do this by next week."

Elda bit the inside of her mouth, holding back her retort. Instead, she picked up her phone and dialed a number. "Yes, he's right here." She handed the phone to the station chief.

"Yes, sir. I understand, sir. No problem here." He tossed the phone back at Elda.

"So, tomorrow?"

"Yes," growled the chief.

Elda stomped toward the door after obtaining his reassurance that the disguises, identities, and train tickets would be ready by tomorrow morning.

"Oh, by the way . . ."

Elda turned back. "Yes?"

"Chatter has it that a Russian assassin is closing in on you." He smirked. "I hope you can handle that."

***

Anatoly caught a cab to Finsbury Park in London, to meet with his Russian contact. He'd left his guns back in Russia, and although a gun was difficult to obtain in England, he could if he had to. He preferred his more silent tools of the trade, however. *They are only women. I will be able to dispose of them quickly, once I find them. I have never failed before, and I will not fail now.*

His contact sent him to a Russian who would be able to hack into Heathrow's security cameras so that Anatoly could see if either of his women had passed through. "This better be productive." Anatoly hated being sent on a wild-goose chase.

The cab dropped him off in front of a row of connected houses. Anatoly slid out of the backseat and rapped on the driver's window, with money in his hand. When the cabdriver rolled down his window, Anatoly ripped out the camera and storage device and added more than enough money to cover the damage. He then threw in even more bills for a tip and took a picture of the driver with his cell phone.

He smiled thinly at the driver. "Okay No trouble?"

"Okay, no trouble, no police, please . . ." the driver stammered.

"Good. I was not here, okay?"

"I never saw you."

The cabdriver grabbed at the additional bills that Anatoly had tossed onto the front seat of the cab.

Anatoly headed to the center of the row of houses and knocked on the door of the basement flat. He entered a dark, windowless room filled with computers, monitors, modems, and a host of other equipment he couldn't identify. The hacker motioned for him to sit in front of one of the monitors and replayed the footage from Heathrow.

Anatoly was tired and almost missed the old woman being wheeled off the plane. *So, the old woman went to London.* He watched the arrivals until the present moment, but no other familiar faces arrived in customs. He could not believe that the old woman would be involved in any operations. She had to be a coincidence.

He sat back and rubbed his tired eyes. He ran his hand over his head and scratched his scalp in an attempt to wake up more.

"Can you show me departing flights from the time of the old woman's arrival to the present moment?"

"Yes, please come back tomorrow morning, and I will have the footage compiled for you to look at." The hacker shrank in his chair when Anatoly scowled.

"You have one hour," Anatoly said.

"*Da.*"

He texted pictures of the three women to the hacker's phone. "*Vot chast' deneg.*" Then, he paid the hacker part of the fee. "There will be much more to come if you find the woman in the footage."

"*Spasibo.*"

Anatoly asked the hacker to call him a cab and hoped he didn't get the same guy again. Anatoly punched in his handler's number, then flung the phone away from his ear and shook his head vigorously.

"*Nyet. Pozhaluysta.* Listen. *Da.* London."

Anatoly smiled. As long as his handler was yelling at him, he was safe from being eliminated. *It is when the chilly niceness creeps in that I should be checking my getaway routes and alternative identities.*

"*Nyet. Nyet.* I have it under control. May I please get more information on the tall, blonde woman? I asked yesterday and have yet to receive any."

Anatoly nodded. "*Khorosho.* By morning. *Da. Spasibo.*"

Anatoly swung the phone away from his ear and then returned it to listen to the rest of his handler's questions.

"*Nyet.* I have tried that. *Da . . . da . . . nyet*! I have also tried that. Please, a few more days."

Anatoly wiped the sweat that was beading on his forehead.

"*Da, spasibo.* I do not need someone to come help me."

*****

A shadowy wisp of a man sitting in a communications room in the Kremlin frowned as he hung up the phone. *I've worked with Anatoly for over twenty years as his handler. He's never failed before. But he has made no progress. How many more days before I send out backup to take over the mission and dispose of Anatoly? I have some time, but I need to be prepared, just in case. This is too important an operation to screw up. Every day she is on the run, we risk her information getting out. The president has been very clear in his wishes to eliminate her. Who else might I be able to tap to do this?*

He scratched his head and looked up at his ceiling, hoping to find the answers mysteriously written there.

It would be hard to lose Anatoly as an operative. Most of all, Anatoly's failure would look badly on me. Mistakes are never well tolerated. Are there other ways to achieve these mission objectives? Perhaps if the woman was on the run and hiding, it would accomplish the same objectives as eliminating her?

He rubbed his face and brought his gaze back down to his desk.

"*Ya podozhdu . . . da . . .* I will wait," Tosh said.

***

Elda slammed her fist against the hotel room door. *Damn, that hurt! I have to learn to stop doing that! That insufferable little man!* It dawned on her that her anger at the station chief had overwhelmed her ability to hear his last words. *The assassin cannot be alive. I witnessed him sink into the freezing water. Damn. There must be another one on his way.*

Wait, wait. How much of this was fear, how much was anger, and how much was left over from seeing Dawn, knowing there were problems there? *Oh, stop being your own shrink!* "Damnit!" That felt good. "You assholes!" Frustrated she looked around the room for something to destroy. *Stop it, Elda. Work it out before they send someone to see what the commotion is.*

She threw herself into a set of brisk exercises to burn off the anger and angst. After ten push-ups, Elda mixed it up and did five clapping and then five one-armed ones. She ran in place for five minutes, did mountain climbers for another five, then jogged into the bathroom to take a hot shower.

225

Red-cheeked from the shower and calmer, she dressed in sneakers and sweats and snagged a bite of breakfast and a strong coffee. *I need to be alert today. I will orientate myself to the city in order to be able to make a quick getaway with Korinna. If another assassin is on his way, I do not have any time to waste.*

She started out the door, realizing how angry she was at the CIA chief. *I have it! I know who I can contact. I* will *get even with you, pudgy one.*

***

The hacker's apartment door bent inward as Anatoly pounded on it. He sprang through the opening, throwing ahead a large bag of new clothing. He stripped off his clothes and tried on his new gear as the hacker stared, wide eyed.

"*Chto ty nashel?*" the hacker stammered.

"What did you find?" Anatoly demanded.

The hacker took off his glasses and polished them, then motioned for Anatoly to come over to the computer screen. "I found one of the women."

The hacker fast-forwarded through the Heathrow departures until he came to a clip of Elda boarding a plane to JFK.

"*Der'mo!*" Anatoly exclaimed.

The hacker gave Anatoly the flight information. "I have managed to screen all incoming and outgoing flights to and from Heathrow up to today. There is no other trace of any of the women. I need more time."

Anatoly snarled at the hacker. "*Nyet.* We have no more time. You better have had done your job well." Anatoly asked the hacker to play the clip again. "Forward… stop… reverse… stop… continue."

The disk drive whirred as the hacker searched back and forth through the footage.

"She's not there, man. I searched all that footage."

"*Der'mo!* Get me footage from JFK," Anatoly demanded.

"*Nyet. Ya ne mogu. Nevozmozhno.* I can't do that. It's not possible," the hacker stuttered back at Anatoly.

"Of course it's possible. If you're able to hack the American elections, then certainly airport camera footage would be child's play."

"I don't have access."

"You what?!"

"Don't have access," whispered the hacker.

"Since when has that stopped you?"

"These systems are not on the internet. They are closed systems."

"So, open them. I need that information now."

"I can't."

"Are you crying? *Der'mo! Der'mo! Der'mo!*" Anatoly pounded the table, glowering at the hacker.

The hacker stood and backed into the corner, not taking his eyes off Anatoly. "I know a man over there. We can call him," he said softly, looking like he might faint.

"*Da, khorosho.*" Anatoly finally grinned.

The hacker passed out cold.

Anatoly marched into the hacker's kitchen and wet a small cloth. He took two ice cubes out of the freezer and wrapped the cloth around the cubes and applied it to the back of the hacker's neck, which revived him. Anatoly picked him up off the floor and sat him on his chair, handed him the cloth in one hand, put that hand to his face, and placed his phone into the other hand.

"Call him now. And give me his name."

The hacker dropped the ice, dialed a number, and reached for a notepad. He wrote the man's name and number on a piece of paper. Anatoly read it out loud and then tore up the paper and handed the pieces back to the hacker, who looked as if he might faint again. Anatoly picked up the cloth and ice from where the hacker had placed it and positioned it on the back of the hacker's neck again.

***

Elda jogged over to the ferry terminal, checking over her shoulder. No sign of a tail. At the terminal, she surveyed the area for surveillance cameras and was pleased to see one broken camera dangling. *Hopefully, they won't fix that anytime soon.* She jogged back toward the consulate, her mind wandering to worry her conflict with Dawn, absently noting the locations of the Hard Rock Café and the U-boat museum.

Suddenly, she heard footsteps running up behind her, at first echoing the cadence of her own

229

footsteps and then increasing in speed. She skidded to a stop, spun around, and squatted to face her attacker while reaching for the stolen hotel steak knife tucked into her right sock. As her hand touched the knife, a man ran past her without a second glance.

Damn, Ainsworth! You are getting jittery. You need to focus on the mission and wipe your mind of your problems at home with Dawn. Compartmentalize. One mission at a time.

After an hour, having gotten a bit lost on the way, she arrived sweaty and out of breath at the consulate.

The CIA chief ambled out and said coolly, "Your disguises and paperwork will be ready within the hour."

As he turned his back on her, Elda asked, "Why didn't you give me more information about the assassin?"

He spun and replied, "Why don't you relinquish the spying to us men?"

Elda's hand twitched toward her knife. She smiled sweetly at him. "Be glad you are on our side. You are, aren't you?"

He stormed away, leaving her standing in the hallway. Elda hurried down to the basement, taking the stairs two at a time to have a chat with communications to get a sitrep on the assassin.

"We don't have much information for you."

"I'll take anything you have."

"A man matching your description was seen at Heathrow airport. We also have evidence that the camera system there was recently hacked into."

"Can you get me pictures of this man?"

"We thought you might want them, and our contact at Heathrow sent us these."

Elda viewed the grainy pictures on the computer screen.

"Yes, that could be the man. It's rather blurry, but his height and body type are correct."

Such efficiency. What a difference from that station chief. And this is a federal office. They are not usually that efficient.

"One other thing."

"Yes?" These doorknob confessions were getting tedious.

"You may want to be careful today. The chief is extremely angry that you pulled rank on him with that phone call."

"Danke schön."

Elda dumped the potentially compromised bag of disguises into a bin and then went on a speedy shopping spree. She ended it carrying two full large shopping bags. Now all she needed were new papers and for Korinna's ship to arrive so they could both catch a train out of Hamburg to Amsterdam—and to protect them both from the assassin, since he would have to remove her to get to Korinna. She shuddered.

She popped into the Hard Rock Café's restroom to change into a man's shirt, suit, and tie. She pulled on leather shoes with slightly larger heels and lifts in them that changed her height by two inches. She added a wig, thick glasses, and a hat and finished with a small mustache. Looking in the mirror, she barely recognized herself. She pulled on a long, wool men's coat to complete the outfit.

She left the café and walked over to the nearby Hotel Hafen Hamburg to book a new room. She didn't trust that the CIA chief wouldn't let out her location in spite for besting him. She made a mental note to dig into his background and find a way to have him transferred to a remote, isolated station.

She sauntered over to her first hotel and ran silently up the stairs to her floor. Taking out a master key, she entered the room that connected to her room. Placing her ear against the door, she heard faint sounds coming from her room, similar to noises made by someone searching it. She inspected the room for a weapon and grabbed a bottle of wine off the sideboard, along with the wine opener. Quietly, she picked the lock on the door between the two suites. She slipped the wine opener under her watch for easy access and, grasping the wine bottle, burst through the door.

The man inside her hotel room spun around as she leaped and tackled him. As they fell to the floor, he yelled, "She's not here. Please don't hurt me."

"Who are you, and why are you in this room?" Elda hissed, pulling his hair and neck backward.

"I'm CIA. Actually, I'm a receptionist at the consulate. But I want to be an agent. So, the chief sent me to place a tracker on Elda's luggage."

"And then what?"

"He's going to give the information to the Russians."

"Get out before I kill you. You will tell your boss you were successful."

The man leaped up and ran as if bulls were chasing him.

Elda removed the tracker from her bag. "Now, pudgy boy, we *really* have a score to settle."

***

8 December, 2018

Natasha and Yuri viewed Aurelio through the one-way mirror. The psychiatrist had explained that it was still too early to visit him.

"I am an important man," he screamed at the psychiatrist. "The CIA and FBI are trying to get me. I evaded forty cars in one chase already. I can evade them again. But I must be free to move! This is a plot. They have all been plotting against me since I was a child. You just don't know what I have overcome!"

He lunged at the psychiatrist, but an orderly intercepted Aurelio and injected him with a strong tranquilizer. He caught Aurelio as he fell and slung him over his shoulder, placing him gently into a wheelchair to be wheeled to his room.

The psychiatrist strutted beaming into the room where Natasha and Yuri were.

"*Doktor, on kazhetsya khuzhe,*" Natasha said, frowning.

"*Da,*" the doctor replied. "Yes, Aurelio does appear to be worse. Patients with his issues usually get worse before they get better… if they *can* get better."

Natasha wiped tears away and looked warmly at the doctor, blinking her big, blue eyes.

"*Kak dolgo?*" she asked.

"*Ya ne znayu,*" the doctor replied. "It's too early to tell how long. We've only been working with him a short while. Every person's journey is unique. Aurelio has been delusional for so long that it might be a while before we can even hope to see any improvement, and he may not ever recover."

"*Da, spasibo.*"

Natasha and Yuri left the room. Yuri put his arm around Natasha, appearing to guide the grief-stricken wife out.

Once they had cleared the hospital doors, the two of them burst out laughing at how pitiful Aurelio was and how wonderfully Natasha acted her role of loyal wife.

"*Poydem pit'*!" Natasha made the universal bent-elbow drinking gesture and steered Yuri toward their favorite bar.

"*Da!* Vodka!"

They walked away hand in hand.

***

Anatoly was angry. His stomach was in a knot, too. These were feelings he didn't recognize. He was usually in control of any situation. He meticulously planned hunting his quarry, and he dispatched them quickly. These women were making a fool of him, and he didn't dare tell his handler the full story until he had located the women again. He had told the Kremlin that he was close to catching the tall woman and just needed to widen the network a bit, so having more pictures of her and her friend would be necessary. They had sent him a picture of the tall one and the passport picture of the shorter one, as well as the information on the tall blonde that he had requested, but his handler did not sound convinced that Anatoly was telling him the truth.

Anatoly contemplated the picture of the tall blonde again, admiring her long neck. His finger traced a line around it on his phone screen. *How perfect for strangulation. I look forward to meeting*

236

you and helping you meet your end. His stomach calmed as he visualized killing her. He breathed a sigh of relief.

The hacker in the UK had talked to his peer in the USA, and just as Anatoly intended to fly to Heathrow to track down his mark, he would also meet this new man in the United States and impress on him the urgency of the situation. The London hacker had sent the New Yorker photos of the three women—the tall one in the red coat that Anatoly had obtained from his superiors, the smaller woman's passport photo, and screenshots of the old woman from the surveillance photos. With the right monetary incentive, this new computer whiz promised to work through the night and have video queued up for Anatoly when he arrived. Anatoly picked up his phone and booked a seat on the afternoon flight out to JFK. He realized his departure would be flagged, and eventually the Kremlin would be notified, but he planned to return before they noticed.

*** *

Anatoly caught a taxi from JFK to the new hacker's apartment in the Bronx. Although Google had said the ride would only take about a half hour, he'd gotten stuck in bumper-to-bumper traffic, and Anatoly was having difficulty keeping calm. The taxi driver kept looking nervously at his passenger in the rearview mirror. Anatoly balled his hands up in fists and brought them down hard on his thighs, muttering "*Chert, der'mo, yebat'*."

The driver held up his cell phone with Google Maps on it. "Soon, man. We're halfway there now. The traffic is unusually heavy for a Saturday. It looks like there's a few accidents. It may clear out soon."

Anatoly leaned forward and looked at the phone through the Plexiglas, took a deep breath in, and relaxed somewhat.

Ya nichego ne mogu sdelat'. Nichego takogo, he repeated over and over to himself, reminding himself that there was nothing he could do.

Anatoly arrived at the address and thanked the driver, tipping him well but not too generously to stand out in the driver's mind for long. He figured the driver would soon forget the large, anxious man he had transported here, since New York seemed to be full of anxious people and the driver would probably see more before his shift was over. *Especially with that traffic! Der'mo!* He located the name on the mailboxes inside the entryway and pressed the buzzer to be let in.

Inside the apartment, a slender, pasty-looking man in his twenties adjusted his glasses at the nosepiece, which was held together with white adhesive tape. He'd set up the monitors and a chair for Anatoly's viewing.

"*Der'mo*! There she is getting off the plane with her backpack and two carry-ons, and there she is getting back on a plane with just the backpack! Is she a courier of some sort?" Anatoly sat back in his chair in bewilderment. The woman's actions made no sense. They did not seem related to the tall woman at all. Perhaps she had been over in Russia to gather something to smuggle back to the States. "But why is she getting onto a plane again? And why had she arranged to meet the tall woman at the Hermitage?" Nothing added up. "Where did that plane go?"

The slender man ran his hands through his greasy hair and then typed a few commands into the computer. "Hamburg."

"Hamburg?" Anatoly shouted. "Why Hamburg?"

The hacker shrank away from Anatoly.

Anatoly's mind filtered through many possibilities, and then he shouted—so loudly the hacker startled and fell off his chair—"Yes!" They might be trying to pull the wool over his eyes. This was the first time she had flown to a central hub for train, ferry, and ship transportation. Hamburg was a major shipping port, and ships regularly traveled there from Russia. What if the tall one traveled there by ship from Russia? There was no record of her on camera at any airport. And perhaps the two women were going to meet and travel from Hamburg via ship? He checked his watch frantically, without pausing to admire it. It was 03:00 in Germany. There was no one at the port that he could contact at this hour. It was also too early in Russia, although they would be awake and in the office before the Germans would.

He paced the room. *"Der'mo!"* Anatoly shouted again. The slender man pushed himself farther away from Anatoly.

Anatoly checked his watch again. He was only a half-hour away from the airport. If he hurried, he could be in Hamburg by tomorrow.

***

9 December, 2018

Damn, he's late. Elda sat in a darkened beer hall waiting for her contact to arrive. To look like a tourist, she kept ordering and taste testing four-ounce shots, just taking a sip or two, to keep her wits about her. She checked her watch. *He may not show. I'm asking him to risk his job.* She took another sip of beer. The unique taste brought her back to her first visit to Germany when she was in the navy. The details were a bit blurry, thanks to the vast amounts of beer she'd consumed every day. She remembered buying a puppet at one of the Oktoberfest halls one evening because she'd thought it was so charming. The beer was just so damn good in Germany.

The group had been staggering out of the hall, marching the puppet in front, when one of the other officers said to Elda, "Put your arms around me."

Elda drew back in shock.

"No, no, not that!" he said. "Just put your arms around me and walk me out, and then you can let go."

When Elda had wrapped her arms around him, there was this clinking sound, as the liter mugs that he had tied to his belt clanked against each other. Elda and the officer drunkenly crab-walked out of the tent.

She still had a picture of the group that evening at the hotel. Elda was sprawled across the officer's lap while each held up a mug. She'd taken one mug for payment and still had it. It was a reminder never to drink that much again.

Elda was sipping her third *dunkles bier* when a man slid into the other side of the booth. He looked nervously around.

"Did you get me my information?"

"*Ja.* Here it is." He slid a brown folder across the table.

"*Vielen dank.*" Elda opened the folder, and inside were pictures of the CIA station chief in compromising positions with the ambassador's wife. "Ah yes, these are perfect."

"You will keep your source confidential, of course."

"Of course. And you will no longer have to suffer him as your boss. Did you bring me the other papers I asked for?"

"*Ja.*" He passed to her a large manila envelope.

"*Danke.*"

"You will take care of this for me?" Elda handed him the tracker.

"*Ja.* I will take it far away and destroy it."

Elda looked up from the folder—the man had disappeared.

***

In a foul mood, Anatoly counseled himself not to attack anyone in his transit to Hamburg. At the airport, he jumped out as the cab rolled to a stop. He hoped that there would be something decent to eat at the airport, but Americans were not globally known for their cuisine. *Bystroye pitaniye. Fast food. The plague brought to every country from America.*

Anatoly landed in Hamburg tired, hungry, and anxious about how much time he had lost. He wasn't thinking as clearly as he usually did. He had been chasing them for eight days now. Usually his operations went like clockwork—done within a few days—and there was never any need to continuously analyze and plan, as he was doing now.

Anatoly memorized the map of Hamburg and located the train station and the piers for the port of call for large ships, as well as the ferries. The hunter licked his lips in anticipation. His spoils awaited him.

***

Elda decoded the message on her phone. *Korinna's ship will arrive this morning, 10 December, 2018, and be unloaded this afternoon.* "Good, but where is the assassin?"

Elda wore her first disguise and packed the others into a large, over-the-shoulder workman's bag that she'd purchased while shopping yesterday. She placed the backpack containing the new papers into another backpack and slung it onto her back, with the other bag over her shoulder. She then called the front desk to check out.

A short man in a workman's uniform left the hotel, carrying a backpack and a large workman's bag. Elda picked up lunch for two and placed it into her backpack. Her informant-provided workman's ID allowed her into the yard. The ship should have just docked. She strolled along the pier until she found a few ships with huge cranes unloading the cargo containers, while others sat just offshore waiting to unload. Checking online, she saw that her ship was one of those waiting offshore. Nervous with the delay, she rapidly walked away and crisscrossed side streets to flush out any followers. Her heart skipped a beat every time a large man approached her.

A few hours later, she returned and switched on her handheld locator to find Korinna's container.

She stomped through the dirt and mud, wandering through rows of stacked containers, turning in the direction of the arrow on the handheld device, until finally, a green light blinked, then turned a steady green as she approached a red container.

There it was, stacked on the bottom, as promised. *Poor Korinna. I wonder how mad she is at me?* Elda tried to open the container with the keys the consulate had given her. The keys didn't work! *What the fuck?* Had he double-crossed her? After a few frustrating attempts, she took out a lockpicking kit from her backpack.

The lock popped open, and Elda flung the door open, leaping into the container and carefully closing the door from the inside. She switched on a headlamp on her hard hat and edged past the heavy equipment to the back. There was no false compartment. She paced off the inside of the compartment as best she could while avoiding the cargo stacked inside. Forty feet. It should be thirty-six-and-a-half feet. Where was she?

Elda was sweating and breathing heavily. She returned to the back of the container and felt along the back wall. No hidden switch, no keypad, no door. She ran outside the compartment and slipped in a patch of mud, falling heavily onto her rear end. She looked up from her new vantage point and groaned.

There had to be hundreds of red cargo containers and at least ten right near the one she had opened. How accurate was the GPS on this tracker?

Elda scaled about seventeen feet to reach the lock on red container number three. She had her toes precariously balanced on an indent in the container and was holding on for dear life to one of the vertical bars while leaning over the lock. Damn! She watched as the keys fell from her sweaty and shaking hand to the ground below. She bowed her head, took a deep breath, and started down to retrieve them.

She scurried back up to try again, hating how exposed she was this high in the air. Again, she dangled midair, held only by one hand and her toes, to fit the keys in the lock.

Success! The container slowly opened, and Elda swung into the dark interior. She ran to the back, pressed a button to access the keypad, and selected the keys for the code. She angled her headlamp down so she wouldn't blind Korinna and pressed ENTER.

Nothing.

"Damn it all!" Elda pressed CLEAR and whipped her sweaty fingers on her pants. She slowly and carefully reentered the numbers. With a soft click, the door slid gently back.

***

Korinna, squinting, rushed out of her hiding place, nearly knocking down the workman standing there, but she stopped short when she recognized Elda's voice.

"Phew, Korinna, that place smells!" Elda said.

Korinna hit her on the arm.

Elda hugged her and then handed her a brown leather carry-on with some clean clothing, work boots, a wig, handy-wipes, and a helmet with a headlamp and sunglasses. "Here. Put these on. I'll wait by the entrance."

Korinna didn't know whether to laugh or cry, but she did know she wanted out of the container! A hot shower and a decent meal were on her bucket list, but that would have to wait. She cleaned up as best she could with the wipes and pulled on the yoga outfit, adding a cargo worker's uniform overtop. She tied her long, blonde hair into a topknot and covered it with the brown wig. She added the hard hat over that and then picked up Privet and placed him into the carry-on. She accessorized with the wraparound sunglasses and activated the light on her hard hat. She squinted again from just that small amount of light. Outdoors would be painful, despite the dark glasses. She felt dizzy after lying down in a moving container for so long. She wondered when she'd get her land legs back. She stiffly limped to the front and hugged Elda again.

"We have to move quickly. Walk out like you own the place. Remember to switch off your headlamp." Elda clipped an ID to the front of Korinna's uniform. "It is a bit tricky getting down. Follow me."

"Eeek! We are way up high, Elda!"

They held on to the poles and climbed and slid down the front of the containers. Once on the ground, Korinna gingerly stepped around the mud holes. Elda led the way. Stopping, she turned, stepped back, and surveyed Korinna in the uniform. "It's so good that they have women working here. You would never pass for a man. The next outfit will be more suited to you."

The two wove quickly through the stacked containers. Once they cleared the yard, Elda picked up the pace.

Korinna sighed. "I really want a long hot shower and a decent meal, but more than that, I want to put miles between me and this damn container."

"I don't think I've ever heard you swear before."

"It's a horrible place. It sucks."

"You go, girl. Let it all out."

"Please, let's move on as quickly as possible. I want to get back to Egor and the troodles."

"I agree with you. We don't have much time to spare. We must hightail it out of Hamburg now. First, we have to make a quick stop at the ferry terminal. Let's go."

"Your shoulder bag is reversible," Elda continued. "After we go to the ferry terminal, we will stop at the Hard Rock Café for a beer. After we order, you'll go change and reverse your bag; throw the old clothes and boots and hard hat into it. Include the ID. You will then immediately slip out of the building without returning to the bar and walk East, away from the ferries and café, to the Museumsschiff Rickmer Rickmers. I will meet you there."

Korinna nodded as tears streamed down her cheeks at the relief of being free from Russia and the container.

"There, there, my friend. I know how hard this must be, but we have a long way to go still."

Korinna dried her eyes and face with the Kleenex tissues that Elda somehow always had on her person.

The two workers purchased tickets on the ferry to Landungsbrucken, to throw off anyone who might be on their trail. From the ferry terminal, they switched disguises at the Hard Rock Café, then purchased train tickets. They caught the S-Bahn from Baumwall station to Haupbanhof Nord, where they walked to Central Station to take the train from there to Amsterdam.

At the station, Elda was startled to get a coded text from the consulate communication center.

"He's in Hamburg."

The assassin had tracked them.

Chapter Thirteen

10 December, 2018

Anatoly was eager to start his search. "*Ya tozhe proveryu aeroport*," he said out loud, reminding himself how that woman had done the hop from the UK to NYC and then to Hamburg. He was leaving the airport for last, since he probably needed a hacker to get the footage from the security cameras. "*Okh i poyezd! Da,* the train*! Der'mo!*" Previous to this stop, one of the women had always traveled by air, probably because they were jumping between continents. Hamburg, however, being a major European port, had multiple means of transportation into and out of Germany. This could end up being a long and tedious evening. *My specialty is killing, not detective work!* He frowned as he stomped toward a taxi.

Anatoly first went to the ferry terminals. At the ticket counter, he flashed a badge and presented a picture of Korinna and another of Elda.

"*Hast du diese Frauen gesehen?*" he asked.

The clerk studied the pictures. *"Nein."*

"Hast du Kameras?"

"Nein."

Anatoly stormed back to catch a taxi over to the shipping yards. He presented himself at the guard shack and again displayed his badge. *"Ich bin ein Polizeibeamter."*

"Ja?"

He threw the two pictures onto the counter.

The guard picked up the pictures.

"Who are they?"

"They are fugitives. Have you seen them?"

"Nein."

Der'mo!

***

Anatoly paced up and down on the street outside the entrance to the shipping yards and called his handler in Russia. "Connect me to a hacker in Hamburg," he said without preamble.

"*Kuda?*" shouted the handler as Anatoly held his phone away from his ear.

"Hamburg."

"*Ya znayu*," replied the handler. "I know. I heard you the first time. What are you trying to do, get us both killed?"

Anatoly heard the sound of the handler's handkerchief brushing against the phone as the handler mopped his sweaty brow. He was betting that there was no way the handler could admit Anatoly's errors to his superiors. He would have to find a way to spin this into success. But there was not much time left. Soon the superiors would ask the handler if Anatoly's mission was successful.

"You have two more days, and then we will see how we can solve this dilemma; be aware that I may have to send someone in to clean everything up."

"*Nyet, nyet*. I can handle this."

"You better."

Anatoly held the phone away from him and viewed it in dismay. He had yet to fail his handler, but now he was disappointing him. His handler was like a second father. He couldn't let him down. And he definitely couldn't get him killed. He knew, from the way his handler was reacting, that this was an important mission. Perhaps there was a way to get them both success in this operation?

He remembered that Elda's luggage had gone to Florence, Italy. Was that a ruse, or should he search there too? He scratched his head. This was far more complicated than his usual cases. For now, he had enough places to search, and he dialed for a cab to take him to the third hacker's apartment. He barely kept his temper in check. He was sick of dealing with those scrawny, pale *botans*! With all this travel, he was grumpy—he hadn't worked out in a while and felt tense. And he was in trouble with his superiors.

Anatoly put his ego to one side momentarily and called his handler back to see if he would approve of a plan to save them both some aggravation. He had been well trained not to take initiative without approval from a higher authority. The success or failure of the operation was at stake. His handler had many more years of experience as to what would and would not work, plus it was his neck on the line too.

The handler answered on the first ring. *"Da?"*

Anatoly explained his plan.

"*Nyet, nyet, nyet*! Are you crazy?"

Anatoly could hear the handler with his phone at arm's length.

"Please listen to me. I will need your help to accomplish this backup plan."

Silence.

Anatoly warily continued. "All I need to do is to find a prostitute who is a tall, Nordic blonde and discreetly kill her. I'll then take a picture of her with her hair covering her face enough that it will be impossible to tell the body is not Korinna's. The assumption would be that it is, especially with you and me testifying that I had eliminated her."

Silence.

"It is a perfect plan. Korinna is on the run and would never be seen in Russia again, and you and I will get to live to do more missions. I'll continue to search for the women and hopefully eliminate them before having to do this, but you do know that if I fail, both of us will probably be eliminated."

"I will consider the plan and call you back tomorrow."

Plan B was surely in his back pocket. If he couldn't find a lead through working with this hacker, he would find a prostitute and have the satisfaction of killing someone and be rid of the worry of his superiors sending someone after him.

***

Anatoly popped into the bathroom at the Hard Rock Café. He ran his hand across his hair stubble. He was still a brunette, and he had been seen by the short woman in this disguise, as well as when he was blonde. He reached into his bag and pulled out black hair dye, a black mustache, and a neatly cut beard. He would also pick up a tourist hat to help hide the shortness of his hair. Should he shave his head completely? *Nyet, I don't like the way I look without hair.* He also took out the brown contact lenses and went back to his natural blue eyes. Black hair and blue eyes were a striking combination, and he never knew who he might have to impress to get information. He reached into the bag again and pulled out a pair of glasses that would make him look studious. He would pick up an intellectual-sounding book at a store to complete this outfit. He hummed as he dyed his hair. Finally, things were going his way again. What was the name of that tune? *Aga!* "Moscow Nights." *I like it, especially when played on a violin. It speaks to me of Mother Russia.*

256

***

The handler sat in the control room, mopping his brow and staring at his phone. He had worked with Anatoly for years, and all the operations had gone off without a hitch. *Perhaps this new plan is a way to get this one back under control?* Saying that made Tosh feel he was running things again and not just doing damage control. More confident now, he'd sleep on the plan and tease out what might go wrong in the morning. If it still held together, then they would move ahead with it.

He located his blood pressure cuff and pumped it up. "*Khorosho,*" he said in relief. Perhaps it was time for him to retire and leave the stress to the younger men. He loved the rush that the jobs gave him, but the toll was getting a bit much on his body.

Shall I quit? No, there is no quitting in this job, only dying. I will see this mission through and win.

***

10 December, 2018

Elda and Korinna ran down the platform with their chests heaving, lungs gasping for air. They stopped short as they recognized the 17:46 train pulling away from the platform. They spun around and, wheezing and coughing, dashed over to board the 18:10. They collapsed into their seats.

Regaining her breath, Elda said, "We are booked into the Mövenpick Hotel Amsterdam City Centre, Piet Heinkade 11, which is an easy walk from the train station."

"Thank goodness! I am not in the shape for running."

"You will like the hotel. It is not the fanciest, but it is far enough away from the hubbub of the tourists and the red-light district, so it is quiet at night, and we can get some sleep."

"*Da. Elda, gde Dasha i Sasha*?"

"*Oni s Dawn*," Elda answered, and then she proceeded to fill Korinna in on the entire operation for saving Dasha and Sasha. Korinna especially loved hearing about their time in the hotel with the special doggie treat bags and little beds and bowls. By the time Elda had finished the story, the drawn look and sadness had gone from Korinna's eyes.

Then she looked at Elda with worry in her eyes. "*I, Egor?*" she asked hesitantly, "*Gde on?*"

"I don't know."

***

Aurelio sat up in bed in a panic. He strained against the restraints on his arms and legs. *They have finally managed to capture me! I must escape.* Sweat rolled down his back as he struggled to free himself. A nurse traveled by his doorway, and he immediately went still. *I must fool them all. I have done it in the past, and I can do it again. I will charm them into believing me and letting me go.*

The nurse returned and entered the room. "*Kak my?*" she asked in that cloyingly sweet voice that nurses used with him.

"*Khorosho! Ochen khorosho,*" he replied maniacally.

The nurse nodded, made a few notes on his clipboard, and then injected him with something that made him drift off.

He woke again with a start. A group of doctors stood in the room, one telling the others Aurelio's history and status. He closed his eyes so they would not notice he was awake. *Manic episodes! Extreme paranoia! Grandiosity! Delusional!* It was all he could do to stay quiet. He opened his eyes and saw a few of them looking at him as if he were an object under a microscope. One young-looking doctor stared at him in fear.

That's the reaction I want! Aurelio assured himself.

"How are you today, Aurelio?" his doctor asked.

"Good, very good," Aurelio replied, glad to be speaking in English with someone.

"Excellent! And is the man with the black truck here?"

"Oh no, Doctor. That was only a product of my mind." Aurelio squinted hopefully at the doctor.

The doctor turned to the group. "See—these new drugs are working! He is starting to be able to differentiate between his delusions and reality."

The group clapped, except for the youngest one, who eyed Aurelio with suspicion.

"Doctor, when can I sit in a chair instead of the bed?"

"Today, Aurelio. You have made great progress."

Aurelio thanked him and giggled to himself. *Excellent. Now I will get my freedom back. And soon I will escape.* Aurelio cleared his throat to get the doctor's attention.

"Yes, Aurelio?"

"And may we have my wife visit, Doctor?"

"Soon, Aurelio. We have more work to do first."

It was all Aurelio could do to stop from frowning. *Who is this man to tell me who can and cannot visit me?* he huffed, but he managed to give the doctor a weak smile.

"See?" the doctor said. "Last week, he would have tried lunging at me from the bed, yelling what a great man he was and how dare I try and control him. But today, he just thanks me. Excellent progress, Aurelio."

Aurelio made a mental note of how the doctor was responding, and how he needed to act to get out of there.

The doctor gathered his minions around him and prepared to go on to the next patient. At the door, the young doctor turned.

Aurelio smiled. The young doctor shuddered as he turned away.

***

Anatoly poked through his collection of nooses. He wanted to strangle the next victim, to feel the body struggling against his and the sudden moment when it went limp, and he was victorious. It was so much better than the impersonal nature of poisoning, and it gave a greater high than sex or drugs. He smiled and repacked the bag after moving a noose and a pair of surgical gloves to his coat pocket, for easy access.

He went down to the restaurant and ordered a *bienenstich*, a custard-filled almond cake, and a cup of coffee. He slowly relished each bite of the cake and sipped his coffee. "The Germans do pastries right," he muttered under his breath, his smile widening as he cut through the cake and custard layers with his fork. He determined he'd wash this down this with a second cup of coffee and a Berliner donut.

He scraped the plate with his fork and debated ordering a second cake instead of the donut but rejected that notion. Rigorous self-control was necessary for success in life. He mentally retrieved his map of Hamburg and compared it against one that

262

he had printed out at the business center. Satisfied that he had it memorized, he returned to his room. Putting on a pair of thin gloves, he scrubbed the tub and the sink and wiped down all the surfaces. He placed his bag by the door, then scrubbed the room key with soap and water to remove fingerprints and left it on the counter. He paced around the room, scrutinizing that everything had been packed up. He pointed and repeated, *"Proveryat', khorosho, ochistite,"* the mantra of "Check, okay, clear," his routine before leaving any room. He studied the trash. He had left nothing behind. Satisfied, he left to catch a taxi to the hacker's apartment. He knew about Uber, but he was only comfortable with routine, and it had been his routine for years to either take the metro or, more commonly, a taxi.

There was a bounce in Anatoly's step for the first time in days. Soon he would feel the release of killing again.

***

Anatoly ducked under the third-floor laundry, which hung right at neck-level on lines strung across the hallway, and knocked on the door of the third hacker's apartment. A baby cried from the apartment across the hall. The faint smell of dirty nappies permeated the stairwell. Anatoly surveyed with disdain the peeling paint and dirt in the hallway. The door cracked open to the length of a thin chain. Anatoly held back the urge to kick the door in and break that silly chain.

"Hallo? Wer ist da?"

Anatoly replied by shoving his hand with a badge in it through the door opening. *"Ich habe dich angerufen,"* he said, repeating in English, "I called you."

The door shut, and Anatoly heard the chain slide off. He was surprised to see an anemic-looking, dark-skinned man open the door.

"Eingeben," the man said, and Anatoly complied by walking into the apartment.

The third hacker closed the door behind Anatoly, turned the doorknob lock, and slid the chain back on. Anatoly shook his head. As if that would keep someone like him out.

His lip curled as he surveyed the large, unfurnished room with two long fold-up tables holding computers, monitors, and printers, all connected to power strips plugged into another power strip plugged into the lone outlet on the furthest wall. Uncovered lightbulbs hung over the computer tables and kitchen area. The kitchen and bathroom cabinets appeared to be the only storage spaces.

"Listen, man, this is only temporary," the hacker stated.

Anatoly turned to him, and he could no longer hold in questioning the hacker's ethnicity.

"*Ty chernyy*?" he said as half question and half statement.

"I'm sorry?"

Anatoly told himself it didn't matter if the hacker was black or white, as long as he could do his job and he wasn't gay.

The hacker recoiled when Anatoly reached into his bag for the pictures.

"Don't worry," Anatoly said. "If I were going to kill you, you'd be dead already. I need you to look at airport and train security camera footage over the last two days to see if we can find these women. How long and how much?"

The hacker named a price.

Anatoly nodded and asked again, "How long?"

"Two days."

Anatoly countered with, "I will be back here tomorrow morning, and you better be done." The hacker reached out a shaking hand for the pictures.

Khorosho, I have him motivated. Anatoly turned to the door and, without unlocking it, pulled on the handle and ripped it open. As he swaggered away, he could feel the hatred of the hacker's stare stabbing him in his back. "I just did you a favor. Buy better locks."

***

The two women blearily stepped off the train and headed east toward the hotel in Amsterdam. Despite their fatigue, they moved at a fast pace, since there was a cold wind coming across the water. Elda was a quick walker, but she had to take three steps for every two of Korinna's. Normally it made them laugh, but tonight they were intent on getting to the hotel under the cover of a night sky—a good thing, since during the day there were so many bicycles clanging their bells and scooters buzzing by that it was hard to focus on where one was walking. When Elda had first visited Amsterdam, she'd wandered into the bike lane by mistake, and that resulted in much yelling, bells clanging, and beeping, causing her to nearly jump out into the road in front of a car.

The lights of the harbor twinkled on the water, and a huge Holland Lines cruise ship was docked at the back of the Mövenpick Hotel. As they trudged along the waterfront, Elda heard the faint sound of footsteps behind them.

"Korinna, we must move faster."

"I can't, Elda."

"There's someone out there. It could be the assassin. Or it could be just a mugger."

"I should feel better knowing that?"

Elda grabbed Korinna's arm and swung her around behind her. She stood peering into the darkness, willing her breath to be still so that she could absorb the sounds of the night. Almost hidden by the slap of water against the docks was the light patter of someone running away.

Chapter Fourteen

11 December, 2018

"On route to the consulate, we to flush out anyone who may be stalking us. We will not be disguised. I had new clothes delivered for you. I hope they fit," Elda said over her second double espresso.

"But wouldn't it be safer to be in disguise now? Didn't you tell me the assassin is close behind?"

"Yes, it would be safer, but only for the moment. It's most important that we find a way to shake this guy for good."

"I don't like this plan, Elda. Can we get another one?"

"No."

***

Heading to the elevators, Elda and Korinna nearly collided with each other as they rushed from their rooms down to the hotel lobby.

Korinna pointed to the sweater she was wearing. "Gee whiz, Elda. How big do you think I am?"

"You tall folks always seem huge to us short ones," Elda retorted. "Would you like for me to return it for you?"

Their laughter sounded forced as the dangerous part of their day began.

They left the hotel and scrutinized the train station in the distance.

"I was sound asleep when we walked this last," Korinna admitted. "Are there muggers here in the daylight?"

"I wouldn't let your guard down."

They kept to the footpath as bicycle bells rang out and cars and scooters rolled past on their left. At the intersection, they gawked at the traffic roaring past in both directions while they waited for the walk signal.

"No way would I jaywalk here!" Elda exclaimed.

Once the light changed, they headed toward the tourist section and soon came close to the first coffee shop, with plumes of smoke coming out the door every time it opened and closed. The familiar smell of pot permeated the streets.

Amsterdam sported a series of concentric circles of canals with "spokes" of streets cutting through them. The officials controlled the water level of the Amstel River and the canals, using a number of dams and levees. They had even dammed up the mouth of the river. Although the layout was symmetrical, there was something about everything looking the same that had Elda feeling lost. She checked the map as they traversed their way across the canals. Finally, Korinna stopped them and held out her hand for the map. Relieved, Elda handed it over.

They found it hard to walk at any decent pace through the streets. People turned sharply, zigzagged, and just stopped, studying their maps or gazing into storefront windows. The crowds limited Elda's visibility of anyone approaching them, and it would be easy to be trapped between two people suddenly stopping.

"It's like the entire city is stoned," Elda observed as she sidestepped a tourist, forcing Korinna to step into the street. "Let's cut up this side street. There might be less foot traffic."

They turned left and walked in the road, around the perimeter of the building. Someone knocked loudly on a window. They glanced up to see an overweight, scantily clad woman pointing at Elda and motioning for her to come in.

"Let's get out of here." Elda grabbed Korinna's arm to spin them around. They jogged a short distance to rejoin the wandering tourists on the more populated street again. As they stopped to catch their breath and regain their bearings, they broke out into a fit of giggling. In front of them was a full window display of condoms of all shapes and sizes and designs.

"Well, I doubt I'll find many souvenirs to bring Dawn in this shop," Elda said, "but do you want to go in and purchase something for Egor?"

That sent the two of them into laughter again. *Definitely a contact high going on here*, Elda thought as tears flowed down her cheeks from the laughter. While Korinna wandered into the shop, Elda bought herself a cup of coffee to attempt to cut the contact high. She could not afford to be stoned right now.

They crossed over the Singelgracht canal, back toward the tourist area. Elda was distracted by all the shops carrying Delftware. Korinna slipped into a shop to buy a chocolate muffin. Returning, she broke off a piece and handed it to Elda, who absentmindedly popped it into her mouth. As she chewed it, she thought she detected a familiar taste, but she was so hungry she couldn't stop herself from swallowing it.

"Korinna," Elda asked, "Where did you get this muffin?"

Korinna pointed to her left. "At the coffee shop. It was terribly smoky in there!"

Elda started laughing and took the bag out of her hand as Korinna licked the crumbs off her fingers. "Let's not eat any more of this until we see how strong it is, Korinna."

"*Pochemu?*"

"Because I think there may be pot or hash in the muffin."

They meandered down side streets and back. Elda stopped at the gates of the Rijksmuseum. She didn't like the look of the dark, arch-covered passageway. A musician played for coins on the opposite side of the pathway. She palmed her knife and walked slightly in front of Korinna.

As she passed the musician, he looked up at her.

She returned his stare.

***

At the US Consulate General, Elda presented her credentials to the front desk and was ushered in to meet with the station chief. Korinna was left in the waiting room.

Elda shook hands with the station chief. His friendly, alert brown eyes were such a contrast to the dull, lifeless ones of the station chief in Hamburg.

"Do you have any information about the Russian assassin?"

"Yes. He was last seen in Hamburg but could be here by now. He is a solidly built Russian with close-cropped dark hair."

"Nothing else?"

"No, unfortunately."

"Can you get me more information?"

"We'll see. Come back in a couple of hours to see if we've found out anything."

"Can we get information to Egor?"

"We will attempt to."

***

Elda returned to the lobby and handed Korinna a pad of paper and a pen.

"Write down a short note to Egor, and we will try to send it to him."

Korinna stared at the blank sheet of paper. All these sentences collided in her mind, competing to be written down. Finally, she simply wrote, *Egor, Ya lyublyu tebya. Ya v poryadke. Lyubit', Korinna.*

Elda translated over her shoulder. *"Egor, I love you. I am okay. Love, Korinna.* That says it all. I do hope we can get it to him." Elda took the pen and paper and left to give it to the chief, to send on to Egor's location.

When she returned, she told Korinna, "If we are going to get an answer at all, it may not be until tomorrow. But we can check back later today before we return to the hotel to see if it has been delivered. *Khorosho?* Our papers will be ready later today, but I've requested special transportation out of here, and we may not have that set up until tomorrow."

Korinna wiped away the tears that had welled up in her eyes at the thought of being apart from Egor and not knowing how he was, and she nodded.

***

Elda and Korinna popped over to the Van Gogh Museum to wait for more information about the assassin's location. The museum was ideal because of its wide-open floor plan, lack of hiding places, and the ability to easily see anyone else in there. There were wide stairs and easy access to the exit from two different staircases.

"This museum is so nicely laid out." Elda pointed to their right. "Look at how far apart the paintings are hung in order to give the viewer enough space. And it's not crowded."

Elda examined her favorite self-portrait, *The Bedroom.* "Look at the detail in it and how he has used perspective to give it just that kind of *off* feeling. I love his colors, too." But she kept coming back to *The Shoes, 1886.* "Korinna, have I ever shown you a picture of my painting of my old leather work boots?"

Korinna shook her head.

"I would love to have this painting and hang them side by side. I wonder if I can get a poster of these shoes. I love them. Just look at his brushstrokes. They are loose and bold. I so wish I could do that!"

The museum had categorized many of the paintings under the years of his life. "It is so clear when he started to go insane. Look at his palette changing and his perspective going wild. Look at the brushstrokes and colors used on his self-portrait with the gray, felt hat."

Korinna silently took in the paintings until she reached the *Head of a Skeleton with a Burning Cigarette*.

"Elda, come over here and look at this one! What a fantastic painting! Sending the correct message for today, but so advanced for that era!"

The museum was small and not at all crowded, so they wandered around twice. Elda vowed to look into whether she could buy a print of Van Gogh's painting of shoes once she got home. They would look great hanging next to the one she had done. She grinned at the thought.

As Elda and Korinna left the museum, the same musician was playing outside this door.

Elda approached the musician, bent, and placed some coins in his case. "Vot." There was no recognition in his eyes as he continued to play. She examined his hands and clothing as she straightened. He did not appear to be a threat.

Elda and Korinna checked back in at the consulate.

"Do you have any information about the assassin?" Elda asked her contact.

"We think he may be in Amsterdam, but we can't confirm that."

"And Egor?"

"No word yet from Egor."

***

Anatoly noted with satisfaction that the hacker's door was repaired, with the addition of a spyhole and new locks. He knocked and stood back slightly so the hacker could better see who he was. Three locks clicked, and the hacker opened the door and motioned him in.

"*Gut, sehr gut.*" Anatoly gestured to the locks and threw a handful of euros down on the floor next to the door. "*Was hast du?*"

The hacker recoiled and inched closer to his computers. "I've examined all the footage from the airport and the train station. I did see where this woman"—with a trembling hand, he pointed to Elda's picture—"arrived at the airport. But there is

277

no sign of any of these three women leaving, either together or separately." He gestured at the picture of Elda again and those of the old woman and the blonde. "My facial recognition software shows no matches and only a fifty percent match between the old woman and this one." He again pointed to the picture of Elda. He then aimed his finger at his computer equipment, where the footage was queued up. "If you don't believe me, you can see for yourself."

Anatoly narrowed his eyes in anger, sighed, and then started laughing from his extreme frustration. The hacker backed up out of his reach.

"*Nyet, nein*, no, no. It's okay," Anatoly said, and he reached into his bag and held out his hand, holding a thick envelope of money. The hacker stayed frozen in position, so Anatoly placed the envelope next to the computer monitors and left the apartment, closing the door behind him. The locks clicked into place as he walked down the hallway.

***

12 December 2018

Anatoly picked up speed and caught up with the woman ahead of him. He reached out his arm and touched her on the shoulder and pointed down at her feet. She gasped and stopped her foot from stepping into a pool of what appeared to be vomit. He jogged by and brushed against a man starting to cross the street. Only a few more blocks and he'd be there.

Anatoly stopped at the Renaissance Amsterdam Hotel on Kattengat. He was proud of himself. Twenty-three in total. He removed the ring from his finger and placed it back into his kit bag. He enjoyed playing games with himself to keep sharp. The games varied, but today it was how many people could he take out with a touch of the poisonous ring. Of course, there wasn't poison in the ring. Tosh would have his head. Anatoly was enraptured at the thought of the streets littered with the make-believe bodies he'd left behind.

Anatoly strode into the Renaissance Amsterdam Hotel lobby. It was centrally located, with a strong brick façade and spacious rooms. The simplicity of the décor appealed to him, and the staff was efficient. Most importantly, the rooms were clean.

Once in his room he made himself an espresso using the in-room machine, since he needed to stay awake for his walk through the red-light district. The smell of the coffee cleared his head as he planned his next steps. He checked his watch: 19:00. *We should get something to eat before I head out*, he said to his stomach, which grumbled in response. He calculated how many calories he had worked off today, not having done his exercises this morning. He headed out to Toscanini for Italian food. The open floor plan of the restaurant would allow him to easily view the other guests.

As Anatoly drew his knife through the meat on his plate, he considered how different it was to cut into a live human being. The juices ran out onto his plate much like blood from a wound, but there was no resistance to cutting up this tender meal, unlike the feel of the knife cutting through muscle and sinew. He'd loved his anatomy classes at the assassin training school. There was a science to killing quickly and silently.

Anatoly finished his ribeye and ordered the panforte to go so he could munch on it while walking around. He didn't trust the sweets sold in the stores. Too much of a chance of getting something with weed in it by mistake.

After paying his bill, Anatoly started off toward the red-light district. He glanced at his watch: 20:56—far too early for peak activity. He was too tired to go at 02:00, and if he had no luck tonight, he would go in the middle of the night the next night. He headed Southeast, walking by a pancake and crepe shop that briefly held his interest, and he bookmarked it in his head to stop at the following day. After crossing over a number of canals, gauging the height of the railings around them so he could calculate the angle and force needed to toss different amounts of body weight over them, he arrived at Dam Square.

"Der'mo!"

He had wandered too far in his musings. He headed back north toward De Oude Kerk, a building whose architecture he admired, on the outskirts of the red-light district. He figured that from the Warmoesstraat area he could roam the streets from Goldbergersteeg and cross the canals and wander from Barndesteeg to Bloedstraat to Monnikenstraat. He was hoping to find an unlicensed streetwalker, since it would be easier to lure her to a hotel room and then later dispose of the body.

He had searched for hours, but he had not yet seen anyone who met his specifications. Although disappointed, he had given himself a timeline of three days in Amsterdam, and if he didn't find anyone by the end of that time, he would fly back to Russia and discreetly use his connections there to find the right double.

Anatoly picked up his pace and hummed to himself in anticipation of finding his prey.

***

"Good news! We have received a message from Egor. Will Korinna please validate its authenticity?"

Korinna reached out her hand for the printout of Egor's message. She read it, and with tears streaming down her cheeks, she handed it to Elda.

Elda translated the Russian into English: "I am okay. I miss you so much. I can't wait for date night again. Hug the troodles for me. Is Sasha still decorating the park? Tell Elda, Honey says hi. Love, Egor."

Elda grinned. Korinna was smiling through her tears. "Yes, that is from Egor," Elda told the station chief.

"Unfortunately, I can't let her keep it," he responded as Korinna hugged the paper to her chest.

"*Ya znayu.*" Korinna reluctantly handed him the paper. "Come, Elda. We must celebrate."

Korinna pulled out the map again and steered them over to the coffee shop. Elda purchased and then pocketed the chocolate muffin.

"You may enjoy it later…"

"*Pozhaluysta*? We must celebrate."

Elda broke off and handed over a small portion of the muffin. She tossed the remaining portion back into the bag and repocketed it. "Only a small bite for you. We are not safe yet, Korinna. We have to get out of Amsterdam. He could be here already."

"Can we pop by the Pancake Bakery first? I would like to see what they carry, and we haven't eaten yet."

Elda's stomach growled in agreement. "Okay. It's on the way, and we can pick up something to take with us for our trip."

Moving toward the Pancake Bakery, Elda spied a man crossing the canal, who could have been a double for the large man at the hotel in St. Petersburg. She stopped dead and put her arm out to halt Korinna.

"Turn around quickly and stoop a bit!"

They spun and took a quick left onto a side street. Elda peered around the corner and saw that the man was crossing the canal and apparently hadn't seen them.

Perhaps I'm imagining things, but I swear that man is the one who was chasing me around St. Petersburg. His hair is darker, and he has facial hair, but he has the same build and moves in the same way. I don't believe in coincidences. Could someone have leaked my location? If it was pudgy boy CIA chief, then I hope he gets what's coming to him.

Elda frowned as the man—possibly the assassin—disappeared around a corner.

They grabbed food to go and walked back to the hotel at a fast clip.

"Korinna, that may have been a different man, but we can't be too careful. We will go back to the consulate when they reopen tomorrow and pick up our papers and depart Amsterdam immediately. We need to get some distance between us and him."

***

The next morning, Elda and Korinna did as much of a beeline to the consulate as the wandering crowds of tourist would allow. After discussing the next leg of their journey with the station chief and collecting their papers, which took far too long in Elda's opinion, they grabbed a sandwich at Lombardo's to take with them. Crossing the canal, Elda was slightly in front of Korinna.

A man rushed out of the crowd at Elda and Korinna.

"Not again." Elda groaned, catching sight of him out of the corner of her eye. "Run Korinna. Run!"

Korinna did an about face and sprinted back toward the consulate. Elda ran behind her while looking over her shoulder. The man was gaining on them.

"Quick, take a left."

Korinna turned left on Prinsengracht.

"Into the garage."

Korinna stumbled breathless into a parking garage. Elda popped in behind her and grabbed her arm, nearly dragging her up the stairs, through the glass doors, and off onto one side to hide behind a parked van. Elda tried the back doors of the van and discovered they were unlocked. She quietly opened one and shoved a panting Korinna inside while holding a finger up to her mouth to signal for silence. She closed the door without a sound and moved over to hide in the bed of a nearby truck. She heard footsteps run by and a few minutes later, a frustrated-sounding *"Chert!"* Then, the footsteps retreated out the way they came.

She peeked over the sides of the truck and observed that the coast was clear. Returning to the van, she let Korinna out. "Okay, the coast is clear. Let's get back to our hotel."

They turned onto Vijzelgracht, heading north, and Elda caught a glimpse of the man ahead, scanning the crowds for them.

"This is going to be a jump and roll, okay? But do try not to roll all the way into the water."

"What?"

Elda grabbed Korinna's arm and pulled her off the side of the road and onto a passing barge. They landed heavily but unharmed in the middle of a small group of tourists. Elda stood and saw that the assassin had jumped onto the following barge and seemed to be negotiating with the captain. "Okay, Korinna, we need to get off before he comes alongside."

Elda found their captain, and after an exchange of money, negotiated a drop off. The barge glided into the side wall with a small bump, and Elda and Korinna jumped up and off the boat. Elda looked over her shoulder to see the second barge pulling over and the man hopping off. He moved swiftly for such a large guy.

"Elda. I cannot do much more of this. I am not in the same shape that you are in," panted Korinna, running down the side of the canal.

Elda stopped short and whirled to face the assassin. He was jumping at her when she bent and put her head down, butting it into his groin, knocking the air out of him. She immediately grabbed his legs and straightened, flipping him over her back into the canal. On the way down, she heard him hit a houseboat with a solid *thunk*, and Korinna gasped in surprise. Elda turned to see him disappear into the canal.

A crowd quickly gathered, which allowed Elda and Korinna to slip away.

"We will have to change into our disguises as soon as we get to the hotel. Hurry."

***

Anatoly, partially dazed, swam underwater to the other side of the road, which bridged over the canal. Climbing onto a houseboat, he reached into his bag, which was somehow still on his shoulder, and picked the lock open, disappearing inside the boat. He stripped off his wet clothes and found towels to dry off with. He then rummaged for clothing, but he found only clothing for a slender man.

Der'mo! Chto eto s etimi toshchimi muzhchinami? How can so many men be so skinny? Glupyye khakery, glupyye zhenshchiny! He cursed the hackers and that woman. He explored the boat and, finding a small washer and dryer combination, he put his clothing in to dry while he calculated his next steps. The boat smelled musty, so it had probably been closed for a while. Anatoly opened the refrigerator, but it had been cleaned out, so the boat's owner was probably on vacation and might would not return immediately.

Anatoly sat at the small dining table and emptied out his kit bag. He found a towel to dry off the knives. Then, he picked up his phone and tried turning it on. The phone stayed dark. *Der'mo! Ne snova! Chert! Not again!* The screen had cracked and let water in. Now he would have to buy a new phone and get this one repaired. He searched for something to take his frustration out on but stopped himself. He could leave no damage—he had to cover his tracks.

He sat at the table with his head in his hands. How on earth could that woman best him twice? Who was she? And how was he ever going to explain this to his handler? His forehead hurt when he touched it. He leaned toward a mirror and concluded that he was going to have a large, ugly bruise. His forehead was turning purple on the right-hand side. He searched in the freezer and snatched an ice pack to hold on his head while he waited for his clothes to dry. He could always cover it with concealer, he reassured himself, alternating between anger and dismay.

He was ready to kill anyone at this point.

***

13 December, 2018

Leaving his hotel, Anatoly walked, with an anticipatory bounce in his step, to the red-light district and obtained a room for a few hours in a nearby hotel—cash, no ID required. He glanced over the desk at the clerk schedule and noted that the sleepy-eyed man currently at the desk was due to go off duty. *Khorosho. He won't remember me.*

After checking that the room keys worked, he jogged down a few streets and returned to a busy part of the red-light district. On either side of the street were buildings with large windows illuminated mainly in red to indicate the woman was available. Those lit with blue indicated a transgender woman or a cross-dresser was working, and the ones with the lights off meant the person inside was currently unavailable. Scantily clad women posed in lingerie, nurse's outfits, and the like. Something to please anyone. The workers in sanctioned brothels were unionized, took frequent health tests, and even paid taxes to the government.

Anatoly strolled by the windows where the women within were knocking and gesturing for him to come in. He ignored them all since he was looking for a freelancer and not a prostitute registered with the government. Turning a corner, he spied a tall, leggy blonde standing on the opposite far corner. Good. She did not have an official window and was on the street, so she would not be missed as soon. Moving closer, he could see she was significantly younger than Korinna, but years of hard living had aged her. *Ona sdelayet. Da, she will do*, he had reassured himself. *This is the one.*

He made a quick negotiation with her and handed her the key to the hotel room. She smiled at him, and in that moment, she was almost pretty. So sad that the years of streetwalking had prematurely aged her. But he would be doing her a favor to end this life for her.

***

Anatoly slipped in through the open door of the hotel room before the tall blonde could close the door. He held his gloved finger up to his lips as she stared at him, wide eyed. He stepped close to her and positioned his hand behind her head, slipping the

290

noose quickly around her neck. He pressed her to his chest with one hand while tightening the noose with the other, covering up any sound by pressing her face into his shirt. She struggled against him, but she finally went limp as the life drained out of her. Satisfaction flowed through his body as he lowered her to the floor. Looking down, he clinically noted that he had a hard-on. He removed the noose, arranged the body on the carpet, covered her face partially with her long hair, and took a number of pictures. He picked up the room key that had fallen from her fingers and backed out of the room.

***

Korinna turned to exit her room and noticed the door was slightly ajar. *Aga, that was it. My brain was searching for the sound of the door latching. Elda will be angry with me.* Korinna chastised herself for not paying better attention. *This is how the assassin will get you.*

***

Tosh looked at his phone. Anatoly's tracker had gone dark. That meant the fool was either dead or had lost his phone. Either way, Tosh needed a contingency plan. If something happened to Anatoly, he might have run into Elda in Amsterdam. Now, why would Elda be in Amsterdam?

Tosh stood in front of his map of the world on the wall of his office. "Aga! That's it!" He traced a line from Amsterdam to the UK. There were US military bases in the UK. Perhaps Elda was heading to one of those bases to fly back to the United States in a government plane. *If he were Elda, how would he go? He wouldn't fly from Amsterdam to London. Nyet, nyet. That would leave too much of a trail.*

Tosh sat back in his chair and pressed his fingers to his forehead. It would have to be via water. Tosh typed into his keyboard and studied the different options for cargo ships, cruise ships, and ferries. A ferry to Newcastle would be the quickest and easiest. No special arrangements were needed.

Tosh leaned back and stared at the ceiling. He really must paint that ceiling. Or at least put a map of the world up there. His thoughts returned to the operation at hand. He would send someone to Newcastle to intercept Elda. Tosh pulled the file on Elda from his cabinet. He copied her picture and dropped it onto his desk. He then set the file back and did the same with a picture of Korinna from her file. He reached back into the file cabinet and pulled out handful of a thick files, which he carried to his desk. *Da, Yaromir.* Yaromir was rather crude in approach, but he had done his jobs well, despite the collateral damage. He was the best of this bunch. Tosh would send him to Newcastle to see if he could terminate

Korinna and, if necessary, Elda too. Yaromir was presently undergoing additional training at the Kremlin.

Tosh picked up the phone and asked that Yaromir be sent to see him.

***

Elda and Korinna met in the hotel lobby. Elda wore a men's shirt, suit, tie, and leather shoes with lifts in them. She had added a black wig, thick glasses, mustache, and hat.

"If I hadn't seen you before, I would not have recognized you," said a tall brown-haired woman in flat shoes, wraparound sunglasses, and a long, flowery skirt, with a matching bag and bandana.

Elda shouldered her bag, and they walked toward the ferry terminal. Elda pointed at the schedule for Thursday, 13 December, 2018.

"If we are lucky, we can catch the 17:30 ferry to Newcastle."

"Do we get a cabin with a window?" Korinna asked.

"Certainly! I bet you don't want to relive your container experience, hey?"

293

"*Da.*"

"It will be fifteen hours on a ship again. I hope it isn't too traumatic."

Korinna shuddered.

"But on the bright side, there will be a flushable toilet!"

Korinna smacked Elda on the arm.

Elda jogged ahead to guarantee they made that ship. They already had the tickets that the consulate had purchased for them.

It was with relief that she stood on the deck with Korinna and watched Amsterdam recede from view. Elda kept an eye on the few passengers who arrived late with them, and none were the man from St. Petersburg.

"He did not board the ferry."

***

As the ferry was docking, Elda received an encrypted message on her phone. She decoded it. Her eyes narrowed in disappointment. Trying to keep any signs of dismay from her voice, she said to Korinna, "There has been a change in plans. We have to finish making our arrangements at the American Embassy in London. They will let the fisherman know that we will be delayed in our crossing with him. So instead of driving to Gourock, we will catch a train from Newcastle to London. This just means we'll be traveling for a few more days instead of heading to the US in a few hours. *Ya proshu proshcheniya.* I am so sorry."

Korinna's face fell. The look of disappointment would have been comical, had it not been so real.

Elda observed her with almost horror, hoping she wouldn't cry again. "I am running low on Kleenex, Korinna."

Korinna laughed and then sighed. "There is no need for you to apologize. It is not your fault. I was so looking forward to wrapping my arms around Egor, feeling his heartbeat in his chest, and truly knowing that he is alive and well."

Elda felt her heart skip a beat and her pulse speed up. The rerouting meant an increase in the amount of time they would face danger from Russian assassins.

Korinna leaned dejectedly on the railing.

"Don't jump, but I have more bad news. The ferry gets in at the Port of Tyne, and we will have to bus to the train station, which is anywhere from a fifty-minute to a two-and-a-half-hour trip, depending on the route. We want the quicker bus—number nineteen—if we can get it, or number eleven, the Blue Arrow. We will be exposed for a long time, and I am not sure how long these disguises will be effective."

Korinna jokingly raised a leg, pretending to climb over the railing, and then laughed at the look of horror on Elda's face. "*Khorosho*. It is what it is."

They both nodded and watched as the ferry gracefully docked. Crew members jumped off and grabbed the lines to help guide it in. It always amazed Elda that they didn't end up in the water between the ship and the dock. She contemplated how many were injured while trying to master that stunt.

As Elda examined the crowd waiting for the ferry, she spotted to one side a large, squarely built man sitting and looking at his phone, holding it strangely. *Is he taking pictures of the ship?*

"Korinna, turn away from the rail. Now."

"*Chto?*"

"There is a man down there who is scanning the crowd and the people on the ship. I recognize him. He chased me on a Jet Ski in Moscow. Tie your scarf around your head and lower your face." Elda reached into her pack and brought out the folding cane. Unfolding it, she handed the cane to Korinna. "Stoop a bit and use this cane."

"I will have to stoop a bit to use this cane. What is it for, short people?"

"Hush, tall one. Just listen to me. I want you to get off the ferry and catch a taxi to the train station. I'll go see what this man wants and meet you at the station. Okay?"

"Elda, please be safe."

"Don't worry about me; catch the first train to London. If I am delayed, I will hop onto a later one. I'm messaging Ed to meet you at King's Cross station."

Elda had removed the inserts in her mouth to make it more comfortable to eat and talk. She now inserted them to help fool facial recognition software. She replaced her regular glasses with a pair of mirrored sunglasses that wrapped around to completely cover her eyes. There was a stiff breeze that would help cover for Korinna's use of the facial scarf.

After they docked, Elda followed Korinna four passengers behind. Korinna did an excellent job of disguising her height and hobbling with the cane. Elda watched as the man scanned each passenger disembarking from the ferry. He passed by Korinna and then by Elda and continued his scanning without changing position.

Elda turned right off the gangplank, away from the gathered crowds and passengers, over to where the man was sitting.

"Excuse me. Could I use your phone, sir?"

The man glanced up and shook his head.

I swear he almost growled at me. Do they grow them all this large and mean looking in Russia? She advanced until she was at his side. "Please. I have lost my phone and need to make a call."

"*Nyet*, no."

The man waved an arm at her, narrowly missing hitting her, as he continued to watch his phone. Elda took advantage of his distracted state and plunged a hypodermic needle into his arm and depressed the plunger. The man jumped up, still holding his phone, and grabbed Elda by the neck with one hand and raised her into the air. *"Malen'kiy chelovek, ya skazal nyet."*

Normally Elda would have taken offense at being called "little man," but at this point she was too busy gasping for air. She had one hand that had managed to sneak in between his hand and her neck, providing her with a limited airway, but the pressure deepened, and she had little time to act. *No means no, I guess.* She wondered why she had such useless thoughts right now, as she willed her other hand to unzip the hidden belt pocket and take out a second syringe. Her feet flailed and ineffectually kicked his knees.

He held her up higher and shook her like a rag doll. Would she throw up or pass out first? She kicked out again, and this time it landed in his groin, causing him to grunt and lower her slightly and loosen his grip. She sucked in a breath of air, then felt his hand tighten again.

She focused on the vein throbbing in his neck and managed to jab the syringe into it and depress the plunger, as her eyesight grew dim and stars danced around in the darkness. *This stuff better work! The first one would have put down a horse.*

His hand loosened. She fell out of his grip with a thump, lying gasping on the ground. She brought her feet up to her chest and explosively threw them straight out, smashing him in the legs. He fell heavily on top of her, knocking the breath out of her, like a tree that had fallen in the wrong direction. His hand slowly reached for her eyeballs. As she turned her head away, she could feel him become a deadweight on top of her.

She inched her way out from underneath him, to find an old lady holding her hat.

"Dear, shall I call the police? Did this ruffian attack you?"

As she brushed off her clothes, Elda reached out and took her hat from the woman. "No need for the police. I know him. He has high blood sugar, and when it gets off, he gets agitated and does not want to take his insulin."

Elda reached into her backpack and unzipped a small black case to show the woman the vial labeled INSULIN. She removed the needle from his neck and, with a bit of a struggle, propped him up against the bench.

"He will be fine in a few minutes, and I will ensure he gets something good to eat."

"You Americans. You are so rough on each other."

"I know. We are. Not at all civilized."

"Quite."

The old woman walked away, satisfied that the situation was under control even though they were crazy Americans. Elda reached down and removed the second syringe from his arm and observed that it all hadn't gone all the way into him. *Ah, that's why. Well, sleep well, my prince.* She emptied the rest of the syringe into his leg. She put his cell phone into her pocket, removed his money from his belt, his ID from his inner coat pocket, and his knife from his leg holster. She then buttoned his coat to keep him warm, checked his pulse, which was strong, and removed his shoes. That should slow him down a bit.

Elda ran over to the nearest dumpster and threw the shoes and phone into it. She checked the pickup schedule and saw that it would be emptied within the hour.

Chapter Fifteen

13 December, 2018

"You are doing so well, Aurelio! And you have been here such a short while. The doctor told me that they will be letting you out with other patients, and that means you are on the road toward coming home." Natasha looked warmly at Aurelio. She had been told that there was a chance he wouldn't survive mingling with the other patients, but it did seem he had improved immensely.

"Yes, Natasha. The doctor has helped me so much. I was in bad shape before this. Thank you for agreeing to have me come here."

Natasha noticed that his eyes had narrowed slightly and did not appear to be expressing the same joy as his mouth, but she smiled tenderly back at him. He really did seem sincere. She must ask the doctor what he thought. "I do hope you are able to come home soon. The apartment seems so empty without you." She hated that place. If he lived, she'd convince him to sell it or rent it out and let them live someplace else. She handed Aurelio a pile of English magazines and a novel from home.

"*Spasibo, Natasha.*"

"Not in English, Aurelio?"

"*Nyet, Natasha.* I must learn to compromise with you."

He has *changed.* "I look forward to being home with you, *moya lyubov'*. I think it might work out this time. Please continue to work hard with this wonderful *doktor*."

She stood, kissed his cheek, and went off in search of the doctor. An attendant who was nearby escorted Aurelio back to his room.

***

"*Doktor*, is he really that much better? Is there any way he could be faking it?"

The doctor shook his head. "No, he is really improving. He will need much more time and therapy, while we continue to monitor and adjust his medications, but I think the time has come for him to mingle with the other patients, and if that goes well, we could consider letting him go home for weekends. From there, it would be an outpatient situation if he can tolerate it. It may be that he will never fully return. At the least, he will need many years of therapy and will always be on medication."

Natasha nodded. She was rather used to living with Aurelio, and if he was healthier and not abusive and manipulative, as he had become, she could put up with him again. And as long as she continued having Yuri's support, perhaps it wouldn't be such a bad life after all. She did like the status that being married to an expat gave her. Not too shabby for a girl who grew up in poverty with no future. She returned her attention to the doctor with a concerned look on her face.

"Narcissistic Personality Disorder, grandiosity, and paranoia often go hand in hand," he explained. "There may be periods of regression. It's almost impossible to cure entirely. But if he can stay sober and clean, there is a chance of normal daily life functioning."

"Spasibo, Doktor."

***

Tosh checked the tracker for Yaromir. It had moved to one spot and then had been stationary ever since. He had not received a phone call from Yaromir either. *Chto proizoshlo? What has happened to Yaromir?*

He mulled over whether this operation was doomed to fail and if he needed to negotiate with Elda to keep Korinna quiet and hidden. *That will be a last-ditch effort.* He pulled three folders out of his file cabinet. Anatoly had finally called him to let him know he was in Moscow and was coming to the Kremlin to debrief with Tosh. Tosh was satisfied that Anatoly sounded nervous. *He should be nervous. I will teach him a lesson and make him a better operative.*

***

Anatoly trudged through Red Square, dreading his meeting with Tosh. Usually, he was impressed by the spectacle of the colorful buildings and the red, brick walls against the white of the snow and the blue of the sky, but today his mind was full and he felt discouraged.

He hoped that Tosh would lend some light on how that woman was able to best him so easily. She had to be an operative of some sort. There is no way a normal, elderly American woman could have done that to him. As he passed the red-and-black, marble-and-granite tomb of Lenin, he thought how Lenin could be ruthless in getting what he wanted. *Eto bylo*

305

tak plokho? My deystvitel'no izmenilis'? He answered his own questions: *Nyet, it wasn't that bad, but we Russians have changed. We have been much more selective about who we choose to eliminate.*

He continued toward St. Basil's Cathedral and the Kremlin. Pride puffed out his chest as he approached. *Imagine how wonderful it is to be part of all this and to be able to help my country.* He hoped he could continue to do so after today's meeting.

Once he arrived, he was escorted into a secure, windowless room with a metal table and two chairs. In the center of the table there was a tray with water, a teapot, and a dish with pastries—a sure sign that Tosh was not totally displeased with him. *Unless the tea and food are poisoned.* He considered that possibility and decided that if they were going to get rid of him, they would succeed anyway, so he poured himself a cup of tea and sat down. Just as he did, the door opened and Tosh walked in, holding three dark-brown folders.

Anatoly sat up straighter. His stomach clenched, and he withdrew his hand, which was reaching for the pastry. He looked directly into Tosh's eyes, trying to read what was going on behind them. Tosh's face showed nothing. Anatoly shrank back farther into his chair as Tosh approached.

Anatoly worried that his read of the food was correct and was grateful he had not yet sipped the tea.

Tosh set a scrambler in the middle of the table. He acknowledged Anatoly's unspoken question of *But isn't this a secure room?* with, "Da. But one can't be too sure." He paced around the perimeter of the room with a bug detector.

Anatoly sat still, like a child afraid of being punished by his parent.

"*Otlichno.* Let's get started," Tosh said as he opened the first folder. He handed Anatoly a picture of Anatoly from when he was first in training to be an operative. "This young man had great potential. As an operative, he never failed. Until now…"

Anatoly looked down at the picture and gulped. *Perhaps the tea and pastries were not such a good sign after all.* He pushed the picture back to Tosh. "*Pozhaluysta …please*! This operation can be saved…"

"*Tikho*, I am not finished," Tosh snapped.

Anatoly shut his mouth.

Tosh placed two more pictures on the table in front of Anatoly, another one of Anatoly as a young operative, and one taken this year. "Is it time for you to retire?"

"No, no. Please hear me out," Anatoly pleaded.

Tosh picked up the pictures and slipped them back into Anatoly's folder and set that folder to one side. He nodded, sat down, poured himself a cup of tea, and took a pastry.

"*Da, khorosho*. Speak."

Anatoly let out a large sigh of relief and selected a pastry from the main plate and put it on a napkin. He handed Tosh his damaged cell phone and asked if someone could fix it for him. Then he handed him his new phone open to the picture of the dead prostitute.

"*Vot*."

Tosh enlarged the picture and examined it, scrolling to see all the parts magnified. He stopped on the face and took out his magnifying glass and stared at it for a number of minutes. He frowned, then smiled and nodded and handed the phone back to Anatoly.

"*Otlichno srabotano!*" Tosh congratulated Anatoly on his initiative.

"*Spasibo*." Anatoly relaxed a bit. They had eliminated the pressure. Now they could talk freely and make plans to ensure there would be no trace of this ruse back to them.

Tosh lifted his teacup and took a sip. Anatoly did the same. They then each bit into their pastries.

"This will get us off the hook for this abysmal mission. But we cannot let another one like this happen. Am I clear on that, Anatoly?"

"*Da, Da, ochen' ponyatno.*"

"Good. Now tell me in detail about the two times you met the short, brown-haired woman."

Anatoly filled him in and included his humiliating splashdowns.

*****

Tosh could barely keep from laughing and celebrating his old adversary, as he now liked to think of her. He considered how few operatives of that generation were left who could manage to thwart Anatoly so nicely. He felt slightly proud of his extended circle of operatives from those earlier years. And she had become the operative that he imagined she would. He was delighted at the thought.

"And what about the old woman? Were they ever seen together?"

"*Nyet*. They were often in the same location, but I never saw them at the same time. I did have the hacker run facial recognition on the two women, and they had less than a fifty percent match."

Tosh nodded. He was well versed in the ways of the old-school operatives.

"They are the same woman, Anatoly."

Anatoly looked at him with surprise on his face. "*Otkuda vy znayete?*"

"I know because I once met this woman. She was young then, but her instincts were good. And her poker face was excellent. She was a good sparring partner, even then." Tosh told Anatoly about the time when he had been assigned to pick her up while her room was searched. "This woman, Elda, is the same woman who sparred with you and won. But I don't know why she has been activated. Perhaps just to get her old friend Korinna out. Ya ne znayu." He shrugged while putting his hands out to each side, as if embracing the uncertainty of it all.

Tosh handed Anatoly the two folders. The one on Elda was slender, but the one on Korinna was thick. Korinna's folder confirmed the information that Tosh had sent Anatoly previously.

"I have seen this information on Korinna, Tosh. She has a spotless record and has served the state well. Why was I sent in to eliminate her?"

"As a translator, Korinna has been in the same room with many powerful men. She knows their secrets."

"But that is true of most of the Kremlin translators. Why her?"

"Korinna was one of our top translators. We used her to help with the discussions between our president and many other high-ranking officials, including the President of the United States. We, of course, taped all the discussions, and the US president had all his transcripts destroyed, as did we. So, the only other remaining record is in Korinna's head. And although her memory is not perfect, as mine is, she has an excellent mind. The consequences of that information getting out will topple the American president and weaken Russia in the eyes of the world. I am not privy to what that information is, but I do know that the order to eliminate her came from our president himself."

Anatoly's face flashed with conflict as he viewed the pictures of Korinna arm-in-arm with Egor as they walked the dogs, and then he looked back up to Tosh.

Tosh easily read what was going on inside of Anatoly and believed that, despite the conflict, Anatoly would do as ordered. Anatoly had been the perfect, unfeeling killing machine. But if Anatoly was to be most effective as an operative, then he needed to be able to see both sides of the coin and still manage his feelings, compartmentalizing them so he could kill even when having empathy for another. He observed as Anatoly opened the thin folder on Elda.

"*Der'mo*! There is really nothing here!"

Tosh nodded. "Yes, but I have a feeling about this woman and a hunch that she has been much more than a mathematics teacher. Now, tell me again everything that you have observed. We need to see what you haven't observed too."

Tosh and Anatoly sat in the room for two hours, while Anatoly repeated each moment of his mission in detail.

"The women are, as far as the Kremlin will be concerned, taken care of," Tosh said. "We may want to find them and persuade them to tell no tales, but for now we need to verify that no one else knows they are alive and that they don't return to Russia while you and I are alive. I want to make sure all traces of them are gone so that no one else can follow them. So, first you must go pick up the luggage in Florence and then report back here to me in Moscow. You and I will work closely together on this. No one else must know about it."

"What about Mr. Ainsworth?"

"I will find Mr. Ainsworth for you while you're gone. When you return with the luggage, we will discuss if he's worth going after or if we should just close the case entirely. But from now on, this mission is only between you and me. Understood?"

"*Da, da, ya ponimayu!*"

"*Khorosho.*"

Anatoly ogled the remaining pastries on the plate.

"Take them! I don't know how you are not fat! And when you return, we will spend some time together in training. There are things I need to teach you."

Anatoly grinned, wrapping the pastries up in napkins and put them in his pockets.

"I have more money and additional identities." Tosh handed Anatoly an envelope of money and another with his paperwork. "You must be careful in spending. I have more from this operation that I allocated, but once I report the successful conclusion, the remaining money will be repurposed. *Ponimayu?*"

"*Da.* I understand."

Chapter Sixteen

14 December, 2018

Aurelio pranced through the recreation room, where some of the other patients sat around playing cards, watching TV, or just staring off into space. He tried to keep a friendly smile on his face. These guys could be violent. As he observed the room, he considered how he could use each one of the residents here. It was important that he get out as quickly as he could, but while he was inside, why not bask in the homage due to him? He was sick of being subservient to everyone.

The room had a faint antiseptic smell and was painted institutional green. The large windows were covered with bars, which broke up the incoming sunlight into strips along the green-and-white linoleum floor. There were no paintings on the walls and only a couch and TV on one side of the room, with card tables and chairs scattered around the room.

He observed the large man on the couch. That one would be a good one to have working for him.

Next to the large man was a short, skinny man with wispy, white hair who was picking at his discolored teeth and staring intently at the TV. Hardly a man at all. Aurelio would work on him first.

"Excuse me. May I join you two?"

The large man snorted and pointed to a nearby chair, and the short man ignored Aurelio entirely. *How dare he ignore me?* Aurelio felt the familiar flush of anger start, but he forced himself to stay calm and smile. They would soon know who the best man here was.

"I'm Aurelio. And you two are?"

A withering look from the large man stopped his attempt at conversation. He bit his tongue and refrained from asking if they had heard who he was.

After watching TV with them for a few minutes, Aurelio bid them both a good day and tiptoed away in search of other marks. To his retreating back, he heard the large man say, "He doesn't have a clue what you're in here for, does he?"

"He will if he tries to talk through my show again," the small man replied.

The large man laughed a cackling high-pitched laugh.

Aurelio turned slightly in their direction, and shivers rolled up his spine. He would be extra careful around that man.

Aurelio stopped by the two who were playing cards and asked if he could watch. Focused on their game, they nodded at another chair around the card table, and he sat down. He didn't recognize the card game, so he asked them what they were playing. One of the men jumped up and lifted a metal folding chair over his head to crash it down on Aurelio's head.

"*Broya, syad'*!" an attendant shrieked.

Broya slammed the chair back down with a clang on the linoleum floor and sat down as the attendant had ordered him to do. Aurelio left the table and pussyfooted back to his room until lunchtime. Clearly, it was more dangerous dealing with these unpredictable people than those he had dealt with in his past. But he was clever and special, and he would soon figure them out.

On the way back to his room, he ran into the doctor, who was coming down the hallway in the opposite direction.

"How are you today, Aurelio?"

"Fine, Doctor. I am so glad you have let me out to see the other patients. I can see how sick I was and how far I have come. It is very instructive. You must have helped so many people in your career."

The doctor puffed up and beamed.

Aurelio scrutinized the doctor. There! He still had it. The doctor had bought Aurelio's act entirely. Now, he just had to manipulate the others there.

One of the interns with the doctor was analyzing Aurelio intently.

Ah, he is impressed with my progress too. Aurelio flashed the intern a large grin. The intern quickly looked away and made notes in his notebook.

***

Tosh stepped off the train in St. Petersburg, which was cleaner, more colorful, and more cosmopolitan than Moscow, but his heart loved Moscow, the heart of the Motherland. Tosh had researched the doctors and nurses at the hospital and had found that Klava Vasiliev, one of the nurses, was in debt and therefore could easily be bribed. He had also checked the nurse's schedule, and she would be on duty this afternoon.

Outside the hospital, Tosh paid the taxi driver, removed his coat, and folded it over one arm to reveal his white scrubs. He attached a badge to his pocket and swept through the front door. He stopped at the gift shop and bought a large box of candy. Presenting this to the women at the information desk, he introduced himself as a visiting doctor and asked them to please keep his coat for him. They readily agreed, knowing the good doctor would probably give them another present for doing so. Giggling, they opened the box of candy and reached in, like little children, biting into a piece and, if they liked it, finishing it. Tosh made a mental note to get them another box on his way out.

He strode down the hallway as if he belonged, capitalizing on his unimposing nature, calm demeanor, and the average features of his wiry build. Those around him often missed seeing him, as he tended to blend in with the background and not stand out in any way.

He stopped at the nurses' station and asked for Klava.

A small gray-haired woman timidly replied, "*Da, Ya Klava.*"

"Klava, do you remember me?"

With a confused look, she replied in the affirmative. "*Da, Ya tebya pomnyu.*"

"*Khorosho! Khorosho!*"

Tosh asked her if there was any place they could talk privately. Klava led him to a small empty lab.

They both sat on metal stools, and Tosh asked her about Mr. Ainsworth's stay at the hospital and showed her an envelope full of money.

"*Ya ne znayu*," Klava said sadly, licking her lips at the thought of so much money.

"*Vy mozhete uznat'*?"

Klava sat up straighter. "Of course I can find out. My friend, Masha Smirnov, works in the medical records department. For a small fee, Masha would readily give me the information."

"Is this Masha discreet?"

"Oh, da. Masha loves to feel she is getting the better of the establishment, and when it lines her own pockets, the better. Da!"

Tosh smiled and passed her a small amount of the money.

"There will be more when you get the information on Mr. Ainsworth. I will be back in an hour. Will that be enough time?"

"Da!" Klava agreed.

Tosh nodded and left to get the layout of the hospital and grab a bite in the cafeteria.

When Tosh returned, Masha took him immediately back into the small lab.

"U menya yest' informatsiya," she said and handed him a slip of paper.

Tosh glanced at and pocketed the paper, passing her the envelope of money. Masha took it with a trembling hand. *"Spasibo.* I will get you any information on patients that you need in the future."

Tosh was pleased. It was good to have someone in his debt. There was no telling when he might use her again.

*****

The day was getting late, and Tosh no longer had the stamina that he'd had had forty years ago, so he called it a day, found a hotel to check in to, and decided to check out the psychiatric hospital the next day. He needed to arrange a contact to leverage at the hospital anyway. He had researched Aurelio's background and current living arrangements. Aurelio was married to Natasha, and Yuri was the operative keeping tabs on the expat. He intended to speak with Yuri before going to the hospital.

Tosh booked himself into the Bridge Hotel, since it was only about a half-hour walk to the psychiatric hospital, but he would stroll through Aleksandrovskiy Garden and view the gold dome of St. Isaac's Cathedral. He wished he had an excuse to visit the State Hermitage Museum while he was in St. Petersburg, and so close to it. He laughed at the thought of poor Anatoly having to visit that museum twice. Anatoly did not appreciate art.

And now I have sent someone with a dislike of art to Florence. What a waste. Tosh loved Filippo Brunelleschi's Duomo and the story behind it. Florence was so rich in the history of architecture and art. Tosh also loved the Cathedral of Florence and looking down over the city from inside it. His favorite museum was the charming Museum Opera del Duomo behind the Cathedral, with its beautiful wooden statue by Donatello.

Tosh remembered that he had helped one of his associates—ex-KGB—get his grandson into medical school. The grandson was smart and had excellent grades but was effeminate and had not made many friends. The young man was interning at a psychiatric hospital in St. Petersburg. Tosh scrolled through his contact list and found his friend's number.

"*Da, da*, certainly we will help you. My grandson, Nikita Lebedev, is doing so well! Yes, he is at the Psychiatric Hospital of St. Nicholas. He has the evening shift tomorrow. Perhaps you will do a late breakfast with him?"

"Yes, have him meet me at the restaurant at the Bridge Hotel at 10:00 a.m. tomorrow morning."

After hanging up, Tosh flipped through his contact list again.

"*Privet, Yuri. Eto Tosh.*"

"*Da, konechno*, Tosh," Yuri said in a surprised tone. "It's been a number of years, *ser*. You were very kind to me in training, and I learned a lot from you. What can I do for you now?"

"I'm in St. Petersburg. Meet me at the Bridge Hotel at eight tomorrow morning."

"*Da*. I'll be there. Do you need me to bring anything?"

"No. Just yourself."

"*Khorosho.*"

"Paka."

"Paka."

Tosh then made arrangements for a doctor's jacket and medical ID for the psychiatric hospital to be delivered to his hotel room in the morning. He lay on the couch and put his feet up to watch the BBC news in English.

As a young man, Yuri had showed potential as an agent, but he had too much heart to be effective, was too eager to please, and acted far too enthusiastic. And his obsession with animals was so gauche and odd among his peers. Yuri had a shaky moral compass, and that made him useful as a gatherer of information, but Tosh had known from the start that Yuri would not be an assassin. Tosh had recommended that they accept him for training, however, to see how his skills could best be used. He eagerly awaited seeing him again and assessing him as an adult.

***

Yuri stopped at the doorway and scanned the room for Tosh. He had good memories of Tosh as a visiting instructor, when Yuri was undergoing his pre-KGB training. The KGB had been disbanded before Yuri could be fully indoctrinated into it, but he had joined the military and had become part of the GSU, transferring over to the SVR afterward. He recognized that he was treading on thin ice as a double agent for the CIA and SVR, but he reveled in the adrenaline rush from the thrill of it all. He was suspicious that he had been assigned expat babysitting duties because someone in the SVR did not feel Yuri was trustworthy. He was aware that someday soon he would have to pick a side.

Yuri saw an old man sitting at a table and did a double take. Was that Tosh? How long had it been? Perhaps twenty-eight years. Tosh had aged significantly. But that alert look was still in his eyes, and Yuri sensed that Tosh had guessed everything that Yuri had been thinking. He took a deep breath. *"Ty Tosh?"*

"Ya Tosh," the man replied, motioning for Yuri to take a seat at the table.

Tosh openly observed Yuri as he sat down. He breathed deeply again to hide his nervousness. He wasn't proud of all he had done since he'd last seen Tosh. He wondered if Tosh knew he was currently working for the Americans as well as the Russians and the mafia.

Tosh asked Yuri to fill him in on Aurelio. Yuri outlined a picture of a man who had become increasingly unstable as he aged, and he'd had a psychotic break after his mother had died. He was estranged from most of his family and was a heavy alcohol and drug user. He and Natasha had a turbulent relationship. Aurelio could no longer hold down a job and was really of no further use for information.

"*I yego sem'ya?*" Tosh inquired, trying to get more information about Aurelio's family and his relationship to his siblings.

Yuri said that apparently there were a number of children from multiple marriages, but Aurelio seemed to only trust one of his full sisters. He desired acceptance and love from his brother and his older half-sister and was angry that they had rejected his, in his terms, "loving" advances. He explained how Aurelio attacked the two of them via email on a regular basis but was most triggered by the holidays, but he understood that was the norm for many people with mental illness. As far as Yuri had observed, neither of them responded nor had anything to do with Aurelio.

"*Interesno.*" Tosh asked a few more questions and left off with, "Is he violent? Would he attack anyone?"

"No, he is too stoned most of the time."

***

Tosh dismissed Yuri. Seeing Aurelio tomorrow could be a waste of time. He was not involved in this. But Tosh did wonder why Aurelio had attacked Anatoly. He replayed the scene on board the train that Anatoly had described. He positioned the players where they were when Anatoly first entered the car and pushed PLAY in his mind.

Aga! That is it! Aurelio was attacking Elda, not Anatoly. I can verify that tomorrow.

Tosh sat sipping his coffee while waiting for the intern Nikita to show up. He looked up as a young, peach-fuzz-faced man of slender build pulled out the chair on the other side of the table. Tosh had spotted him enter the restaurant and listened to his footsteps as they approached his table, so he wasn't surprised by the man's arrival.

Tosh introduced himself as an old friend of Nikita's grandfather and said he had been helpful in arranging Nikita's admission to medical school. He pointedly mentioned that he was aware of the difficulties Nikita had had, despite his good grades. Nikita blushed from his neck up and across his wide cheeks. He sat tensely with his hands on the edge of the table, clearly ready to push his chair away and run if need be.

"Relax. I don't bite."

Nikita gave a stilted laugh and folded his hands in his lap.

"I just want some information about—and to see—a patient at your clinic."

"*Kto*?"

"Mr. Aurelio Ainsworth."

Nikita blinked. "I knew it!"

"Knew what?"

"I have been watching Mr. Ainsworth, and I feel he is acting a part and may be dangerous."

"Tell me more."

"Mr. Ainsworth has a diagnosis of grandiosity, narcissism, and extreme paranoia. Because he feels guilty about having had life so good, he has created fantasies that he has been targeted by the CIA, FBI, and DEA since he was a small child. He gives himself a sense of self-worth by telling himself that he has outsmarted them all, but he also believes they are still trying to set him up and/or to kill him. He suspects his wife, who he says is a prostitute, is also involved in this plot against him. He has recently been hanging around with two other patients, each with a similar diagnosis. The doctor is saying Mr. Ainsworth is better and may be able to be released soon. I think that he is manipulating the doctor into believing this. But now you show up. Could any of Mr. Ainsworth's tales be true?"

"*Nyet.* His tales are a product of his own mind. I think he may have seen something that I would like to get more information on, but we have limited interest in him otherwise."

Nikita nodded and exclaimed, "I knew it! *On choknutyy.*"

"Perhaps it's not good form for a doctor to call a patient 'nuts?'" Tosh inquired, while trying to hold back his laughter.

"But you see, I have been trying to tell the doctor that Mr. Ainsworth is faking it and manipulating him, but the doctor will not listen to me."

"It is also bad form for a junior to tell a superior that he is being manipulated."

"*Chto ya dolzhen delat'?*"

Nikita looked so forlorn as he asked Tosh what he should do, that Tosh spent the next ten minutes giving Nikita advice on how to better handle his superior. He then told Nikita to give him full access to Aurelio's records when he returned.

After Nikita left, Tosh picked up a package from the front desk. He went to his room and donned his new, long, white doctor's jacket and hospital ID. He was uncertain if he would check out of the hotel. He had booked the room for two nights. Just in case he had to scram, he wiped everything clean and packed up what little he had brought. Old habits were deeply ingrained.

Tosh left the hotel and started his walk to the park.

Tosh felt responsible for Anatoly. Anatoly's parents had died when he was a young boy, and he had no family, except for Tosh and the state. Throughout the years, Tosh had studied Anatoly, looking for cracks in his armor, weighing whether Anatoly would make a good replacement for him when he retired. Anatoly's need for perfection could be his downfall, and Tosh was heartened to see Anatoly, for the first time, find a workaround solution to an engagement. It meant he was ready to look at the politics behind their assignments and to operate at a higher level. He didn't tell Anatoly that the pictures would fail a facial recognition scan, because he didn't want to discourage Anatoly's newfound initiative. He hoped no one would look that closely.

Tosh wanted to teach Anatoly how to think more before leaping into action. Anatoly was insightful, but his desire to have everything in its rightful place, combined with his need for perfection, had stopped him from rising any further.

Once Anatoly returned, Tosh would find someone who could help him look at the root cause for his anger. It might limit his effectiveness as an assassin in the future, but it would allow him to better handle others like him. Tosh would also spend more time himself mentoring Anatoly and seeing how far he could grow. *I must do all this quickly. Who knows how much time I have left, since I have lived a hard life, and it has taken its toll on my body.*

Tosh's phone beeped. He read his message and started laughing. "Yaromir is stuck in Newcastle without any money!" He shook his head at the absurd turn this case had taken. He quickly dialed a number.

"Da... da... da. Idi za nim. Spasibo." He hung up, having told the agent on the other end of the line to fetch Yaromir. Apparently, a small man had attacked him with a hypodermic needle when he was

using the facial recognition software on his app to scan the crowd. He had tried to strangle the man but failed when the man stuck him with a second needle. He woke up to find his phone, fake ID, knife, money, and shoes gone. He finally had managed to steal a pair of shoes, some money, and a phone to call in, but he had no ID, so he couldn't fly back.

Tosh sighed. This operation couldn't get much worse, though it helped that Yaromir hadn't been arrested. But he would bet that the small man was Elda in disguise. Too bad his cell phone was missing. He could review the video of the passengers disembarking. He could have someone pick it up. Da, he would have the agent also pick up Yaromir's phone, since the tracker appeared to still be working. Tosh typed an encrypted message to the agent.

Chapter Seventeen

14 December, 2018

Aurelio tried to make inroads with the other patients again. He was looking for an easy mark. He enjoyed manipulating others to buy him necessities at the commissary. Not that he couldn't afford to do so on his own. Natasha and Yuri regularly brought him items and deposited money into his account. He liked the feeling of power that ripping people off and making them do his bidding gave him. He would have to be careful, however. He did not want to get caught doing anything that would lose him any privileges.

The large man and the little man were back on the couch, watching TV. The volatile man was playing the same strange card game with his buddy. One patient stood looking at the wall. Two men sat at a table engaged in conversation. Another man sat on the floor, rocking back and forth. And one paced in a circle, muttering to himself. Aurelio concluded that the two men talking to each other were his best bet. He tramped over to that corner of the room, with two sets of eyes tracking him from the couch and the cardplayers watching him over the top of their cards.

"*Privet.*"

"*Privet.*"

"*Menya zovut Aurelio.*"

"*Menya zovut Stanislav, and I yego zovut Yevgeni.*"

Finally, here was someone who could talk civilly and not throw a chair for no reason.

"May I sit down and join you two gentlemen?"

"I would be happy to have you join the conversation that Yevgeni and I are having," Stanislav replied.

"Perhaps you could illuminate some of the darker areas for us?" Yevgeni said.

Aurelio puffed out his chest. "I would be honored to do so. What is the topic of conversation?"

"It is not right that we are here. We have been unfairly judged and trapped in here. There are those who do not know and do not understand. We have tried to elucidate the matter for them to no avail. The darkness is still there," Stanislav pontificated.

"I definitely do not belong here, nor does Stanislav," Yevgeni chimed in.

"Exactly! I do not belong here either. My wife, Natasha, has been working with the Russian and US agencies to eliminate me. There are forces conniving against me. I used to think they were misguided, but now I feel that evil lurks behind them."

"Stanislav and I were sure you would be a kindred spirit."

"How would you know that? Where do you get your information? Are they telling you things about me?"

"No, no. Stanislav and I can identify those like us. We have ways that others do not."

"They are out to take my money and are envious of my position," Stanislav added.

"Very much my story too! What is your position, Stanislav?"

"I am the ruler of the world, and Yevgeni holds a high position in my cabinet."

"Are you trying to entrap me? If you are the ruler of the world, then wouldn't I, an important man, know of you already?"

"They don't want you to know the truth. They have hidden me in here to keep the others from finding out about me. Yevgeni was captured after I was sent here. It was thick-witted of them to incarcerate us both in the same place."

"Why are you telling me this? How do you know to trust me, a stranger to you?"

"Ah, but aren't we all strangers to each other? And because we are strangers, we are comrades in familiarity. Our sources are the same."

Aurelio leaned in to whisper, "We must be careful. The others are watching and listening. They are jealous and out to get us. But if you are the ruler of the world, then who appointed you?"

"God, of course. I am one of the chosen ones."

"Of course! That makes sense. I can see that because I am special too. Did you know that once the FBI tried to trap me on a highway, but I flew over all of them and escaped?"

"Yes, yes, we can tell you are special. We welcome you. You could be one of the leaders of the world once we escape from here."

Aurelio felt like crying. After all these years, could it be that he had finally found others who understood him? Elated, he cackled at the beauty of the truths they had presented to him. "Well, I am better than them all. It is clear that you are also superior and have been persecuted as I have been. I'm delighted to work with you two."

The three men shook hands. Yevgeni gripped Aurelio's shoulder and cautioned, "Watch what they do to you here. I once was associated with a man who had to have all his teeth removed because they had inserted transmitters into them."

"They have the technology. My half-sister and brother practice mind manipulation from afar."

The three men looked warily around the room.

***

When the attendant came in and told them it was time to go back to their rooms, Aurelio pranced back along the corridor. The large man from the couch passed him and hip-checked him into the wall.

"*Izvitite menya,*" said the man as he stomped past with his small companion.

Aurelio rubbed his probably bruised arm and stared at their backs. Clearly that was a man to be avoided. He would have to talk to his new companions tomorrow and see what his story was.

Information was power. He was glad he was not yet allowed to have meals with the rest and would have supper in his room.

Holding his crotch and rocking back and forth in his chair, Aurelio remembered that Natasha had not been to see him for a few days, nor had Yuri. He wondered when either of them would come again. He would like to get a new book in English. The library only had books written in Russian. His Russian was good enough that he could read and speak it fluently, but it wasn't relaxing. English was his native language. He was relieved when Natasha had wanted to learn it. He was also impressed at how quickly she'd picked it up. She now spoke it like a native. She was a smart woman when it came to learning languages, apparently. He didn't expect that in her, since women were inferior to men, and few were capable of going through life without a man to help them. Natasha needed his help and would come to see him soon.

***

Anatoly caught the Lufthansa flight to Florence. He had taken Tosh's cost-savings advice to heart and booked an economy seat. *Der'mo!* He was flying first class back. These seats were far too small. And the food. *Eto der'mo!* He frowned at the man in the window seat next to him when the man's elbow

338

tried to take the armrest. The man quickly withdrew his arm, turned to the left, and curled up as small as he could in his seat. Anatoly grinned at the woman with the aisle seat, and she recoiled slightly.

After close to four hours, Anatoly was ready for the stopover in Frankfurt. He followed the smell of freshly baked bread to Heberer's Bakery, where after much deliberation and discussions with his stomach and taste buds, he selected a chocolate cream croissant and a strawberry Danish.

When the plane landed, Anatoly brushed the crumbs from his lap. He hoped that the return flight would also go through Frankfort.

Anatoly drove away from the airport and immediately was assaulted by an angry Italian driving inches away from Anatoly's back bumper and beeping the car horn.

"*Der'mo*! Bezumnyy! These Italians are nuts!"

He contemplated slamming on his brakes, when the car zipped by him with the driver throwing an obscene gesture with one hand and steering with the other, all at high speeds. The driver zipped back in front, barely missing the front bumper of Anatoly's car and of the car speeding toward them in the opposite direction. Anatoly took a deep breath, remembering all that Tosh had said about keeping his anger in check and having this operation go off smoothly. He swore almost continuously as he drove, itching to bump one of them with his car, but he continued his breathing exercise that Tosh had taught him and arrived at the print shop without incident.

Anatoly located a men's clothing store and bought a dark suit with a white shirt and tie. It was hard to find shirts that fit him well off the rack, since his neck and shoulders were so large. This one, like the others he'd tried on, bunched at the waist when he tucked it into his pants. The pants also didn't fit well, because his thighs were so muscular. Usually, he had his suits tailored for him, but he did not have time for that. He cinched his belt tight to hold up the pants and buttoned his jacket to hide the fact that nothing fit him well around the waist. *I hope these pants don't split when I sit down.* He sat in a chair in the store to test the flex. His thighs strained at the material, but nothing ripped. He was ready for action.

***

Anatoly pulled the black Alfa Romeo up in front of the Hotel Brunelleschi and paraded into the hotel.

340

"*Ciao*. I am Elda Ainsworth's personal assistant, sent here to pick up the luggage that she and her traveling companion had sent in anticipation of their stay here." He handed the clerk his business card.

"*Ciao*, Mr. Smith. How can we help you today?"

"Unfortunately, Mrs. Ainsworth had urgent work matters and had to delay her vacation to Italy. She had her luggage sent on in advance, so it is already here. We will rebook her at a later date."

The desk clerk let out a loud dramatic sigh and reluctantly checked the records online.

"*Scusami*, Signor Smith, but there are no reservation under that name."

"*Per favore*, please check under the name Korinna Fedorov."

The clerk rolled his eyes and waved his hands in the air and then typed the name into his computer. "*Scusate*. There is no reservation. *Niente*." He shrugged.

Anatoly sighed and passed some money across the desk. "Perhaps there is someone else who might know where the luggage is?"

The clerk quickly palmed the money and called over the bellhop. *"Bagaglio della signora Ainsworth?"*

"Sí! La signora Ainsworth did not show up. *Il bagaglio è qui."* The bellhop pointed toward the luggage room.

Anatoly offered to pay the hotel for the storage, but the clerk declined with a knowing smile, so Anatoly passed him more money, which quickly disappeared. He followed the bellhop, who went into the luggage room and returned with two bags, which he passed over to Anatoly with a flourish. *"Qui."*

Anatoly nodded and checked the bag tags. *"Grazie.* These are the bags."

Chapter Eighteen

15 December, 2018

Elda felt pressured by the need to get home to Dawn and have that chat. And she felt tired.

Usually, she was enchanted by the English countryside, but not today and not on this train. "Damn, I'm getting too old for this shit."

Korinna snorted.

"Oh crap. Was that my outside voice?"

Korinna nodded. "*Da*, Elda, it was."

Elda looked at the other end of the car and spotted a large man in an ill-fitting brown suit stepping into their car.

"Korinna, get down under the table now."

With a faint squeak of protest, Korinna wedged herself under the table, and Elda reached up overhead and brought down backpacks and luggage to scatter over Korinna's huddled form. The large man meandered down the aisle, holding his cell phone and studying each person he passed.

"Crap. Stay down there, Korinna, until I tell you all is clear. No matter what you hear."

"*Chert.*"

"Quiet!"

The man passed by Elda and then turned around to reexamine her. She sprang out of her seat, raced to the end of the car, and whipped around. He drew a weapon and started firing. Glass shattered in the sandwich case. People screamed and ducked. Elda threw herself through the doorway and jumped up to hold onto the top of the rubber material around the door. The door slid open, and as his face came through it, Elda brought her heels down sharply onto the bridge of his nose and then dropped and wrapped her legs around his neck. He lurched forward, bringing Elda swinging around with him. What had she been thinking with that move?

Elda twisted and grabbed a handhold on the other side. She thrust forward, slamming his damaged nose into the door. He screamed, grabbed his face, and dropped his gun. Elda dropped from his neck and back and grabbed for the gun.

Just then, a British Transport Constable sprang through the door and onto the wounded man. He quickly cuffed one wrist and secured the other cuff to a handhold. Elda pocketed the gun and flashed her credentials so he would not jump on her next. Blood was spattered everywhere.

"You're hurt, love?"

"No, no, that's from his nose."

"Yes, you are. Look at your arm."

Elda was suddenly aware of a very painful stinging sensation in her left arm. "Ouch. Damn. You're right." She willed herself not to diminish all womankind by passing out at the thought.

"Let's get you to a seat, and then I can finish with him."

"He's very dangerous, you know?"

"People always underestimate us Brits."

He guided Elda into the car and sat her down. Just then Elda heard the creaking sound of metal separating from metal coming from the gangway connection. She shifted to jump up, but the constable ordered her to stay put.

"I have this." He entered the gangway and returned a moment later. "He's gone."

Elda walked into the gangway. The handhold had been completely ripped away, and a large cut was now in the rubber connecting the two cars, with streaks of blood leading to the outside. She could see glimpses of the bucolic English countryside with gridded green fields and hedgerows flash by. There was no blood leading through the next door. "Yes, he's gone."

***

Elda tenderly touched the sore spot on her upper arm. "You know, in all those movies where the hero says 'Don't worry. It's just a flesh wound' and struts off to battle again? That's bull. Flesh wounds hurt!"

"It does look like a small scrape."

Elda stuck her tongue out at Korinna and sank into her chair.

"But haven't you been shot before, Elda?"

"Only once. I usually get the bad guy first. And when I got shot, it was a clean, in-and-out wound. A few stitches, some pain meds, and I was up and running again. Not like this tiny, annoying thing that stings like the devil. A Band-Aid covers the entire wound. But look at my shirt and jacket. That was an excellent disguise, and now it's ruined. And he got away. Plus, I have no idea where or when the next assassin will show up. It's my duty to protect you and get you home."

"This is just duty?"

"This is duty, love, and friendship. There's also the honor of winning and proving the United States as being the most powerful. Failure is not an option here."

Korinna patted Elda's good arm, and they sat listening to the train move smoothly over the tracks.

"I'm sorry. I know you've been through so much. You are separated now from your home, your country, your husband, and your dogs. I'm just tired. And sick of looking over my shoulder. I thought these days were far behind me."

"I'm so sorry to have brought you into this, Elda, but I didn't know who else to ask for help. And you have to admit, so far you have been successful."

"Just lucky and grateful that I still have fast reflexes." Elda sighed. "There's such an adrenaline rush at the beginning of an operation and then periodic highs, but I've done enough, and at this age, the surge of activity and constant alertness takes its toll on my body. It's hard to give up, though. It's like giving up my youth and, in a way, my capabilities. It's hard to think of my past accomplishments and a future with less time and less energy for any new ones."

Korinna nodded. "It's almost addicting. But look at what too often happens to addicts. You have a fuller life now. And you deserve to let go and relax."

It was so like Korinna to understand and be compassionate even when she had given up so much herself. Elda felt selfish.

"No, no, Elda. Your pain is valid."

Elda forced a smile. "Okay, Korinna, it's time for me to get off my pity pot and get strong and serious again to bring us both home in one piece."

"I would appreciate that."

Elda brought up a map on her phone and located the American Embassy in London. She laughed at a memory. "Korinna, did I ever tell you about the time we had to pick up stamps at the embassy in London?"

"*Nyet.*"

"We had been driving in a four-ton truck for two days, without sleep, and we had just finished burning classified trash and had to go into London to pick up stamps. We dropped off the petty officer to run in and get the stamps while we circled the block. We ended up in a fender bender with another large truck from a nearby farm. The driver asked us if we could just forget it happened, so he didn't get into trouble. I readily agreed. I felt guilty about that for years."

"You did something off the straight and narrow?"

"*Da, da*, Korinna. I did."

They both laughed.

"I think it's time you let go of that guilt."

"*Khorosho*, but I may have PTSD about going to the embassy again!"

"Perhaps you can apply for a driving disability?"

Laughing, Elda returned to the map on her phone. "We'll be getting into King's Cross station. We'll have to catch a bus to Vauxhall station. From there, it's only about a fifteen-minute walk to the embassy."

As the train pulled into King's Cross, Elda received an incoming encrypted message on her phone. She opened it, typed in her password, and viewed a real-time video feed.

"Oh, there you are," she said to her screen. "You are quite the survivor."

The man's face looked back at her as the camera recorded him lifting her bag up and into the trunk of a car. The feed turned dark as he lowered the trunk.

"Well, now we'll know where you are."

***

Tosh answered his phone. "You're in Grimsby, England, at a Russian-allied doctor's office? *Da*… uh-huh. They removed the handcuffs? *Nyet. Da.* You *shot* at her? And lost your gun! After he sets and packs your nose, you're going to get a boat ride out to a Soviet trawler and head back here. Uh-huh… *Da. Da. Nyet. Da.*"

He sighed and hung up. He'd thrown all he had at her. Perhaps it was time to talk with Elda.

He made another phone call. "Da. Accident at sea. He has outlived his usefulness."

"We will move quickly through the station, Korinna. We are not out of the woods yet. I will update Ed." Elda sent a short, encrypted message to her boss to let him know where Anatoly was and that the pressure-activated camera embedded in the handle was doing its job.

When they disembarked the train at King's Cross, Elda took in the changes that had happened since she was last there. If it hadn't been for the Harry Potter movies, she wouldn't have recognized it. She rapidly took in the station layout. The new station was encased in a spaceship-style steel roof, and the inside had vaulted arches that formed a steel grid. She jogged over to join Korinna.

"I really don't like all this modernization. The old station had character and mystery. This one gives the impression that we will be beamed aboard and flown off into outer space."

"You have quite the imagination. I like that it is so clean. But it does lack the character of the Russian stations."

Elda's stomach growled. "It doesn't look like they have caught up to us yet. I'm hungry. Shall we find someplace near the station where we can grab a bite to eat before heading over to the embassy?"

Korinna agreed, and Elda searched for places using her phone.

"The Gilbert Scott Bar in the St. Pancras Renaissance Hotel is only a short walk from here. They claim to have a lovely afternoon tea. Perhaps we can even ask for some jam butties to be added to your plate."

Korinna hit Elda on the arm, which caused Elda to almost drop her phone.

"Okay, I deserved that. But let's try it. It looks lovely."

As they paced their way to the Gilbert Scott Bar, Elda checked the feed on her phone. It was still dark. The pin on the map had not moved significantly since the luggage was dropped into the trunk. Perhaps he was staying overnight at the hotel? Was the tracker still working, and if so, where was he going next? Was he still after them? Or would they again send someone new?

***

Tosh ambled through the Aleksandrovskiy Garden in St. Petersburg and admired the sun illuminating the gold dome of St. Isaac's Cathedral. It was a bright day with a blue sky and light winds blowing the snow in circles around his feet. It was nice to be out in the field again. *Zhizn' khorosha*! *Da, Life is good*. He cautioned himself to pay attention. "You are an operative again, not an old man admiring the scenery."

His mind took him back to his first operation in St. Petersburg. It was a simple operation to turn a married expat, Robert Clark, into a conduit for information. Robert worked at Boeing in the United States and was at an aeronautics conference in St. Petersburg. Tosh had arranged for a prostitute to pick Robert up at the hotel bar by posing as a single woman looking for a fun night. After a few drinks, they both ended up in Robert's room, which had been wired for video and sound. As the prostitute undressed, she asked him about his family, and later, after they'd had sex twice and Robert was in a drowsy state, she asked for information about his job. While he was sleeping, she snuck out of bed, photographed the documents in his briefcase, and then fled the room.

The next morning, when Robert was on his way down to breakfast, Tosh intercepted him and asked for a moment of his time. They sat together in the lobby while Tosh handed him a picture of the night's activities and told him he also had video and audio that could easily be sent to Robert's wife, Helen, and his boss at Boeing. He passed Robert another picture that was a schematic from the new plane that Boeing was working on. After seeing that, sweat broke out on Robert's brow, and he begged Tosh not to tell his wife or boss. Tosh told Robert he owed him and that when a man came to see him in the United States, he would have to cooperate and give that man some information. Robert readily agreed.

That operation pushed Tosh up the ranks to more important roles.

However, Tosh was most proud of his first operation as an assassin, which also took place in St. Petersburg. He'd been sent to kill a double agent who could not be turned into a triple agent. He tracked the man down and shadowed him for days, until he was sure of his routine. Then, after a huge snow and ice storm, Tosh intercepted him in an isolated place on his normal route. He broke off a large icicle and pushed it up under the ribs and into the spy's heart. He watched the life drain from his victim as he lowered him facedown into the snow.

He then took off the spy's coat—with his wallet in the inner pocket—and boots, to imply a robbery, and used the boots to obscure his own tracks in the snow. When he was about a mile away, he tossed the boots into the canal, gave the coat to a wandering homeless man, and threw the wallet into a canal about two miles away from the incident. It was the perfect kill and established Tosh as an accomplished assassin.

Tosh recalled those days as a time period when spies cooperated with each other and only killed if necessary, not to cover their tracks or protect their careers. It was like the old days of mafia and police. Gentlemen agreements.

That was the way Cold War spies had operated. They helped each other unless they got in each other's way. And if one couldn't turn, temporarily remove, or scare off the other, the other spy was eliminated. But it was a sad occasion. There was a lot of mutual respect in those days.

Tosh returned his attention to the present day. He picked up the pace and turned onto Yulitsa Yakubovicha. He then turned left onto Ulitsa Truda, toward the Naval Museum. He crossed over the Moyka River near the Marine Barracks, turned right, and continued on the embankment.

He entered the psychiatric hospital and folded his coat over his arm so that his white doctor's jacket and badge were visible. Nikita hovered in the lobby. Tosh waved him over and asked to see the records first. Nikita led Tosh to a room with a computer and logged in. He pulled up Aurelio's record. Tosh, with his photographic memory and his ability to speed read, had all the information he needed in a matter of minutes. He nodded and stood up, and Nikita logged out.

"Please take me to see Aurelio now. Is the other doctor here?"

"*Nyet, on ushel.*"

"*Khorosho*; it's very good he is gone. Now please take me to Aurelio's room and wait outside to prevent us from being interrupted."

The blush faded from Nikita's normally rosy cheeks, and he gulped and nodded. Turning, he led Tosh to Aurelio's room.

Tosh quietly opened door and slipped in. Aurelio, who'd been pacing, paused.

"Aurelio?"

He jumped. "Yes…"

"You are an important man, you know." Tosh studied Aurelio. It was apparent he had lost touch with reality, but with every word, he began accepting

Tosh into his delusional world. "I need to punish the man who did this to you."

"Huh?" Aurelio was confused.

Tosh realized that Aurelio felt put upon by so many that he hadn't connected it to the attack. "Do you remember, Aurelio, when the jealous, angry man stabbed you?"

"Yes. I remember! Why did he stab me?"

"I will tell you, Aurelio, but can you first tell me what happened that day, in detail?"

That opened the floodgates. Aurelio told his tale from the time he woke up that day, including a description of feeling so angry when he saw his half-sister, Elda, that he'd rushed at her, only to be stabbed by that man.

Tosh nodded and encouraged Aurelio to continue, only stopping him so he could fill in his family background and the roots of his anger toward his brother and half-sister. When he finally finished, Tosh said, "It is as I thought, Aurelio. This man was jealous of you and overcome with his own inadequacies. He observed you coming from first class, when he was only in the economy section, and became enraged. It was a sudden act, stemming from passionate emotions."

Aurelio nodded. "But tell me, who was the man connected to?"

"That is the nub of the issue, Aurelio. This man was such a nobody. He has no connections. He was jealous of you because he viewed you as upper class, with many connections."

"Ah yes, that would be true. I have found many who have been jealous of me, especially when they see my lovely wife on my arm."

"I believe that is so true, and we need to stop people like him from attacking people like you. I will make sure he knows what he has done."

Aurelio viewed Tosh suspiciously. "But why do you care? What's in it for you? Were you killed by someone like him?"

Tosh realized that, for some reason, Aurelio assumed that he was a ghost. "Yes, Aurelio, I was, and I want to avenge my killer and all others like him. Your importance has drawn me here. I was told I could get the information I needed from you."

Aurelio puffed his chest out and stood straighter. "Ghost, can you help get me out of here?"

"Unfortunately, no—but others in the living world will bend to your will and help you out."

Aurelio punched the air in a victorious gesture, and Tosh snuck out unnoticed.

***

Aurelio peered all around the room and saw no sign of the ghost. *Wow! I can't wait to tell my friends!* He opened his door, checked the hallway for more ghosts, and then went into the rec room.

Stanislav and Yevgeni were shouting at each other and pounding the table. The attendant was over at their table, trying to quiet them down. The large man jumped up from the couch and intercepted Aurelio.

"My friend would like to see you."

"I'm busy right now. He can wait."

The large man put his hand on Aurelio's arm. It felt like a vice was cutting off his blood supply. He stopped in his tracks.

"Now."

"Well, I seem to have found some time in my schedule," Aurelio said, and he followed his arm to the couch.

When they sat down, the large man released Aurelio. Aurelio gently rubbed his arm. It would definitely be bruised by morning.

"You need to understand our rules," the small man said.

"What rules? I don't attend to anyone's rules. I am a very important man."

The large man took Aurelio's face gently in one hand, with his thumb on one side and his fingers on the other, and turned his head toward the small man. Aurelio tried to free his chin, but when he did, the fingers and thumb tightened ever so slowly. Aurelio stopped struggling and looked directly at the small man.

"Do you know why I am in here?" the small man asked.

"No, I don't."

"My large friend here has murdered many men, but I make him look like a gentle soul. Do not be thrown off by my size, and do not cross me. Understand?"

Aurelio sat frozen in fear. He had always had control of anyone by paying them off or by being able to run away. Here, he had no money of any consequence and could not get away from these two.

"Y-y-yes," he stuttered. "I understand."

"You will follow our rules, correct?"

"Y-y-yes, I-I will." Aurelio felt like crying, but he discerned that would weaken his position even further, so he blinked rapidly to hold back the tears. He fretted about why the ghost did not appear to help save him now. It was all so unfair.

"Now, go back to your room. You are not to return here tonight."

Aurelio glanced at his new friends, who had stopped talking and were watching the interchange with great interest. It appeared that they were betting on the outcome, as they placed broken toothpicks in the middle of the table. They lowered their eyes when Aurelio glanced their way. He would receive no help from them, so he slowly stood up and minced away toward his room, while rubbing his arm and moving his jaw around to make sure it still worked.

"You will pay for this. I have connections," he muttered as he left, but he was helpless here and speculated if he could go back into solitary for protection.

Tosh returned to his hotel room, now realizing that Elda was Aurelio's half-sister and not his wife, Mrs. Ainsworth. He sat on the chair next to the bed, took his shoes off, and rubbed his feet. He checked his phone and discovered that he had an encrypted video feed to view. A note accompanying the feed explained that it came from Yaromir's phone, which had been found in a landfill.

He played and replayed the video feed. *Aga!* This was where facial recognition was still not good enough. He stopped when he saw the small man walk down the gangplank. *That is her walk. I would know it anywhere.* He spoke to the frozen image of Elda on his screen. "Well done. You have changed the shape of your face and hidden your eyes. What am I going to do about you, and how are we going to end Korinna's story?"

He closed his eyes. And what should he do about Yuri? He was hiding something. Tosh would dig into it more and see how he could use him. But first they needed to finish this mission.

He picked up his cell phone. "Yuri, meet me in fifteen minutes in the Aleksandrovskiy Garden, next to the monument to Nikolay Przhevalsky."

Tosh was at the arranged meeting place in ten minutes and spent the extra five checking that there was no one suspicious around. Yuri showed up exactly on time.

"Yuri, would you know how to get a message to the Americans? I would like to get a message to Aurelio's half-sister, Elda."

Yuri's eyes opened wide, and his mouth fell open in astonishment. "*No pochemu?*" he blurted out.

So, he does know the Americans. And it appears that he also knows Elda. How close is he to them? This could definitely be used to my advantage. "Vy?"

"*Da*, yes, I do," Yuri stammered. "I can get a message to Elda."

Aga! That's what he has been hiding. "Khorosho," Tosh said, "now listen carefully."

Tosh slowly told Yuri his message for Elda and asked him to repeat it back so Yuri had it word for word. "*Khorosho*, Yuri. I would like for her to get that immediately, *pozhaluysta*. And remember, in this you work for me. *Ponimayu?*"

"*Da, ya ponimayu.*"

"*Khorosho.* When you're done, leave a message at this number to let me know she has been given the message."

Yuri nodded his understanding and agreement.

"*Poka.*"

"*Dobryy vecher.*"

Tosh went back to his hotel room, satisfied he had set the right wheels in motion. He was looking forward to dealing with Elda again. His phone rang, and it was Anatoly reporting that he had the bags and was staying the night in Florence.

"How are the pastries there, Anatoly?" Tosh laughed at Anatoly's description of the beautiful pastries he had seen. "The artwork is lost on you, but food is your art!"

He asked Anatoly to check in first thing in the morning before he started out again. He would decide then whether he needed Anatoly to stay in Florence to eliminate Elda.

Tosh needed to hurry to Florence and meet with Elda. *And all I really want to do is order room service and turn on the TV to BBC again.* Seeing how the rest of the world thought helped him with his analysis of the targets. He was loyal to his country, but not stupid. He would switch between that and the Russian news to get a comparison view. Feeling the pressure of time, he phoned the desk to have a taxi take him to the airport for his trip to Florence. The two of them would meet in Florence, but would they both leave?

***

15 December, 2018

Elda and Korinna walked into the American Embassy and were immediately brought into a small conference room. A man with a square jaw, aquiline nose, and dark-brown eyes greeted them. As he stood up, he ran his hand to neaten his salt-and-pepper hair, a mass of cowlicks sticking up in different directions.

"Ed! Ed Wilson! What are you doing here?" Elda asked, smiling broadly as she moved forward to give him a hug.

Ed gave her a warm hug back. "I hope that's not politically incorrect now."

"Don't worry, Ed. We both know there's nothing intended."

Ed smiled back at Elda. The two of them had known about each other's sexuality for years but kept it under wraps. Korinna stood to one side with a puzzled look.

"Korinna, this is my boss, Ed. He is the one who received your message and sent me to find you. Ed and I have worked together for many years. His father, Ed senior, originally recruited me into the CIA, but I credit Ed for being the one who found me first. It's a longer story that dates back to my days stationed in Wales. But I digress. We must help Korinna get to the United States."

"*Spasibo*, Ed. I am so grateful you sent Elda to help me. Now can you help get us home?"

"Korinna is always direct, Ed. So please fill me in. Why were we sent here instead of to the sub?"

"Your sub was sent out on a fleet exercise in the Mediterranean, intended as a show of strength, so will not be available for at least a week. However, there have been new developments, and we will take good advantage of this extra time. We have received a secret message from a handler in Moscow, via Yuri."

"Via Yuri? A message from a handler?"

"Yes. We don't have much information on this man, but his name is Tosh. All we have is an old picture of him on file." Ed put down a picture on the table.

"That's Tosh? That is Tosh?" Elda said wide eyed, shaking her head and pointing at the picture.

"Yes. Do you know him?"

"Yes! That is the man who picked me up that day in Moscow many, many years ago. What's his message?"

"Tosh wants to talk with you."

"With me? He mentioned my name? And how did he get to Yuri?"

Ed repeated Tosh's message word for word. He wanted to meet with Elda away from Moscow. Tosh had added: *Since your luggage is already in Florence, would you like to meet there? I will have Anatoly stand down while we meet.*

"Amazing. He still is a master operative. Anatoly must be the name of the large man who has been trying to kill us."

"Elda, you are not thinking of going, are you? We are finally safe."

"You do not have to go, you know that," Ed added.

"Yes, Korinna, and yes, Ed. I know we've come a long way to get to here, but if we don't get complete closure on this, Korinna and Egor will live their lives in fear. And I have no way of guaranteeing that Dawn and I will be safe."

Korinna sat down heavily in a chair and shook her head. Ed looked at Elda expectantly.

"Yes, I'm going. Send a message back to Yuri that I will meet Tosh at the hotel in Florence. And tell him to ask Anatoly to remove the luggage from the boot of his Alfa Romeo and give it back to the bellhop."

Elda and Korinna asked for food to be brought in, and they used the shower and bathroom at the embassy to freshen up while waiting for the reply. Ed booked them two rooms at the London Marriott Hotel Grosvenor Square Hotel near the embassy. When the message from Tosh came back an hour later, it read, *Touché. I will see you there on the fifteenth of December.*

Elda noted his wording. Apparently, Tosh also remembered the day he'd picked her up in the car.

"I should only be gone a couple of days. Then, hopefully, we can continue our journey to the United States. Ed, if something does happen to me, you will make sure that Korinna gets to the US safely? And you will take good care of Dawn?"

"Yes, of course, but we will also be sending backup."

"Please tell the backup that they are to stand down and do nothing unless it is on my command. And as long as I'm alive and well, Tosh and Anatoly are to get safe passage back to Moscow. Correct?"

"Correct."

"Okay. I will hit the road tomorrow for Florence. Ed, can you please arrange for my ticket, some money, and a passport?"

"I'll take care of all of that."

"Are you sure you are going to see Tosh and find out what he needs, or are you going for the art?" Korinna asked.

"Ah, you do know me well. If I only get to see one thing, I want to see the wooden statue of Mary Magdalene by Donatello. The last time I went to Florence, the Museum Opera del Duomo was closed for renovations. I was heartbroken. Plus, I do want to get the best cup of hot chocolate in the world, in that little café across from the fake statue of David. What was the name of that place? Riverori?"

"Rivoire," Ed said, "I know it well. They start with melted hot chocolate and top it all off with whipped cream. I wish you could bring me back some."

"Seriously? Elda is off to get herself killed, and all the two of you can talk about is hot chocolate? Gheesh!"

"Don't worry, Korinna. Tosh is old school. There is an unwritten pact between spies of our era. As long as Tosh still adheres to the old rules, the meet will be held sacred." To distract Korinna from worrying, Elda added, "While we're here, would you like to send another message to Egor?"

"Oh, *da!*"

***

When Elda entered her room, Sobaka was perched on top of a pile of pillows, reading a book about the history of the Soviet Union. *Subtle, Ed. Real subtle.* She reached under the mattress and found a plastic knife, a Canadian passport, plane tickets for tomorrow with an open return, and some additional euros and rubles. She dialed the special line at the embassy, and after a few soft clicks, it switched over to Ed's secure line.

"Thanks."

Ed inquired, "Do you need anything else?"

"Can you take Korinna touring tomorrow?"

"Certainly. By the way, we have heard back from Egor. He is in the United States and has been reunited with his dogs. We are debriefing him and arranging his new identity."

"Wonderful! I can't wait to tell Korinna. Thank you!"

At dinner, Elda passed the message on to Korinna, who had tears in her eyes.

To deflect her from crying, Elda asked, "I never asked you, how did you meet Egor?"

Korinna immediately brightened and replied, "We were both at a special school, but I was in intensified courses for languages, and he was learning more and more about music. He had a reputation of being a heartbreaker and a bit of a wild young man. He used to sneak out of the boy's dorm on Saturday nights with a few others to get laid. He thought it was all a big secret, but I learned later on that the school officials allowed it and even set the boys up with some gorgeous women so they would not stray too far and catch something. As government workers, they were well taken care of. I never told Egor I was aware of what he had done, nor did I tell him that it was set up. He was proud of his antics at the time. All I know is when I met him, I fell for him the moment I gazed into those baby-blue eyes and saw that rakish grin. He was such a prankster. I pretended not to like him, because I didn't want to end up a part of his long line of women left behind."

Sincerely curious Elda queried, "So how did you get together?"

Her eyes sparkling with her memories, Korinna filled Elda in, "Years later, we were both at an event for the Kremlin. I was a young translator, and he had just started playing for the orchestra. When we were both on break, he strode over to me and said, 'Hi, Korinna.' I swooned at hearing him say my name. But I kept my face impassive and asked who he was. After that, we met for dinner, and two years later I finally was sure he wouldn't stray, and we were married. We've been together ever since. He is my funny, gentle, yet strong, giant, and *moy drug*."

Elda reassured Korinna, "You will be back together with 'Honey' and the troodles soon."

Chapter Nineteen

15 December, 2018

Elda settled into the back of the taxi at Firenze Airport and wondered if she would take a taxi or a hearse back to the airport. She popped an antacid tablet into her mouth and chewed it, in hopes that it would settle her nervous stomach. She wanted no trace of nerves when she met with Tosh.

I hope to be in Dawn's arms again. And to hold my squirming little puppy, and to snuggle with my cat. She flashed back to when Dawn and she first met.

Dawn was stunning. Elda took one look into her eyes and was immediately lost. She didn't usually sleep with anyone on the first date, but she'd felt it in her bones when she left the bar with Dawn to go back to her apartment, that this was the woman she wanted to spend the rest of her life with. They didn't leave the apartment for two days.

She'd been exhausted and happy as she'd wandered home, with memories of their steamy sex and Dawn's phone number in her pocket. She called her the minute she was home and arranged a date that evening. They had not been separated since, except for Elda's trips for work.

Why was she doing this? It was time to give up the adrenaline rush of the old days of spying. *I pray to get out alive and return home safely to my family. I am lucky to have Dawn as my wife. It is time to agree to her demands that I retire.*

***

Elda dumped her baggage at the Brunelleschi Hotel and set off for one more walk around Florence before the games with Tosh began. Wandering southward toward the Ponte Vecchio, she turned a corner near the Fontana del Procellino and bounced off what felt like a brick wall.

"*Chert!*"

"Shit!"

Elda whirled around and took off like the sprinter she never was, while Anatoly took a few more seconds to absorb whom he had just run into and then took off after her. She vaulted up the stairs and ducked under a row of leather jackets, whipped by a table selling silk scarves, and managed to throw money at a vendor to grab one on her way. She tied

374

it around her head for a quick disguise. She could hear Anatoly bouncing off people behind her. *"Chert! Scusi... Der'mo!"* She cut out the side of the market and ran her hand over the snout of the bronze boar as she scooted by.

Galloping full steam ahead down the Via Calimada, she looked behind her and saw him squeezing his way out of the market. She twirled left onto Via Vacchereccia, running all out toward the Piazza della Signore, bumping into tourists as she ran. Thank goodness it wasn't peak season right now. The streets would be almost impassable.

Glancing over her shoulder, she saw that Anatoly was gaining on her. She should know by now she could not outrun that man. Ahead of her were two teenagers stepping onto e-scooters. *Aha!* The ZTL was not in effect right now. With a burst of speed, she caught them before they left and held out more than enough money for the scooter next to her, which the teen gladly took. She swung right at the replica statue of David and opened the throttle to take her to the river. She hoped the gates were open at the end of this street. Again she glanced behind her and observed that Anatoly had commandeered the second scooter. *Damn I need something faster.*

She turned onto the Lungarno delle Gracie and motored along the river, where she spotted a woman settling onto her Vespa. "Please. I need it. Help me!" She jumped off the e-scooter, shoved a wad of bills into the woman's hand, grabbed the keys, and jumped onto the larger, more powerful scooter.

She looked over her shoulder to see Anatoly grab the handlebars of a man's scooter, throw the man from the scooter, fling it around to the correct direction, hop on, and take off after her. *Damn that man.*

Elda took a quick left over the St. Trinity Bridge, passing other Vespas and cars. She checked as she skidded right onto Lungarno Soderini. Anatoly was still there. The Vespa was at full throttle. Elda cruised at full speed along the far side of the river on Lungarno Soderini and then whipped the bike right over the Ponte alla Carraia. *Damn. He's still there!* She continued on the riverside road, straight past the St. Trinity Bridge, directly into the one-way traffic coming at her along the Lungarno degli Acciaiuoli. Horns blasted, fists raised, and middle fingers were thrown at Elda as she wove her way around the oncoming traffic. She glanced back. Anatoly was slowly gaining ground.

Elda steered right over the Ponte Alle Grazie and raced around the curvy roads up to the Piazzale Michelangelo with Anatoly on her bumper. The Vespa roared its raspy rich cadence with the engine revving up. The wheels skidded on the gravel by the edges as she worked to use every inch of the road, leaning into the curves so much that the footrest nearly touched the ground.

At the top of the steps leading up to the Church of San Miniato, she skidded the Vespa around and bounced back down, holding on for dear life. Tourists screamed and jumped out of the way. Anatoly shook his fist at her as she buzzed by him on his way up the stairs. He had to get to the top before he had room to turn around. She could hear police sirens in the distance. *Damn! I have to ditch them, too.*

Elda careened down the side of the hill to the Scalea del Monte alle Croce and then continued to cut through yards, alleys, and side roads and took a sharp left onto Lungarno Torrigiani to follow the river to cross with traffic over the Ponte alla Carraia. She glanced behind her, and Anatoly was nowhere to be seen. She was soaked with sweat and breathing heavily but was not going to stop until she was back at the hotel.

***

"Chert! Der'mo!" Anatoly had the throttle fully open, but the bike was standing still and sputtering. He pulled the beat-up, black Vespa over

to the side in the parking lot of the Piazzale Michelangelo and threw it to the ground. *"Kusok der'ma!"* He kicked at it and then grimaced in pain as the vibrations from the kick traveled from his steel-toed shoe to his knee.

Just then, his phone rang. *"Privet?"* He listened as Tosh told him to stand down. Tosh was in Florence and would soon be meeting Elda at the hotel. *"Chert.* No, no problem. Yes. I will return to Moscow."

***

Elda figured the clerk had probably been bribed by Tosh to tell him when she arrived, so she asked him to stay at the desk, saying she had a question for him but needed to check in first with a fellow traveler at the hotel. She borrowed the clerk's desk phone and asked to be connected to Tosh's room, to tell him she was there.

The voice on phone was so familiar, it startled her. *Perhaps a bit older, but it's that same man who was in the car.* Her mind flashed back to that day when Tosh had picked her up. She'd been in Moscow as a tourist, but she was in the US Navy at that time. She had been asked to get some information over at the American Embassy, from her old college dorm mother, whose son worked at the embassy. She had been returning to her hotel after visiting with her former dorm mother for a few hours, when Tosh picked her up. With her clearance and knowledge of Russia, she probably should not have been in Moscow, and she'd kissed the ground when her plane from Moscow landed at Heathrow.

After finishing the call, Elda thanked the clerk and handed him back the phone. He immediately picked it up again and whispered into it.

"Do say hi to Tosh for me," Elda told the clerk as she turned and left the hotel.

Tosh had asked Elda to meet him at the Museum de Opera, next to the wooden Donatello statue of Mary Magdalene. She strolled there, composing herself while drinking in the ambiance of Florence.

When Elda arrived, she found that Tosh was already there. *Ah, the devil.* He'd probably been there all the time but had managed to have his hotel phone rerouted to his cell phone. That meant he had connections here.

Elda reminded herself to be extra cautious. He was older than the man she remembered, paler and thinner. He blended in well with the background, rather ghostlike, but when he turned to face her, she recognized his eyes with that intelligent, piercing look.

He volleyed first. "Elda Ainsworth. It is a pleasure to see you again."

Elda nearly froze in place as his gaze reached inside her to bare her inner thoughts, but she showed no outward sign that he had shaken her with his knowledge of her full name. She willed her feet to keep moving and her voice not to crack. As she marched toward him, projecting confidence, keeping eye contact, Elda responded, "Hello, Tosh. Shall I call you Tosh, or is there another name that you prefer?"

"Tosh will do, Elda."

"I never did ask you what you were studying at the university."

"It was mathematics, of course."

"I know where you could have found a good mathematics teacher."

They laughed and shook hands.

As they stood together looking at Donatello's statue, Tosh said, "This is one of my favorite pieces of art in Florence. Have you seen it before?"

Ah, you devil. You know the answer already. "It is my favorite piece also. When I was last in Florence, I specifically came right here to see this piece, only to discover that the museum was closed for renovations."

"What year was that?"

"Not that long ago."

"Were you here for business or pleasure?"

"Ah, that would be telling, wouldn't it?"

Tosh smiled thinly. "Have you seen Donatello's Bronze David in the Bargello Museum? It is oddly out of proportion and effeminate in hair, stance, and musculature. Quite different than the determined young man Michelangelo depicted in his statue of David."

"Yes, I have. It is wonderful how artists see the world and bring us into their mindsets. The art experts postulate that Leonardo da Vinci was the model for that statue. Verrocchio's David is slightly in between those two depictions. Have you seen that one? It also has a slightly effeminate stance, a skirt, and a fluffy hairdo—but it also has a square jaw and look of determination."

"So, you are an art lover too?"

"Yes. Florence is one of my favorite places in the world. I am glad of the opportunity to come back here one more time."

They stood admiring the wonderful detail in the statue of the rags, the gauntness of the body, and the haunted look on her face.

Tosh was the first to break the silence. "I asked you to come here because you know the old codes of honor among spies. The world has changed, and there are no such rules anymore. In the old days, killings were justified, but the hit on Korinna was ordered to save a politician's reputation, not to protect our wonderful countries. I executed the orders given to me, and I wish to conclude this mission well. I worry that if we don't take care of all the loose ends, then our future safety will be at risk."

He took out his phone and showed Elda the pictures that Anatoly had taken of the dead prostitute in Amsterdam. "Anatoly shows great promise as a senior operative or handler. He will need to work on his temper and become more political than either you or I could ever become. He proposed this as a solution to our mutual problem."

"May I?"

Tosh nodded, and Elda took the phone away from him and enlarged the photograph. She could see where Anatoly had done a good job selecting the double to kill, but also where the face differed—facial recognition software might pick up on it.

"I see." She handed the phone back to Tosh. "I may have a solution that would be satisfactory to all. You do know that Korinna lost her husband, Egor, in a tragic bus accident in Canada."

"Yes, I do. Those roads can be so dangerous. A shame the body couldn't be recovered."

Elda caught his implication that the death had been staged. "Yes, it was such a shame. I know that often widows cannot go on living without their husbands. Egor was the love of Korinna's life. And did you know her dogs were also stolen? I fear that she may not have enough to keep her going." Elda blinked her eyelashes at Tosh and put on a sad expression.

Tosh commented dryly, "Ah, that would be such a shame. Her body would need to be sent back to Russia, however."

"Yes, it would. If the DNA matched in the database and the dental records matched, I would suppose that would be all you'd need for verification?"

"Yes, that would be what we would check."

Elda nodded. "How can I get in touch with you again?"

"Shall we use Yuri?"

Elda concurred, "Yes, that would be good."

Tosh spoke to Elda like a colleague, inquiring, "Tell me more about Yuri. I have not worked with him since he was a pre-cadet. He had too soft a heart and not a strong moral compass at that time, but I thought he could be useful in the KGB."

"Yuri has been helping both sides of the pond keep an eye on expats. He also has strong connections with the Mafia, so he is able to move in many circles. He does have a soft heart, especially for animals. He is driven by acquisition of money and his own sense of doing good."

Tosh nodded. That added up to his own assessment. Yuri would be a good addition to Tosh's operatives. He said as much to Elda.

Elda encouraged Tosh's line of thinking, "He would probably welcome an excuse to get out of St. Petersburg and babysitting stoned expats."

Tosh sent another shot over the bow of their verbal sparring. "What about your half-brother?"

Elda was careful not to show any signs of surprise that Tosh had heard of the relationship between her and Aurelio. "He was dead to me many years ago. I mourned his passing, after he lost his brain to drugs. I have no emotional connection left there."

"Good. Then we will pull his watchers off and use them elsewhere."

"Yes. He is of no use to any government." Diverting the conversation from her family, Elda asked, "If Yuri can go to London for a couple of days, it would be helpful…"

"Yes, he can be useful to both of us. I will call him to Moscow and make arrangements for him. He will give you what you need."

Elda concluded their plans, "And he will come back with what you need."

***

Anatoly packed his bag. He went down to the car in the garage and removed the two suitcases from the trunk. He carried them back up and, using a duplicate key, unlocked the door to Elda's room. Placing the bags on her bed, he turned and left the room again, with a touch of regret that he would not be able to get his revenge on her for having tossed him into the canal twice. Just to toss her into the canal in return would be satisfying. Of course, it would be more fun to strangle her. But Tosh had given him orders not to kill her and to bring Yuri to Moscow.

Anatoly dialed a number on his phone and told the rental place where to pick up the car. He checked out at the desk and had them call him a cab so he could catch a plane to St. Petersburg. There, he would pick up Yuri and bring him to Moscow to meet with Tosh again. What was Tosh thinking of doing with Yuri? If he had wanted Anatoly to kill him, he wouldn't have Anatoly bring him to Moscow—that left too much of a trail. Tosh would either let him know or he wouldn't. Anatoly just wanted a good, clean assignment again. Preferably one where he could kill someone. Throwing that man in the canal after poisoning him had felt so good.

Anatoly was pleased at his memory of a quick kill. He nodded in satisfaction, recalling the pleasant feeling as he'd strangled the prostitute. Although he hadn't killed the main target, he considered it a service to have eliminated a drain on society. Plus, it had saved her from a hard life on the streets. He threw his kit bag over his shoulder and left the hotel. As he rode off in the back of a cab, he caught sight of Elda approaching the hotel. He raised his hand and threw her a figa, sticking his thumb between his knuckles. It was the equivalent of a middle finger, and he sneered at her.

Elda blew a kiss back at him.

I have a feeling you and I are not finished.

***

Elda felt drunk on the overwhelming amount of art and architecture that surrounded her. Being in Florence was like being a kid in Disney World. At the hotel, she frowned when she noted the tell was missing from her door. She stood to one side as she unlocked the door and kicked it open.

The small room was entirely visible from the doorway, and no one was there, but she recognized the luggage on the bed. She slipped into the room with her back against the wall and kicked the door shut. She double locked the door and then placed her own lock on it.

Elda checked through the luggage. It was all as she had left it back in St. Petersburg. Korinna's luggage was there too. She scanned the bags for bugs and found one placed in hers, as well as another tracker in Korinna's. Interesting. Was the message that they had tracked the luggage here and wanted her to know? Elda shrugged, crushed the bugs beneath the heel of her shoe, flushed the remains down the toilet, picked up the luggage, and took it down to the front desk, where she asked that they send it to the embassy in London. She checked her watch and calculated that she could not catch the 14:45 British Airways afternoon flight back to London. *Oh, what a pity. I'll have to stay in Florence for the night.* She asked the clerk at the desk to make her a reservation for dinner at the Osteria Santo Spirito. She'd enjoy the walk over the Ponte Vecchio and would perhaps pick up a small gift for Dawn.

Elda sensed a presence behind her. She berated herself for not having heard Tosh approach.

A soft voice spoke near her ear, "I appear to have missed the 14:35 to Moscow. Perhaps we could change that reservation to be for two? That is one of my favorite restaurants too."

Without turning, Elda stated, "We appear to have a lot in common."

Elda addressed the desk clerk and asked him to call the restaurant back and change the reservation from one to two people. She then swiveled to Tosh, "I am planning on cleaning up and then wandering around a bit. Perhaps do some shopping. Would you like to join me, and then we can end up together at the restaurant?"

"That would be interesting."

Yes. It would be.

***

Elda towel dried her hair and slipped a shank—made from the plastic knife Ed had given her—into her sock. It was good to have a weapon, just in case. She decided against wearing a scarf and put a short piece of rope into her pocket. As she automatically performed these actions, she recalled the years of government training in hand-to-hand combat and stealth skills. She felt fortunate that she didn't have to use these skills often, but she appreciated how instinctively her reflexes performed after all that training.

Flipping Anatoly over her shoulder was only part of what she could do. One day, years ago, when she had been informed that an assassin was on her trail, she'd slipped into an alleyway, knowing that the temptation of trapping her in a dead-end alley would be too much for the assassin to ignore. She'd bent to tie her shoe, and as she did, with her gloved hand she removed her knife from its ankle holder. She quickly rolled out of the way as the assassin leaped at her with his knife in hand, narrowly missing her. That he would go for a more silent method and not shoot at her had been her bet.

It was a good thing the odds were with me that day.

He fell hard, and Elda jumped on him and thrust her knife into his neck before he could get up. He dropped his knife and held his hand to his neck in a vain attempt to stop the bleeding. Elda kicked the knife away and stood back from him, watching him die. It was worthless to search him, since he would have no ID on him. His eyes closed, and his body went limp. If he wasn't already dead, he would soon be. She turned and walked away. It was getting easier to not feel about these killings and to forget them and move on. That had scared her, and she had worried about who she was becoming.

Elda now quickly finished dressing and went downstairs to meet Tosh, sure he also had secreted away useful weapons. At least they were ready in case someone tried to mug us. Unless Tosh was here to terminate her.

***

Although Florence was beautiful in the light of the full moon that evening, Elda tensely observed the killer spy at her side.

"Is Florence at all like your hometown?" Tosh asked.

"There is no place that can hold a candle to Florence."

"Is that a British accent I detect?"

"Could be."

"Or perhaps a midwestern one?"

"I've been to many places in my lifetime. My accent is a hodgepodge by now. Have you always lived in Moscow?"

"I love Moscow. It is the heart and soul of Russia."

"Did you like being in the KGB?"

"Why are you part of the CIA?"

They laughed at each other's obvious attempts to get information.

"May we stop here on the Ponte Vecchio and look at the jewelry in the shops?"

"I wouldn't take you for a woman who liked jewelry."

"You just never know, do you?"

They stopped at several jewelry shops on the Ponte Vecchio. Elda bought a solid-gold bracelet for Dawn, at which had Tosh raised his eyebrows.

Elda also bought a thin gold necklace for Korinna and a small solid-gold cross for herself to keep in her wallet. She'd never wear distinctive jewelry. In her line of business that would be hazardous.

Since they had been zigzagging and looking on both sides of the bridge, Tosh spotted the cross in Elda's hand and asked her where she bought it. She took him over to a shop on the other side of the bridge, where he purchased a similar one. She noted he also purchased a gold watch.

"I wouldn't take you as a man who liked jewelry."

"You just never know, do you?"

"Touché."

Elda pointed up at a small, gridded spyhole in the Vasari Corridor. "Have you ever done the tour of the corridor?"

"No."

"Are you flying out tomorrow?"

"Yes. Are you?"

"Yes, I am. Too bad you cannot stay and take the tour. It is a wonderful experience. The art is beautiful in there, but most of all, it brings back an age where the nobles spied on the commoners below and made safe passage through to the church and to the Pitti Palace."

"Ah, our type of place, hey?"

"Are you of noble blood or a spy, Tosh?"

Tosh laughed and put his arm around her and steered the two of them around a gaggle of approaching tourists.

Elda respected Tosh. He was smart, charming, and smooth—a worthy adversary. As in their first meeting, they seemingly spoke of nothing of consequence but were sparring to see who would win the war of words.

At the restaurant, Elda stared at Tosh's hands.

"Why do you look at my hands that way?"

"I have found that hands in general are indicative of the person. When I first met you, I discovered that your hands were large and probably quite adept at strangulation. Your hands are strong and capable. I can imagine that, had your life gone in a different direction, you might have become an artist or a craftsman."

"Ah yes, and sell paintings at that market you like to visit?"

Elda blinked. Was there nothing that Tosh missed?

"Perhaps being a handler at the Kremlin was a better path for you."

He laughed. "How nice it is to be able to work together in peace. It is a shame our countries never really stopped the Cold War," Tosh said.

"And the rules of engagement have changed too. There are not many left who would find a mutually beneficial solution."

"When I am back in Moscow, I will send Yuri to you. Perhaps in the coming weeks, you might send me a *London Times*? I look forward to reading the obituaries."

"I will make sure you are kept up to date on the news from London."

The waiter came with the tab, and Tosh picked it up. Elda raised an eyebrow.

"I wish to celebrate our successful business negotiation."

"To staying alive for as many years as we have."

"May we continue to do so. Our paths may cross again."

***

The next day Elda grabbed a slice of coffee cake from the café in case she became hungry on the flight back to London and then took a quick walk to stop at the Museum de Opera one more time, to see the statue of Mary Magdalene.

"Well, why am I not surprised?" Elda said as she stepped to stand next to a slender man also viewing the statue, for perhaps his last time.

"Fly safely, Elda."

“Goodbye, Tosh.”

“Let’s say farewell. Perhaps I will come visit you some day.”

“Or I you.”

Chapter Twenty

16 December, 2018

Elda strolled into the embassy and was hugged by Korinna and Ed. They moved quickly into a secure area, where Elda could brief them on the plans.

"Let me get this straight. We get the prostitute's body from Amsterdam. Yuri brings us the dental records from Moscow so we can match the dental work to the records the Kremlin has on file for Korinna. We send back the blood type and DNA from the prostitute, and Tosh will have Korinna's records changed. We then publish an account of Korinna's tragic suicide and car explosion, which parallels the death of her dear departed husband. We offer to send the charred body back to Moscow, and they accept the offer. Her face is too damaged for facial recognition to tell that this is not Korinna. Did I get that right?" Ed ran his hands through his hair with a look of horror on his face. "My God! Who thought of this scheme?"

"I did. With Tosh's help, of course. Think about it, Ed. Can you see an issue with it? And why should that prostitute have died in vain? Her death will protect Korinna and me and Tosh and Anatoly. It's a win-win for both sides."

Korinna sat in a chair with a stunned look.

"Don't worry, Korinna. This is how we protected Egor too, only there, we didn't need to supply a body. Here, we are supplying a body that's already dead."

Ed laughed. "Yes, it will work, Elda. There is nothing like the creativity of the combined brains of two old Cold War–era spies."

"Watch who you are calling old there, Ed."

"I will be back. I need to speak with some agents and get this started. When will Yuri be here?"

"I'm not sure, but probably within a day or two."

"Good. We should have the body here by then."

"Ed, before you go, can you please arrange a visit for me to MI6? I want to see what gadgets they'll let me have from the lab."

***

The ambulance screeched to a halt and cut its sirens at the Amerikanskaya Klinika. An attendant was holding an oxygen mask on Aurelio's face, and the psychiatrist was holding pressure on Aurelio's wound. The policeman, also crammed into the back of the ambulance, was jotting notes in his notebook.

The doctor and Natasha took a step back as the gurney with Aurelio loaded onto it rushed by and rapidly disappeared down the corridor. The doctor commented, "I think the psychiatric hospital may not be conducive to his recovery. He tends to anger the other patients. And the friends he was making were stirring up his illness again. If he lives, Natasha, I'd like for him to go home and do outpatient treatment on a daily basis."

"Can we get a live-in nurse for him, Doktor? You see, I finally decided to divorce him, but I am just waiting for him to be more on his feet before I move on. It's the least I can do for him."

"Aga, well yes, we can arrange that. Would you stay to help him settle in?"

"No, I think it's best that I not be there when he comes home. Don't you agree?" She put her hand

399

on his arm and gave him a look that spoke of many possibilities.

Natasha didn't add that she had worked with an orderly at the hospital and had finally found the right combination of drugs that caused Aurelio to spill the location of his money and the passwords to access it. She had removed two-thirds of the money in Aurelio's accounts. The remainder was more than enough to keep Aurelio comfortable for the rest of his life. She had paid off the orderly and her debt to the government, and she'd given a small but significant percentage to Yuri, as a thank-you for his company. The remaining money would allow her to live a good life abroad in a warmer climate. She planned on starting that life soon. She was getting too old to use her charms for money anymore.

The doctor gulped and nodded. "Yes, it is best if you are not there. I will make some phone calls and arrange for both medical and psychiatric home care to start after he's released from this hospital. Then I'll arrange the outpatient care once he's well enough to leave the apartment. Will you wait to see how the operation goes?"

"Yes, I will wait. Do you wish to wait with me?"

"No, I'll call later. I need to get back to the hospital and see how the attackers are and if my staff is okay."

Natasha settled into one of the waiting room chairs and called Yuri. She was sad that she and Yuri would be parting ways, but he had told her he had a new job and was going to Moscow. She had no idea when, or if, he would return. It was all good timing for her move.

***

Yuri closed his apartment door behind him. Out of the shadows, a disembodied voice commanded Yuri to come in. In panic Yuri spun around looking for anything he could use as a weapon.

"You should have seen your face, man."

"How did you get in?"

"Your locks are child's play. *Vot*." Anatoly handed Yuri a packed bag.

"This is my bag."

"*Da*. You are going to Moscow."

401

Yuri looked around the apartment that had been his home for many years, took a step into the hallway, and locked the door. "Will I be returning?"

"*Ya ne znayu.*" Anatoly shrugged, clearly bored with having to pick up Yuri.

At the airport, Yuri hopped out of the taxi first and let Anatoly pay the bill. He then led Yuri to a place where they could get pastry and tea.

"*Ty lyubish' sochniki?*" Yuri asked Anatoly.

Anatoly perked up at that and responded with a smile. "*Da!*"

"*Dve chashki Chaya I dve sochniki, pozhaluysta.*" Yuri ordered two teas and pastries.

"*Spasibo.* I may not like killing you, if I have to."

***

Finally home at his own apartment, Anatoly was upset to see so much dust had gathered. He washed off the kitchen table and swept the floor. He then sat at the table and methodically unpacked his kit bag and laid each piece out. After cleaning and ensuring all were in working order, he placed everything carefully back in the bag and added the guns he'd left behind. He would not need the bag again until Tosh gave him his next assignment, but he wanted to have it ready. It was midnight when he finished organizing, cleaning, and dusting.

He went to his closet and opened a secret compartment in the interior bench and placed his bag inside. He then checked that his bedside gun was loaded and placed it on the table next to him.

***

Surprised by the sound of a paper bag being ripped open, Yuri flinched and stepped backward, then spun around. *Anatoly!*

"*Chto? Eto sochnik!*" Anatoly handed Yuri a pastry with a big grin.

Yuri was thankful that his hand was not shaking as he took the pastry, and he forced a grin. "*Spasibo!*" He took a huge bite to mask his expression.

Anatoly pointed at Yuri's sugarcoated mouth and made a circle around his own mouth. Yuri wiped his mouth off on his sleeve as they trotted into Tosh's office. Tosh was sitting waiting for them. Anatoly handed Tosh the paper bag.

"*Eto vam*, Tosh."

403

Tosh peeked in the bag and grinned when he saw what it was. "*Sochnik*. A childhood favorite. *Spasibo*!"

The two men sat down across from Tosh, and Yuri pointed at the empty third seat. "*Kto*?"

"Someone who will help round out our team here," Tosh answered, "but first, I wanted to talk to the two of you. You both have different and complementary skills. Anatoly, you are a skilled assassin with dedication to the Motherland, wonderful attention to detail, and a zest for killing. You carry out plans and orders well, but you have little empathy and limited communication skills.

"Yuri, you are a broad-brush thinker, a creative and effective communicator, and a man who can read and manipulate others well—but you have a soft heart and changing loyalties and tend to make up your own rules.

"I was thinking of having Anatoly replace me when I retire, but I know now from him that he does not want that job."

Anatoly nodded vigorously in agreement.

"If I could combine the two of you, I would have the perfect solution here. So, I am bringing in some glue."

"Chto?"

"Kley?"

Yuri wrinkled his forehead, frowned, and narrowed his gaze at Tosh. He then glanced to see if Anatoly had figured out what was going on but saw his own expression mirrored there.

Tosh laughed. "We will discuss that when you return. But first, we must finish this other operation. Yuri, here are Korinna's dental records. You will go to London and give them to Elda. You will bring back a thumb drive with information for me. Anatoly, you will go to Wales and leave a trail of where you went, and return here, while Yuri is in London. When Yuri returns, I will set you up with a hacker, and you will have this information placed into Korinna's records."

"Der'mo! Khaker? Der'mo!"

Yuri cleared his throat and pointed at Tosh's frown.

Anatoly quickly changed his tune. *"Ya lyublyu khakerov!"* he said, while smiling sweetly and making the symbol of a heart with his hands.

Tosh laughed, and the tension was broken.

"You are both booked on the 18:35 British Airway flight to London. It will arrive at 19:55. Yuri, you have a room at the London Marriott Hotel Grosvenor Square Hotel near the embassy. We will get a message to the American Embassy letting them know that Elda will have a visitor tomorrow. After you are done, Yuri, you are booked on the 21:35 flight back to Moscow the day after. Enjoy London without the dogs."

Yuri jerked to attention.

"No, Yuri, I didn't know, but now I do. *Spasibo*. You really must work on your poker face, Yuri."

"*Da*," Yuri answered, giving a sheepdog look.

Tosh chuckled. "Anatoly, you will catch the direct rail to Paddington station and jump on the train to Cardiff Central. In Cardiff you will stay at the Sleeperz Hotel near the station. Do not do anything to get arrested, but be sure they remember you. You will get a nap and catch the 05:33 to Haverfordwest. You will noticeably eat breakfast at the Platform One Diner in Haverfordwest. You will then return to Cardiff and catch a train to Paddington station. You will take the Heathrow Express train to the airport and join Yuri on the 21:35 flight back to Moscow. Yuri will pass you the USB drive then."

Tosh handed Anatoly and Yuri their plane tickets and gave Anatoly a train pass to and from Wales. "Anatoly, you will report that you sabotaged the brake lines in Korinna's rental car. That, combined with the report from the UK, would give credit for the kill to you, and it will keep anyone from getting suspicious and looking too closely at the body."

"Anatoly, here is the name and address of the hacker. You will have the hacker place the corpse's DNA information into Korinna's records. *Ponimayu?*"

"*Da, ya ponimayu.*"

"Yuri, here is the address of your new apartment. You can settle in there when you get back. I am giving the address to Anatoly too in case he needs to find you there. When this operation is done, we will meet here again, and that third chair will be filled. *Ponimayu?*"

"*Da, ya ponimayu.*"

"*Idti.*" Tosh dismissed them both with a wave of his hand.

***

After the door closed, a secret door opened on the side wall. A tall, athletic, but feminine woman sashayed into the room and sat across from Tosh in the third chair.

"Well, Snezhana, what do you think of your new teammates?"

Snezhana Chelovek crossed her muscular legs and smoothed down her slacks. She sat up straight in her chair. "They both bring a lot to the table, Uncle Tosh. But they do need someone to plan and organize and bring their creativity together with attention to detail, to help them stay on track during their operations."

"That is why I have brought you in. You have shown through your training that you are extremely loyal to Russia, good at follow-through, and expert at planning and organization. You have inherited our familial photographic memory and have ranked top in all your classes. Although you can eliminate others when required, it is not where your true strengths lie."

"Very true."

"But you have the family connections and respect of others. I think, combined with these two, you will be successful as my replacement. I had resisted filling it with a family member, but you have shown yourself to be worthy of it. Now, we need to train you to grow into this position, with help from myself, Yuri, and Anatoly."

"*Da, dyadya* Tosh."

"Good. When Anatoly and Yuri come back, I will set the three of you up on an operation. I have a short mission for you now." Tosh placed a folder on the desk.

Snezhana reached back and tightened the tie holding her long, brown hair in place. Tosh was aware that it doubled as a strangulation device, but also wished his niece would cut her hair, since long hair was a liability as an operative. He could order her to do it but was hoping that she would come to that decision on her own. She picked up the folder Tosh had pushed across his desk to her.

"*Spasibo, dyadya.*"

"We must have you stop calling me 'uncle.' It is now not appropriate in the office."

"*Da, ya ponimayu.*"

Tosh sighed heavily as he watched her flounce away. *Youth is so wasted on the young.* He envied her naivety and energy and longed to return to the beginning of his career and escape the end. He pondered if he was doing the right thing in using his own niece this way.

Elda owed him now. He wondered if she would help him train this generation. Perhaps the two of them could work together to instill ethics and old-school skills on both sides of the pond. He shelved that thought and went to his files to select a mission for the three to work on when this one was done. Something achievable, but one that would need all three of their skills.

"Aga!"

That might do it. He placed the case file to one side and continued his search through the paper files. Tosh could computerize his whole office, as many of his younger colleagues had, but he believed, having employed the use of many hackers, that nothing placed online was safe. Old-school paper records were the most secure way to store and transmit information. He believed that the use of dead drops would return, and spies with boots on the ground would be the most effective in these days of cybercrimes. He did admire the use of cyber terrorism for a quick way to immobilize an entire region, but the retaliation was massive. Stealth was usually much better.

"*Stels, eto khorosho*," he muttered.

Tosh took off his glasses, sat back for a moment, and surveyed the room. There was nothing personal in his office. When he was gone, there would be no trace that he was ever here, except for the many file cabinets full of information. He regretted not being able to talk to Elda about her opinion on online storage and the days of the Cold War. *If we weren't still in the continuance of a form of Cold War, we might even be friends.*

He sensed, although he had no proof, that neither of them could ever be romantically attracted to the other. Those made for the best friendships. This line of work was a lonely one. There was no one you could trust. No one you *should* trust. And those you did like were trained thieves and assassins. They used each other for the greater good, or one of them killed the other. *How will this end?*

He put his glasses back on and continued his hunt for the perfect mission to break in Yuri, Anatoly, and most of all, Snezhana. She was now just an operative to him. That she was also his niece was no longer a concern.

Chapter Twenty-One

17 December, 2018

Will I be arrested on sight? Can I trust Elda? Yuri nervously stepped up to the embassy gates. "Elda, please," Yuri asked at the guard shack by the gates, realizing he didn't even know Elda's last name. He breathed a sigh of relief when she appeared to escort him into a secure area via a side entrance.

"Did you bring the records?"

"*Da.*" Yuri handed the records to Elda.

She looked inside and nodded. "Here is the flash drive to bring back to Tosh. He will know what to do with it. Please safeguard it well."

Yuri nodded and waited.

Elda handed him a thick envelop across the table. "This is a thank-you for all the fine work you have done for me. I expect that Tosh will have you rather busy from now on." Elda looked at him compassionately. "Our paths could cross again. If they do, I hope we're on the same side."

Yuri startled and frowned. He hadn't realized that by working for Tosh, he and Elda were now enemies.

"The troodles are well and send their love to you." Elda passed a picture of the two troodles to Yuri. "You can keep that if you want to."

Yuri fondly stroked the picture with his forefinger and tucked the picture into the inside pocket of his jacket. "*Spasibo.*"

Elda stood and shook his hand. "Please remind Tosh that I will be waiting for his go ahead."

Yuri had so much he wanted to say to Elda but kept his tongue. "*Da, ya budu.*"

Elda walked Yuri back out to the gates, and the guards opened the small side gate for Yuri to walk out. He took the short walk away from their relationship.

"*Poka, Elda. Spasibo.*"

"*Poka, Yuri. Spasibo. Vsego khoroshego.*"

Yuri quickly dashed away to his new life. He hoped he never had to harm Elda.

***

Elda tossed the records on the table in front of Ed. "Can these please be scanned for micro-transmitters before we use them?" She then went downstairs into the embassy morgue, usually just a holding place for bodies to be transferred back to the United States. But on occasion, autopsies were done here, so the facility had a competent doctor on call, as well as a dentist who could check dental records. She asked him to call in the dentist and the doctor so they could prepare the body for transport to Russia.

Once the dental work had been completed and modified to appear as old as the dates in Korinna's dental records, the doctor was to replicate bruises and burns that would occur from a flaming car crash. It was complicated work. They also performed a facial scan at the end to see if the face structure matched Korinna's. If not, they would have to damage the face more, mimicking the damage that would be found if she had gone through the car window. It would be best if they could get the match, since a facial match, combined with the dental records, would convince the Kremlin that Korinna was dead and the mission was completed.

Elda next went over to the copywriter's desk to review the stories that would be placed in the papers and sent to the Kremlin. She summarized bits out loud.

"A car crashed off the cliffs in Wales, in between Haverfordwest and St. David's. The car bounced off the cliffs and exploded. It was low tide, so the car landed in the mud flats and continued to burn. When they found the body, it was unrecognizable, and any paper ID had burned. They traced the car by the VIN back to the car rental place and discovered that it had been rented to a Russian citizen, Korinna Fedorov. Does the Kremlin want the body back?"

She turned toward the copywriter. "Excellent! Good work."

Elda then read the second story, which was a summary of the previous and prepared as a press release.

"Perfect." She thanked the writer and ran upstairs.

"Hi, Ed. Where's Korinna today?"

"I have a bodyguard with her, and she should be here shortly so we can plan the next stage of this operation."

"Yuri will head back tonight with the information for Tosh, so we should have word soon that the DNA has been planted in Korinna's records, and we can then send the notification to the Kremlin.

If we wait another day, we should get notification from Tosh that the case has been closed and it's safe to return to the States with Korinna. I know she's getting anxious to be reunited with Egor and the troodles."

"Did you have fun in Florence?"

Elda already was aware that Ed had a full report of her activities in Florence on his desk. She had spotted agents following her and Tosh. It had been quite the West-East gathering in Italy.

"It was good to finally come face to face with Tosh. I had heard so much about him through the years. I can see where he is to be respected. He may appear friendly on the outside, but there's a steely core and dedication to his country inside that man."

"I'm glad that you met Tosh. We know so little about him. With your instincts, combined with your training as a therapist, you can see things inside people that others often miss. It's in your folder that you are an empath. Is that true?"

"Yes. I am deeply attuned to what a person thinks and feels. Part of my training was to help me not absorb these feelings but to understand them and let them go."

"I would like a full report that includes your intuition about Tosh."

"I'm going to go write up my report while waiting for Korinna."

"Thanks."

Elda went into the windowless room that they had converted into a makeshift office for her. She could tell that it was partially used as a storeroom, with boxes piled up in one corner and a temporary desk and two chairs placed against one wall. She took a paper and pen and wrote out her notes on Tosh in longhand for later entry into a computer. She disagreed with the practice of storing sensitive information on computers. Backup drives often failed, and anything on a network that had connectivity to the internet was not secure. At home, she had the handwritten copies of all her important cases. Dawn had instructions to burn them if Elda died before her.

Hmm. I may need to rethink my death plans. What if I outlive Dawn? Who will take care of my home office? Everything is secure, but someone should destroy it after my death. She made a mental note to chat with Ed about it before she left London.

Her phone pinged to alert her to a text. Korinna had arrived at the embassy. Elda texted Ed, asking him to entertain Korinna for the next half hour. She hated having Korinna wait, but she had to write everything down while it was still fresh in her mind. After rereading her report and ensuring it contained every detail of the operation in Florence, she put down her pen and jogged up the stairs to go see Korinna.

"Elda, look. They gave me a picture of Egor holding the troodles! Isn't it wonderful? He is safe in Maine with Dawn!"

Korinna held out her phone to show Elda the picture. Elda glanced at it, but she couldn't focus. Something nagged her, like she was missing an element in her notes on the operation. She handed the phone back to Korinna, who kissed the picture. Elda presumed she would do that all day.

"Don't wear out the glass on your phone."

"When can we go?"

"Soon. I'm waiting for Tosh. Ed, what are the logistics for getting us home?"

"Well, if you trust Tosh, then we can fly you home British Airways and let you drive from Logan Airport, where you left your car, back to your home."

"That's it! That's what has been bothering me! Ed, will you please have someone pick up all my clothing from the hotel and go to wherever they stored the suitcases from Italy, and bring it all here to a secure room for scanning? I did a preliminary scan, but I think I may have missed something, and we may need to use more sophisticated equipment. I am suspicious that Tosh may have inserted a micro-transmitter somewhere. Be sure to check around the back of the neck area of my clothing. I must have sensed something was not right, as I didn't wear any clothing today that I'd worn in Italy."

Elda paced and chewed at her fingernails as she waited to hear the results.

"Stop doing that, Elda. You'll have no nails left."

"I know, Korinna. Dawn hates it when I do it, too. It's a bad habit. Let's get some candy from the machine and eat while we wait."

"I don't know why you are so slender. You eat like a horse."

Elda was just finishing up her second KitKat bar when Ed received a text from the scanner technician.

"You were right not to trust Tosh, Elda. Korinna, please excuse us for a few minutes?"

"*Da, konechno.*" Korinna settled into an armchair and opened a book.

Ed led Elda downstairs. "They found a micro-transmitter slipped into the luggage lining and another on the collar of the jacket you wore in Italy."

"Ah yes. Tosh put his arm around me when we were shopping on the Ponte Vecchio, and when we were walking back from the restaurant, Tosh reached over to brush something off my collar. I figured at the time that it was the same habit that I have from the military, of brushing lint off others, but something seemed off. Perhaps it was the pressure or duration of the touch. I scanned my clothing and the luggage when I got back to the hotel but found nothing."

"This is a very sophisticated tracker. It is extremely small and powerful. It does not appear to transmit visual or audio, but it does transmit GPS location. I expect that it bounces signals off of satellites for retrieval in Moscow. I imagine that Tosh is trying to find out where you live so he can have leverage over you."

"My first impulse is to burn it and all the clothing, but that would be too easy an ending for this chapter between Tosh and myself. Do burn the clothing and the luggage, but I have another plan for the trackers."

Elda filled Ed in on her idea as they entered a secure room and were joined by the technicians.

"I have never seen anything like this. I have not dismantled it and have left it operational," a technician said.

"Good. We will take the trackers. Please burn the rest of the clothing. It will be an excuse for me to go shopping before I go home. Too bad we're not still in Italy. I could use an Italian leather jacket."

The technician reluctantly handed Elda a plastic bag with two pinhead-sized trackers in it. "Here you go."

"Thanks." Elda handed the bag to Ed. "You know what to do."

Ed chuckled. "Yes, I do. Devious, and Peter Pan-like." Ed marched out the door to send the trackers on the next leg of their journey.

***

Yuri arrived at Heathrow and picked up a Bakewell tart and a Chorley cake to give to Anatoly, as well as a custard tart and some Empire biscuits for himself. He spotted Anatoly sitting at the gate and sat down next to him, placing one of the food bags in between them. Anatoly rose, and as he did, he picked up the food bag with the thumb drive inside. He reached in and withdrew and pocketed the device.

Regarding Anatoly as he passed him on his way to his seat in the last row of first class, Yuri smiled at the sight of Anatoly chewing slowly with his eyes closed. This would be a good partnership.

After landing and going through customs and immigration, Yuri took a taxi from the airport to his new apartment. Tosh would call him when he needed him. Until then, there was no harm in getting comfortable. The taxi passed a man walking a dog.

Vozmozhno, sobaka? He reflected on if he should get a dog. Perhaps even he could have a cover as a dog walker when he was in between cases. No, that wouldn't work. His clients would be mad if he left for long periods of time. But if he had a good dog walker and dog sitter, he could get a dog. Perhaps a girlfriend who liked dogs too? Then she could take care of the dog.

Yuri daydreamed as he ambled toward his apartment. Perhaps just two cats? They would be easier to care for when he was away.

He missed his connections in St. Petersburg and would have to rebuild an entire network again here in Moscow. He suddenly realized he had not told Tosh he had returned and took his phone out of his pocket and entered Tosh's number. Tosh did not pick up, so Yuri left a message.

Perhaps Tosh would let me live in St. Petersburg? Nyet, it's better if I get a new start. He flew up the stairs to his apartment, hoping they had rented him a decent place.

"*Khorosho*!" He felt lighthearted seeing that the apartment was bright and open and already furnished. He put his bag down in the inside hallway and closed the door behind him. The next stage of his life had begun.

***

Anatoly hiked up to the door of a ramshackle, multistory high-rise apartment building that had been built in the Soviet era. He had left his kit bag at his apartment but had enough weapons with his bare hands and belt, if he needed them. He checked the address on the slip of paper Tosh had given him: *804*.

He entered the main lobby and curled his lip at the obvious dirt, filth, and lack of repairs. On the elevator was a large sign that declared, *Ne rabotayet*.

Der'mo! This is starting out badly already! When will this bad-luck operation end? Anatoly fumed as he jogged the stairs, barely out of breath by the time he reached the top step. "*Khorosho!*" He allowed a self-satisfied smile, which quickly disappeared when he observed the clutter and dirt in the hallway. He stepped around toys and garbage bags and knocked on 804. He was gratified to see someone peer out of the peephole and heard the click of multiple locks being flipped.

"*Khorosho.* This one at least has some common sense." He thought back to how gratifying it was, though, to have ripped that other hacker's door off.

The hacker let Anatoly into his front room, and Anatoly was again pleased. There was no sign of dirt or clutter, and the computers and monitors were neatly aligned, with the cords tidily wrapped up and covered where they snaked across the floor to the outlet. He nodded. This was more like it.

"Satisfied?" the hacker asked.

"*Da.*"

Anatoly took in his view of the hacker. Another slender, pale-faced young man who looked like someone should feed him and make him play outside every once in a while. His eyes were clear and intelligent, and he had the smarts not to interrupt Anatoly in the middle of his assessment. Anatoly handed the hacker the thumb drive and an envelope from Tosh. The hacker opened the envelope and took out the instructions, laying them on the table next to the keyboard. He then pocketed the money without counting it.

Another good sign. He'd let Tosh know this one was okay.

"What is your name?"

"Stas."

Stas read the instructions and then sat down at his computer. He typed a few passwords into fields before he accessed the Kremlin system.

"Aha. I have located Korinna's personnel file and found the accompanying data files. Here is her medical file, and this field holds the DNA information. I will replace the DNA information with the new data."

Before Stas closed the file, he ran his finger along the screen, tracing the characters in the field, and then read it out loud the second time while Anatoly checked the results. All had been entered correctly, and the hacker removed all traces of his entrance into the system and disconnected. The entire operation took minutes.

"Gotovo."

Anatoly was impressed by the efficiency of the entire operation.

***

Aurelio woke up in the recovery room after his surgery. He tried to move but was tied to the bed rails and had an oxygen mask on, and he was connected to many monitoring devices. He licked his parched lips and tried to call for a nurse, but his throat was so dry that the sound was muffled by the mask. He breathed in, and if he hadn't been restrained, he would have doubled over from the pain in his abdomen. He gasped, inhaling the antiseptic taste of the oxygen mask, coughed, and panicked. Alarms went off on the monitors.

A nurse rushed in, turned off the alarms, and increased the morphine drip rate.

***

The doctor walked into the waiting room to see Natasha.

"He woke up, but we had to sedate him again because he was in distress. The wound was surprisingly deep and ragged. He will have to be monitored here carefully so that the wound does not get infected and that he doesn't pull out his stitches like he did last time. This is a critical time for him."

"I understand, Doktor. I wanted to arrange home care for him when he finally does get discharged. I am leaving him, and there will be no one to take care of him after this hospital stay."

"That is unfortunate news for Aurelio, but you do have to do the best for yourself. Let me take you to a woman who can work with you to fill out all the necessary paperwork to have home care kick in after his discharge. That is, if he makes it that far. Do you know what should be done with his remains if he doesn't?"

Natasha was a bit thrown by that question. Aurelio had a family plot back in the United States, but it would also be costly to send him there. She did not want to waste money transporting a dead body from one country to another. "His wishes used to be to be buried back in the United States, but that was many years ago, Doktor, and now he lives in Russia and is a part of my family. He will get a good burial here. Can you help me make those arrangements for his future, even if he does survive?"

She had the will he had signed that left everything to her, but if he made a new will, it could negate that. She didn't want to be on the hook for taking care of anything to do with him in the future. Best to do all the arrangements now and prepay for them with his money.

"This woman can help you arrange all that too."

Natasha placed a hand on his arm. "*Spasibo, Doktor*. Thank you very much."

***

Tosh received messages from Anatoly and Yuri that both their missions were successful. He slipped on gloves and picked up a burner phone.

"*Privet*, Elda. It is done. I must ask that you use the date 17 December in the release."

He then took out and shredded the SIM card and dropped the phone into his pocket, to be thrown away later. He removed his gloves and picked up his office phone.

428

He called Anatoly to tell him to pick up his next assignment.

"*Da, seychas, Anatoly*. Now." He hung up halfway through Anatoly's response.

Anatoly would be crabby since he had not had much sleep. Tosh then called and ordered some pastries to be delivered, since he had observed that Anatoly did not like being an errand boy and had expressed his dislike of hackers, so the pastries would hopefully brighten up his day a bit.

You are getting soft, Tosh, he told himself. *Myagkiy v golove. Da, soft in the head is right!*

He laughed and then pulled out a record to show Anatoly. This was a second kill authorized by the Kremlin, and the target was a double agent who had turned on the United States by giving the Russians classified information and now was trying to get back in good graces with the United States by attempting to pass them information about the Russian military. Russia, however, had already figured out that someone who spies on their own country is not to be trusted and was feeding this person fake information. They would have kept the double agent in place, but the United States didn't take the bait, so the person was useless to Russia as an operative.

Tosh approved of this kill. And it would be an easy one for Anatoly to get his confidence back. The target was never an operative while in the United States. In fact, he was only a desk clerk at the NSA, handling minor bits of information, but he had hacked into the computer before he defected and had left with more damaging information. Many in the United States stupidly admired this person as a whistleblower, since some of the information had been gathered on private citizens. Those people did not understand what it took to keep a country safe and that this person's actions were those of a traitor. *Da, eto khorosho.*

Tosh placed the folder on Anatoly's chair. He viewed his monitor and noted that the trackers had gone from the hotel to the embassy and now were heading away from the embassy. He was a bit disappointed that Elda had not discovered his ruse but gratified to have outsmarted her. *Soon, Elda, I will know where you live. Then it will be only a matter of time before I have much more information on you.*

There was a knock on his door.

"*Vkhodit',*" he said, and the door opened, showing a tired and grumpy-looking Anatoly. "*Vvedite, Anatoly.*"

Anatoly entered the room as commanded and sat in his chair. He brightened up at the sight of a plate of pastries on the desk.

"*Dlya, menya?*"

"*Da, dlya tebya.*"

"*Spasibo!*" Anatoly picked up the one closest to him and raised it in the air. "*Eto sochnik!*" He lowered the pastry to his mouth and took a bite. He performed a visual sweep of the room and, not seeing what he was looking for, asked in between chews, "*Chay?*"

"*Prikhod.*"

"*Spasibo.*"

Anatoly scanned the desk, clearly looking for a folder. Tosh pointed to his butt. "Aha!" Anatoly jumped up, removed the folder from his chair, and sat down again. He nodded as he read through the information.

"*Ustranit'?*"

"Yes, eliminate."

Anatoly smiled. "*Spasibo, Tosh.*"

"*Pozhaluysta.*"

A staff member entered the office with the tea.

"*Spasibo*." Tosh poured a cup for himself and one for Anatoly. He told Anatoly to go home and rest for a couple of days and then move forward with this operation. Before he left, however, Tosh needed him to sign his report about the recent operation in Wales, stating how Anatoly had tracked Korinna to Wales and modified her steering and brakes, which resulted in her crash over the cliff. Her car had burst into flames, and Anatoly had driven on before the police arrived.

"How did you know that the prostitute in my picture would not have passed a close inspection?" Anatoly asked.

"I have a photographic memory, as good as, if not better than, any computerized facial recognition system. I have seen enough pictures of Korinna to know that the prostitute was a close match, but not close enough if anyone had run facial recognition on that picture. They may have to break one of the cheekbones to make a better match, even with burning the corpse. But you did well, Anatoly. She was the exact height and weight. Now go home and get some sleep."

Anatoly stood up and then looked longingly at the plate of pastries.

"Here." Tosh held out the bag they'd come in.

Anatoly smiled widely and emptied the plate into the bag. "*Spasibo*." He nodded at Tosh as he went out the door.

He gives new meaning to the way to a man's heart is through his stomach! Tosh again checked his monitor. The trackers were headed toward Heathrow airport. *Khorosho.*

***

They were being followed.

"Korinna, let's go into this shop. I like that leather jacket in the window."

"*Da.* That would look good on you, Elda."

Elda checked the reflection in the mirror as she ambled around examining the jackets. There! She was almost certain that was a tail.

"I don't see what I need here. Let's go to that store we passed by that carries jeans and cool shirts and pick up some clothing for me there."

"Oh yes, the one with the mirrored balls hanging from the ceiling and the huge dressing rooms. I know what shirt I want you to try on." Korinna nearly ran to the shop.

Elda wandered from rack to rack, checking the mirrors. She randomly gathered up a selection of shirts. "Korinna, can you look over there for a new jacket for me? I'll quickly try these on and meet you in the pants department?"

"*Da.*"

As Elda had hoped, her tail followed her into the fitting rooms. Elda left her door open a crack. A woman crept toward her room while checking the other rooms along the way. Elda stood back behind her door. The woman looked in to check for an occupant. Elda reached out and grabbed her by her ponytail and yanked her into the dressing room. To cover the tail's shriek, Elda said loudly, "I know. I know. These are atrocious!" She then whispered in the woman's ear, "One more shriek like that and I'll cut your throat. I know you. You were the driver in Moscow. Who are you? And why are you following me?"

"I will tell you nothing."

Elda increased the pressure of the knife on her throat. Blood welled up at the cut.

"I ask you again. Who are you?"

"I am Snezhana Chelovek. You will get nothing more from me. I doubt that you will kill me."

"Do not doubt me, young pup. Hmm… Chelovek. You are related to Tosh then? I thought you reminded me of him."

"He is my uncle."

***

Where are they? They should have been back an hour ago. Ed glanced at his watch. He texted Elda again. Still no answer.

Ed picked up his desk phone and dialed a number. "Yes, that's correct. You will meet the Air France flight from Heathrow and hold up a sign that says *James Jones*. James will identify himself and hand you a manila envelope. You take it to 999 Anastasia Boulevard, St. Augustine, Florida, where you will ask for one of the handlers, Fred. He will take the envelope so that it gets to the right spot…Yes, yes, I know what that place is. It is all arranged."

Elda and Korinna walked in just as he hung up. Elda was carrying a bag of clothes and wearing a new leather jacket, as well as new jeans, a shirt, and leather gloves. She had a pair of new sneakers on and topped the outfit off with a bowler hat.

"I always wanted one of these!" Elda lifted a hand to her hat. "Korinna convinced me to buy it."

"You can pull it off. The hat complements the shape of your face."

Ed squinted warily at Elda and Korinna. "What else happened?"

"Tosh sent us another present. Elda sent it back to him."

"Dead or alive?"

"Oh, definitely alive. She may be missing something, however." Elda reached into the bag and pulled out a long, brown ponytail and held her trophy aloft.

"Oh my God, Elda. Who did that belong to?"

"Apparently, Tosh's niece. I did her a favor. It's a liability for a budding spy. And she's lucky I didn't scalp her."

Ed frowned, but his eyes were smiling. "We'd better get you out of here before they send a more competent person after you. I have heard from the fleet, and we still cannot get you back via submarine."

"Rats. That would have been fun!"

"Too claustrophobic. I've had enough of being in dark, enclosed, cramped spaces for a while," Korinna said.

"What about getting us on a fishing vessel and then transferring to a US ship when we are off the coast? That should cover our tracks."

"You really don't ask for much, do you?" Ed sighed. "Okay, let me see what I can do. Meanwhile, we have sent the press release out and notified the Kremlin that we identified Korinna's body through the rental car company information. They have asked that we send the body back to Moscow for proper burial, so it is on its way."

"Great! Can Korinna sit with you for about an hour while I pop over to MI6 to pick up my goodie bag?"

"Sure. Since they already know you're both here, Korinna, do you want to place a phone call to Egor? We can bounce it around enough, so they won't be able to trace it to the destination."

"*Da!* Yes, please!"

"Say hi to Honey for me," Elda said, heading out to pick up her new toys.

Chapter Twenty-Two

19 December, 2018

Tosh stood at the open grave and scanned the area as the casket was lowered into the ground. Across from him stood an older woman dressed in black. *Who is she? Aga! The neighbor.* He trudged over to her as the dirt was being shoveled on top of the casket. *There is no sound quite like that one.*

"I knew Korinna for many years, through our work together," he said to the woman,

"I'm Anna. I have been Korinna and Egor's neighbor for many years. I loved taking care of the dogs for them. How tragic this all is. First the dogs disappear, then Egor dies in Canada, and now Korinna is dead. Do you know what happened?"

"Yes, a tragic end to a love story. She couldn't live without him and drove her car off a cliff in Wales."

The neighbor started crying. "I will miss that entire family."

"I hope you have good neighbors again," Tosh said as he patted her shoulder.

He walked away satisfied that only the neighbor had shown up at the burial and that she was no one to worry about.

He checked his phone to view the trackers. They were in Florida and wandering around a small area. *Khorosho*! *That must be where Elda lived. I have you now, Elda.* He took his burner phone from his pocket and called an agent in Florida and passed the coordinates over to him. "*Da, da, pozvonite mne.*"

He hung up. The agent would call when he was at the exact location. Tosh only wanted more information. Where she lived, who she lived with, where she went every day. Things that he could leverage later on.

Tosh's feet crunched on the packed snow and ice on his way to the metro. It was a cold, breezy day in Moscow. Deaths always made him reflect. He considered his life a good one, even if it was at times lonely. Perhaps that was why he felt the need to continue a connection to Elda. Even though Elda was younger than him, they shared a past of sorts. Few from that era were still alive, let alone in the spy business.

As Tosh stepped into his office, his phone beeped to let him know he had a message. *Aga! From Florida already.* He used his burner phone to call the agent back. It was important to leave no trace of this for others to find. This was between Elda and himself.

"*Kakiye? Ferma alligatorov?*" He listened as the agent described the St. Augustine, Florida, Alligator Farm and Zoological Park. He looked at his phone to see a picture of an albino alligator. "*Oni tam*? The trackers are there?" He hung up, shaking his head in admiration. "Good one, Elda."

***

Aurelio sat in his living room, listening to the emptiness that surrounded him. He was so used to hearing small sounds of Natasha wandering in and out, of Yuri barging in with his large presence, of his own voice yelling at Natasha. Now, there was no one to yell at. He moved gingerly off the couch, holding his side, which still hurt after the operation, and went into the kitchen to pour himself a scotch. *I don't care what they say about not drinking or doing drugs. Who are they to tell me, a grown man, what to do?* He returned to the living room and turned on the television, to have some background noise.

Sitting back down, he opened his computer and thought of emailing his siblings, but he found he had nothing to say. He didn't like the new medication that they had him on. It robbed him of those wonderful spurts of energy when he could do so much. And not being able to do meth, bath salts, or cocaine robbed him of his edge. He wondered if he could get them to prescribe him something like Ritalin or Adderall or even Dexedrine. The Abilify was causing him to gain weight. He burped and drank again from his scotch while licking his lips. He blinked his eyes a few times to clear the blurriness, closed his computer, and placed it to one side.

He picked up his phone and dialed Yuri's number.

"Etot nomer bol'she ne obsluzhivayetsya."

He hung up and dialed Natasha's cell phone.

"Etot nomer bol'she ne obsluzhivayetsya."

He threw the phone across the room. "This number is not in service. Damn, I am sick of hearing that!" He was more irritable lately. He needed some pot to calm him down.

He stumbled across the room, picked up his phone, and dialed Olav's number.

"Olav, buddy, it's Aurelio. I need your help, man."

He held the phone away from his head as Olav yelled.

"No, man, I would never take your hash! What do you take me for anyway?"

More yelling from Olav.

"Olav, buddy, remember we had prostitutes in the room that night. They cleaned the money out of my wallet. I'm sure they went through our bags too."

Olav spoke again, and Aurelio brought the phone closer to his ear.

"Good. You see the truth now. I need your help. I was let out yesterday just to find that Natasha has left me. Yuri is gone too. I have no contacts here anymore." He nodded, satisfied that he had hooked Olav into helping him. Olav was still angry that his own wife had left him. "Yeah, buddy, I need some pot."

Aurelio grabbed a pen and paper off the table and wrote down a number that Olav gave him.

"Thanks, man! Any chance this guy has any coke or other speed?"

Aurelio listened and nodded again. "Okay, I'll see what he has. I owe you one, man. Come to St. Petersburg soon, hey? I have the place to myself. I have to go to the nuthouse for daycare during the week, but on weekends, they don't even check in on me."

Aurelio and Olav arranged a weekend a few months from then, when Aurelio no longer would have to go to his daylong outpatient sessions, for Olav to come up to St. Petersburg. He hung up, satisfied that he would soon have his life back on track again.

I am a great man, he told himself. *Then why do I feel like this? The doctor tells me that it's all inside of me, and all I have to do is connect to it and talk about it, but I think he's wrong. All I have to do is keep agreeing with him for another couple of months, and then I will be free to live my life again.*

He meandered into the kitchen and poured himself another scotch, then plopped onto the couch in the living room and propped his feet onto the coffee table. As he sipped his scotch, he felt a flash of how successful he was. *Just look at this apartment. It is worth millions. My mother always told me I would be the most successful of her children.* He sighed contentedly. *Yes, life is good. I am better off without that bitch Natasha.*

An hour later he was passed out and drooling on the couch.

***

Elda and Korinna boarded the fishing boat at the dock in Brixham, England. Elda shook hands with the captain, who then motioned for them to go inside the cockpit while the crew cast away.

"I wish we'd had some time to explore the village. Did you know that this town has a long fishing history and was one of the staging areas where the American servicemen left for the D-Day landings?"

Elda was always impressed by Korinna's vast knowledge of history, but she was amazed that she had knowledge of this small town in the UK. "How on earth do you know *that* piece of information?"

Korinna shrugged. "*Ne znayu.* It just comes to me from something I once read."

"Brain burps."

"*Kakiye? Chto takoye*, 'brain burp?'" Korinna asked.

"You know, when your synapse misfires and something comes out of your mouth before you realize where it came from."

"*Aga*! Brain burp."

The trip was choppier than either had hoped for.

"I am glad we haven't eaten lunch," Elda said.

Korinna just looked at her with a pale face.

As they exited the English Channel, the boat settled into a rhythm of rocking over the waves that Elda found almost comforting.

Once darkness fell, the captain turned on the running lights, and when daylight broke on 20 December, they were in the Atlantic. On the horizon, steaming toward them, was a destroyer. Elda had been immediately alert when she'd heard the lookout spy the ship. The captain handed her a pair of binoculars.

"Yes, that's definitely a United States Navy destroyer." She waited until the dot had turned into a recognizable ship. "It may be the USS *Michael Monsoor* out of San Diego."

"Okay, how would you know that, Elda? Can you read the name from here?"

"No, but most of the destroyers are of the Arleigh Burke class. The newest class of destroyers are the Zumwalt class. There are only two in the fleet so far. They have had a lot of electrical problems, and neither ship can use their AGS guns, so they are not any good for far-reaching munitions coverage. They can be used for ship-to-ship protection, and this one was loaned to the Atlantic Fleet for an exercise in the Mediterranean, partly to see how far they can stretch the capabilities of a ship that is basically a lemon. That's probably why they sent it to be our bus."

Korinna looked a bit horrified at the thought of a malfunctioning ship being their ride for the next few days.

"The US doesn't plan on making anymore Zumwalt-class ships. Too bad they used Admiral Zumwalt's name on these ships. Zumwalt was the chief of Naval Operations just before I served, and he was highly respected, if not revered. He pushed for equal rights for women in the navy and sent a Z-Gram on it that started the full integration of women into the regular navy."

"Did you serve under him?"

"No, I served under Admiral Hayward. He presented as a bit dweeb-y, but he had a sharp mind and believed that the Soviets were a threat to the United States. He dealt with a lot to rebuild the forces after the end of the Vietnam War. I liked him and Admiral Watkins, who succeeded him. It was under their leadership that I recognized how I could help keep America strong from the Soviet threat. It was the beginning of my long career in studying the profession of being a spy."

The ship traveled closer. Elda judged the size of the waves, and for a moment regretted this way of creating subterfuge and obscuring their trail.

"Korinna, here, put on this life vest." Elda handed her a military-grade vest. "We are going to have to make a ship-to-ship transfer. You are going to go first so you are sure to get there in case the seas get any worse. The two vessels will steam side by side at the same rate of speed, keeping an even distance between them. The destroyer personnel will use one of their deck cranes to lower a basket down to the deck of this fishing boat. You will climb in, sit down, and hold on, and they'll lift you to the deck of the destroyer, where they will help you out of the basket."

The captain approached. "Here, Korinna, wear this helmet. They are doing a test run of lowering and raising the PTB now."

"PTB?" Korinna asked.

"Personnel Transfer Basket. Look out toward the stern, and you can watch them lower and raise the basket."

"Is this dangerous?"

"Well, it could crash against the side of the boat on the way up, or drop too fast, but don't worry—the navy trains for this a lot."

Korinna put on her helmet, and Elda checked the straps of her life jacket and helmet. She then stepped back and took a picture of Korinna with her iPhone. "Just in case I ever have to blackmail you."

Korinna laughed and hit Elda on the arm.

"Ouch!" Elda smiled. That reaction was what she wanted Korinna to have, to get her mind off the dangers of the transfer. At least it wasn't dark or stormy.

"We have a lot going positively for us in this transfer. Good daylight and rhythmic seas, which will allow them to time the raising and lowering of the basket." She didn't tell Korinna of the danger of the winch motor giving out and the basket getting stuck in the air or crashing down into the deck.

Korinna sat in the PTB looking terrified as the basket jerked off the deck of the fishing boat. The two ships were rocking at different cadences and lurched at each other with each swell. The basket swung from side to side as it slowly moved up, and then suddenly stopped. Elda held her breath and looked over at the frowning winch operator. Korinna screamed as it dropped suddenly and stopped again.

"Aha! Got it!" the winch operator said, and the basket moved up again.

Elda let out her breath. The PTB moved smoothly over the gap between the two ships.

"Drat!"

The basket stopped, and Elda held her breath again.

"Okay. We're good."

The basket jerked with starts and stops until it finally came down hard onto the deck of the receiving ship. A shaking Korinna was lifted out, and the PTB returned for Elda.

The winch operator made some adjustments to his machinery. "Come on, dear. You can do it," he said to the winch. "Okay, let's try it!"

Elda took a deep breath, squared her shoulders, and marched to the basket. She threw the luggage into the PTB, shouldered her precious to-go and goodie bags, put her life jacket and helmet on, and climbed in. The basket jerked, but this time it went up smoothly and was lowered to the deck of the destroyer.

"Permission to come aboard, sir?"

"Pergra."

The captain, once she was out of the basket, shook her hand.

"Welcome to the USS *Michael Monsoor*."

"You're a long way from home, Captain."

"Yes. Once we drop you off, we will be heading back to San Diego for repairs."

Well, how comforting. "Thank you for picking us up, Captain. We will stay out of your way."

"I hear you're ex-navy. Would you both like a tour of the ship?"

"Yes, definitely. Thank you, sir."

After their tour they settled into a small cabin.

"Why do you choose the top bunk, Elda?"

"Easy choice. If I fart or throw up, it floats downward. And when I climb in or out of bed, I disturb you, whereas, when you climb in and out, I don't wake up. Also, I don't hit my head when I sit up suddenly, and in the military, the top bunk was easier to make. I guess if the compartment starts filling up with water, I'd be safer longer too."

"Geesh! Seriously?" Korinna threw a pillow at Elda and missed.

"And it's harder to throw upward and easier to throw down." Elda lobbed her pillow at Korinna, hitting her on the arm. "I hope the breakfast is good on this ship."

"How can you even think of food, after that ride and the swinging basket!"

Elda laughed and then handed Korinna her small bag that held the book she was reading.

"Spasibo," Korinna said.

The days at sea fell into a rhythm, with Elda waking up at dawn and doing her exercises in the cabin, taking a brisk walk around the deck, showering, and then shaking Korinna awake for her shower.

When they were in the cabin together, they fell into their old way of easy conversations.

"So, why did you become a translator, Korinna?"

"We had no choice about our careers when I was growing up. You hoped that you would have some talent or skill that Mother Russia would need so that you could obtain more comfortable living arrangements for yourself and your parents. We didn't have much at all. My father was a minor clerk in the government. That, at least, helped us get an apartment where we had two bedrooms. When I was young, my mother perceived I was picking up languages easily. She was a schoolteacher, so she worked with the language teacher to start me learning French, as well as Russian. When it became clear that learning two languages at once was not a problem for me, they added English to the mix, and in a year, German. By the time I was in third grade, I was fluent in four languages. My teachers pointed it out to the government, and I started fourth grade in a special school for talented children. My parents were delighted."

"Did you like the school?"

"It was not my role to like or dislike the school. I was to attend and get good grades, and I was happy to be doing what I loved.

"Did you think at any time that it was wrong for you?"

"We were not trained to think, Elda. We had no choice. It was an honor to be given the opportunity."

"Did you ever regret it and wish you had done something else?"

"Why? I met Egor at the school. We fell in love and got married. I had a great career where I traveled to many different places, as did Egor. We shared our stories when we returned, which deepened our relationship. I met fascinating people and dealt at high levels. It was actually a lot of fun."

Elda nodded, trying to absorb a world where you weren't encouraged to think freely and make choices. She had been so many things in her life. Would she have been more successful if she had been forced to just do one thing, or would she have gotten so bored that she would have done poorly at the end?

"So why did you do what you do, Elda?"

"It's so hard to describe what I do. I have done so many things. I dream of doing something, or being something, and if the feeling persists, I go do it. I've been pretty successful in all that I have tackled. As an artist, I have been in six galleries. I have three published books. I was a C-level executive in corporate America. I received an early promotion in the navy. My movie at least was shown to a sold-out audience. I helped rescue my friend, and all of this has made me happy. I guess I like being busy. I definitely like doing projects. I love doing construction work. It's so tactile, as is painting—and like painting or writing a book, you start with nothing, a demolished room, a blank canvas, an empty page, and voila, you create something out of that nothingness! My life has been like that—a blank canvas on which to create possibilities."

Korinna frowned and nodded, probably trying to wrap her head around Elda's life where nothing was decided for her.

"Do you feel this has been your destiny? This life of many things, many careers, many projects?"

"Yes, I do, and perhaps that's a similarity between the two of us. You had a destiny to do languages. It was a God-given talent. I have creativity as my God-given talent, and it takes many forms. It appears to be haphazard, but there is a theme for me. A theme of seeing the whole and creating something that only lives in my brain. Even with this mission. I pictured what would happen, like a play, and gave it many different forks in the road along the way, to see which had the best ending for us."

"I look forward to many more of these talks, Elda."

"Me too, Korinna."

To stave off boredom, Elda made herself helpful as an understudy to a few of the crew, offloading minor tasks, while Korinna read or gazed contemplatively out to sea. The water stayed relatively calm, much to Elda's and Korinna's relief. Before they knew it, the shipping traffic had picked up around them, and soon they were sailing into the port.

"We are almost home, Korinna."

***

The door shut with a click behind her. Tosh frowned, tossed the Kleenex left on his desk, and then sat back in his chair and contemplated his ceiling. *Damn it, Elda.* She'd bested him with the alligator trick, and although she'd done him a favor with cutting off Snezhana's ponytail, she'd shamed his niece. He needed to send her a clear message.

He drummed his fingers on his desk. They'd covered the airports and the shipping ports in the UK. If he were Elda, where would he go and how would he get there?

Tosh's chair came down with a thump, and he sat up straight. "*Aga!*" He'd bet her accent was either Canadian or American. So, she would take Korinna to North America. She knew Tosh's reach was mainly political in the United States, so she would be safest there. So, he guessed the United States. The most direct way in was through the East Coast. And she'd have to have had a military transport, since they'd been unable to find her on the cameras in the airports.

Tosh drummed his fingers on his desk some more, then picked up his secure line and dialed.

***

Slap. The lines hit the dock, and sailors ran to pick them up and secure them to the mooring cleats. In the shadow of a nearby ship, a civilian contractor observed as the ship slowly settled into the dock. He adjusted his glasses so the camera embedded in the frame could get the best pictures. A large group of sailors departed the ship for shore leave. He patiently waited.

∗∗∗

Tosh grabbed his phone. He listened to the man on the other end and hung up.

"Chert."

Chapter Twenty-Three

24 December, 2018

Elda's Honda Ridgeline truck turned off the side road onto a dirt track.

"Where on earth do you live, Elda? It seems like we've been driving for days and now are out in the woods somewhere!"

Elda laughed. "We are almost there. This is the last part of the trip. I promise."

It had been a long trip from Boston. They had stopped at Portsmouth, New Hampshire, to eat and were on their last leg of driving. They had left 95 North in Newport, Maine, and gone onto minor highways and side roads and were now closing in on home. Elda could feel the tension drain from her body.

When they'd arrived at Logan, Elda had circled the car with two different types of scanners before getting into it—MI6 had given her a portable scanner that would even detect the new tracking devices. She felt confident they had not been followed. They would soon pass over one more scanner hidden in the road, before turning into her driveway.

She chuckled.

"*Kakiye*?" Korinna asked.

"Oh, I was just thinking how Tosh's face must have looked when he received the news that an alligator had eaten his trackers."

The two of them laughed.

"A dingo's got my baby," Korinna said.

Elda cracked up. "Meryl Streep was, of course, wonderful, but I didn't like that movie. And I always remember the quote as 'A dingo ate my baby.'"

"Oh, that fits even better."

A conversation scattered with "brain burp" and "a dingo ate my baby" carried them home to the cabin by the cliffs. Elda parked the car and slid out and stretched, to be nearly bowled over by a little ball of fur jumping up and barking, and two others attacked Korinna. Elda picked Vee up and, as she straightened, nearly was bowled over again by Dawn. Elda looked to her right, and Korinna had one dog in her arms and Egor had the other, and the two of them were in a doggie-human embrace.

Elda kissed Dawn, trying not to squash Vee in the process. A contentment washed over her. She joined in as everyone grabbed the bags with what free hands they had and walked to the cabin.

"Be careful of that bag, Dawn. I'm not sure yet what's in it and what my new toys do."

"Gads!" Dawn frowned and gingerly passed the shoulder bag over to Elda.

"Thanks, dear."

The four humans and three dogs bounced into the cabin. They placed the bags inside the front door.

"I like it up here. The snow reminds me of home. There is more beauty, though, with the woods and the cliffs and the sea." Korinna sighed. "Elda, would it be possible? Could we live up here too?"

"I don't see why not. This is a community of many operatives, military, ex-operatives, and retirees. We all know each other, and it's safe and secure. There would be a lot for you to do, and we have dog friendly places, including restaurants. And I would love to have you guys nearby. I'll call Ed in the morning."

"Tomorrow is Christmas, Elda," Dawn said gently.

"Really? Wow! How did that happen? What a wonderful Christmas Eve!"

Dawn put on some Christmas music and made hot chocolate. The four of them sat chatting and watching the twinkling Christmas lights. The cat settled down by the woodstove, and the dogs lay cuddled next to their owners.

"Oh, I nearly forgot," Dawn said. "There's a huge box that came here for you, Korinna."

"*Chto eto?*"

Elda read the return address of the American Embassy in London and grinned broadly. "Oh good. It arrived."

Dawn went into the side sitting room and came back, pushing a large box toward Korinna. She offered a pair of scissors to Korinna, to help remove the massive amounts of tape around the box.

"I gather that Yuri wanted to make sure everything was still in the box after its journey from Russia to London and then on to here. I had left instructions at the embassy for them to forward the package on when it arrived."

"*Da*, there are problems with mailing things to or from Russia and having them all arrive at their destination."

Korinna frowned as she struggled with the tape. Finally, she lifted the top flap and removed the paper covering the contents. Her tears overflowed.

"*Chto eto*?" Egor asked, coming over to where Korinna was kneeling on the floor next to the box and putting his arm around her.

She reached in and handed him the family photo album, and then reached in again and screamed in delight. "My grandmother's throws! Elda, how did you do this?"

"I have my ways . . ."

Korinna danced around the room in delight, with one of her grandmother's throws around her shoulders and two troodles and Vee excitedly dancing on their hind legs around her.

Elda laughed to see her friend so happy. "Life is good, hey?"

"*Zhizn' khorosho.*"

"Look, it's snowing. How wonderful," Dawn said.

They all sat watching the snow fall and reflecting on how lucky they were to have their family and friends.

"Would you do it again?"

"For you, Korinna, of course."

Dawn sighed heavily and frowned.

"You okay, honey?"

"Sure," Dawn replied in a tone that didn't sound that okay. A long silence ensued.

Finally, Elda said, "Did you know that the spare room is also used as a debriefing room, so it's quite soundproof?" She gave a leering smile to Korinna and Egor.

Egor blushed, and Korinna punched Elda in the arm again. Trying to not appear too anxious, Egor and Korinna placed their cups in the sink, gathered up Korinna's belongings, and disappeared into the spare room with the troodles barking and dancing behind them.

"Shall we?" Dawn reached out her hand and led Elda upstairs, with Vee wagging her tail and leading the way.